At night . . .
alone . . .
at sea

It was not a sound, exactly; it was a sense of movement somewhere near Sue that roused her from her sleep. Her heart began to thump so hard that, oddly, she was afraid someone might hear it. In the dark she could not see at all . . .

There was the sound of the engines, the steady wash of waves. There were the tiny creaks and sighs of the yacht, which could be heard only at night. And the small yet definite noise that came again: the faint click in the tiny chest of drawers very near her bed.

She tried to steady her breathing in the hope that would steady her wildly thudding heart. She had an impulse to thrust her head under the blanket and was so frozen with terror that she couldn't move. If she made the slightest move, then whoever was there, so near her, would instantly know that she was awake and aware of him and would instantly—no, no, her mind cried; not murder me! No, no!

MIGNON G. EBERHART

"ONE OF THE MOST POPULAR WRITERS OF OUR ERA."
—*San Diego Union*

* * *

"ONE OF THE LAST GIANTS OF THE ERA."
—*West Coast Review of Books*

Also by Mignon G. Eberhart

Published by
WARNER BOOKS

MIGNON G. EBERHART

THE PATIENT IN CABIN C

WARNER BOOKS

A Warner Communications Company

The author wishes to acknowledge with gratitude the sailing friends who did their best to keep her on course: Jackie Preis, Gwynne and Bill Pfeifer, Carlene Roberts Lawrence, Charles Teetor; also, with most sincere remembrance, Lothair Teetor's fine boatmanship and hostmanship on his yacht the *Barbara*. The *Barbara*, however, bears no likeness to the *Felice*, and all the characters in this novel are entirely fictional. If an error has occurred in marking charts, it is due only to the author's steering.

WARNER BOOKS EDITION

This Warner Books Edition is published by arrangement with Random House, Inc., 201 East 50 Street, New York, N.Y. 10022

Warner Books, Inc.
666 Fifth Avenue
New York, N.Y. 10103

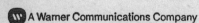 A Warner Communications Company

Printed in the United States of America

First Warner Books Printing: January, 1985
Reissued: May, 1990
10 9 8 7 6 5 4

One

The sunset gun boomed over the ultramarine waters of the Sound. The great flag began to descend slowly, its red, white and blue startlingly bright against the deeper blues and purples of the sky. Only a faint rose color cast a glow over the dining room. A tightness always caught at Sue's throat with the sound of this traditional formality at the Sea Cove Club. She could barely see the dark gray strip across the water that was Long Island.

The red-white-and-blue dropped and dropped and was gathered expertly into waiting arms before it could touch the ground.

A mellow-toned ship's bell struck three times. It was a signal; seats and dinners were resumed.

Monty pulled Sue's chair farther out, seated her, and resumed his own seat.

"Nice, isn't it?" Sue said.

Monty nodded, looked up and across her shoulder. His handsome, rather broad face broadened further in a wide smile. He sprang up again. "Hey, Stan! Over here." Sue glanced around quickly. It was—it must be Stan Brooke, making his way to the small terrace table. She hadn't seen him for years. He was older; so was Sue, but he was as she remembered him, slim, tanned, with black hair and deep gray eyes, smiling, too, as he neared the table. Then he recognized Sue.

"Sue! Hello."

He took her hand.

"Stan!"

"What are you doing here?" Monty asked. "Sit down. Have a drink with us. Have dinner with us."

"Thank you." Stan lowered himself into a chair that a pretty and attentive waitress had instantly pushed toward the little table. "Actually I thought I might run into somebody to crew for me."

Monty laughed. "That little sailboat of yours."

"She's good," Stan said. "And she's mine." He grinned. "Who owns that whacking great yacht tied up down there?"

"Oh—" Monty tried to look embarrassed but did not succeed in hiding his pride—"she's mine."

"Good God!" said Stan.

Monty nodded, smiling, so his excellent teeth flashed.

"Good God!" said Stan again. "Is he telling the truth?" he asked Sue.

She answered, "Oh, yes. And she really must be splendid."

"I know. This is, I can guess. I stopped to take a look at what I could see of her a few minutes ago. Some little brown man in a white jacket didn't exactly order me off, but he was certainly prepared to do so if I put a foot on the gangway."

"That was Juan. He came with the yacht, actually." Monty motioned to the waitress, although he needn't have, for she had already established herself almost at Stan's elbow.

"What'll you have?" Monty asked.

"Oh . . ." Stan glanced at Sue's martini and Monty's short whiskey. "Martini, I think. Thank you."

"You are not in uniform," Monty said. "Have you given up the navy?"

"Well, it didn't give me up, I'm thankful to say." Stan grinned again. "Fact is, I'm on leave. Two weeks. So I decided to have a thoroughly good time—"

Sue laughed. "And go to sea again!"

"Well, yes. But different." Stan gave his turtleneck sweater a hitch and pulled his blue jacket straighter. "I seem to have grown some the past few years," he said. "Mom put away all my civvie clothes, but none of them fit."

"That's life in the navy for you." Monty tipped up his drink and, with a nod, ordered another. "What boat were you on?"

"Pardon me," Stan said with a chuckle. "Ship."

"Well, then, ship."

"The *Lancaster*. A destroyer. Home base San Diego."

Monty nodded. "Let's see. You graduated from the Naval Academy. When do you expect to make admiral?" He was laughing in a friendly way.

Stan shook his head good-naturedly. "That might take a little time. Day or so."

Monty always liked facts. "Seriously, what is your status now?"

"Two stripes," Stan replied rather shortly. Sue had always known something of his reverence and love for the navy; she could see that while he took Monty's questioning casually, Stan really didn't like joking about it. He added soberly, "It's a great service, Monty."

"Yes, I suppose. In a war. But in peacetime—"

"In peacetime we have to try to keep the peace," Stan said, again shortly, and changed the subject. "How are you, Sue? I haven't seen you since . . . since . . ."

"Since ages ago, when you invited me to a dance at Annapolis. Remember? Aunt Addie took me. Chaperone." Sue lifted her eyebrows. "But it was a fine dance, and you did look handsome in your uniform."

Monty put down his empty glass with a click. "Look, Stan, I could use a crew, too. On the yacht."

"You mean *me*?"

"Sure. We're just starting on a short cruise. You'd be back here long before your leave is up. Come on Stan. Do you good. Did you get a look at the diesel engines on the *Felice*?''

"Nope. Only saw some fancy mahogany. *Felice*? Is that her name?" There was a twinkle in Stan's eyes. "Should have called her the *QE Three*."

Just for an instant Monty's face hardened in thought; Sue had the fantastic impression that he found something attractive about Stan's humorous suggestion. And he did. Monty said, "That's not a bad idea."

Stan was taken aback. "I was joking."

"Oh, I know. Fact is, though, sometimes people say things in jest that offer some damn good notions." Monty's eyebrows were drawn together thoughtfully.

Stan stared for a moment; then he rallied. "Thinking about leasing her for world cruises? Extra special cuisine, trips, clienteles?"

Monty took up his drink. "Oh, no. But sometimes— well, I'm always alert for ideas. In my business."

"What exactly is your business, Monty? I know you buy and sell real estate and factories and everything."

Monty didn't really care for the implied flippancy. "I have been called an entrepreneur," he said rather stiffly. "Some people say business consultant." Then the chill vanished. "Personally, I call myself a peddler."

"But then, what do you peddle?"

"Oh, anything; as you say, everything." He moved his glass in a thoughtful circle. "Fact is simple, Stan. I find, or see, or hear of a business that is not doing well but has potential. Then I get in touch with people who can and are prepared to spend money to make that business a better-going concern. Put the two together. That's all. Simple."

"Well," Stan said, "It must pay you."

Monty became rather sober again. "Oh, sure. I get my percentage and sometimes invest a dime or two myself."

"It sounds just great. Honestly." There was real admiration in Stan's voice.

Monty nodded. "I like it. I like the money, too. No

getting around that," he added frankly. "The *Felice*, for instance. I always wanted a yacht."

"A change from the traditional sailing yacht? Not a bad idea, really," Stan said. "Although me, I like sailing when I'm on my own. Naturally."

"Not for me," Monty sensed no criticism, if indeed there was any. "I don't sail, never have. But I admit I like to feel a wheel under my hands—I mean," he added quickly, "the kind of wheel—it's almost like an automobile. Lots of power under you. Don't have to wait and try to judge the wind. Just watch out for other shipping and mark the buoys at the chart desk and—all there is to it."

Stan's face was amused, half-admiring. "You do get what you want, Monty, don't you?"

Monty agreed. "I try. Have a small house and nine acres in the Weston hills. Lalie is there now—you remember my sister. Half sister." Stan nodded rather vaguely. Monty went on, "An apartment in New York. A tiny house on Eleuthera. But somehow I always wanted a yacht, and I finally got one. Actually I bought her from a friend in Palm Beach. Juan, the little man you saw, came along as steward. Helps out as crew in a pinch. The *Felice* practically sails herself. She moves like—well, come on with us, Stan."

Stan's frowning face was thoughtful. "It's a temptation. She looks like a beautiful ship."

Sue watched him, thinking of the days—so long ago, it seemed to her—when she and Stan had sailed, gone swimming, fishing, sledding, skating with a group of other children—then, later, teenagers. Suddenly all of them had widely separated. She remembered, though, distinctly, the various expressions in his gray eyes. His dark eyebrows were drawn slightly together; she knew he was weighing a cruise on the luxurious yacht, with her fine engines, against some days of sailing, never very far from Sea Cove in his own little boat, the wayward little boat that had been Stan's pride and joy since he was fourteen.

"All right," he said suddenly. "I'll go. I'd like to, Monty. I have a long leave—long enough, I think. When do you sail?"

"Not till morning. There's a party of us. Sue and I are having dinner here at the Club. The others are joining us later tonight—anytime. We sail in the morning. Can you make it?"

"Sure. I'll just hustle over to Stratford and get some clothes."

"Don't bother. There're plenty of extra jeans and sweat shirts in the yacht."

"All the same—" Sue guessed what Stan was about to say; he had very strong ideas of what a lieutenant in the navy should wear on any kind of boat—ship, she corrected herself.

"Okay." Monty was always agreeable, at least almost always. "No, wait, I invited you to have dinner with us."

"Thank you. I guess not. Mom expects me home."

"Well, then, see you when? About eight or nine in the morning?"

Stan nodded briskly. "Sure. See you then. Good night, Sue. You're prettier than ever."

"Thank you, Stan."

Monty cut in. "Guess what she's been doing while you were running the navy."

"Being herself, I imagine. What have you been doing, Sue? Monty here looks as if he had a great secret."

"I *have*. That is, I expect I have," said Monty with an inner glow that Sue felt she might, just might, understand. Then another whiskey silently appeared on the table and diverted Monty.

A slightly puzzled look came into Stan's face. Sue said quickly, "I've taken training as a nurse—"

"A nurse!"

"Yes, of course. Why not? I didn't want to do nothing but sit around and—and do nothing," she finished inadequately.

"But—but a nurse? Has anything happened to your aunt?" He was too polite to add, "and the Gates money?"

Sue put him straight. "No, no. Aunt Addie is very well. Everything is fine. I'm a graduate nurse and like it and—" And feel as if I'm doing something important, she thought, but didn't say it.

"Well," said Stan, "good for you."

"You'll see Aunt Addie. She's going on this cruise. And some friends of Monty's. I've not seen the *Felice* yet—only from the pier. I'm very glad you are coming, too, Stan."

They rose as Sue saw from the corner of her eye yet another whiskey approaching. Monty was never really drunk, but sometimes he did, rather absently, drink a little too much. "We'd better eat," she said. "Your guests will be arriving, Monty."

He beckoned to a pleasant hovering waitress.

Stan was speaking to Monty. " . . . of course all the charts?"

"Oh, sure! We had intended just to jaunt along toward Montauk. Taking our time. Stopping whenever we wanted to. But with you I believe we can take the *Felice* out farther. The weather forecast is good. Now that I have a crew I think it would be more interesting to go around Montauk and then Cape Hatteras and—wait a minute! I've an idea! Now you are going to spell me, we'll go to Eleuthera. I told you I have a small place there."

Stan looked a little stunned. Monty was all but chortling. "I've been there only a few times. We may have to tie up at Nassau. Depends upon—oh, never mind. I'll phone right now to my caretaker and tell him to prepare for us. Get in supplies from Nassau, all that."

Stan said, "Well, I—that sounds a little ambitious. But with an ocean-going yacht, fine. You mean the outside ocean trip? Not the Inland Waterway?"

Winnie, without whom, Sue sometimes thought, the

Club couldn't function properly, came forward. "Your menu, Mr. Montgomery."

"Oh, yes. Thank you, Winnie." Monty was always polite. He replied to Stan, "Sure. The ocean. Not the Inland Waterway."

Stan looked serious. "What about your equipment? Besides the diesels," he added with a half-teasing, half-serious smile.

"Oh, everything's in order, I believe." Monty gestured expansively with one arm.

"Of course Eleuthera will mean quite a voyage."

"Oh, sure. But with good weather! Eight or nine in the morning?"

"Right, Captain," Stan bestowed the honorary title upon Monty, accompanied by a fine salute. Monty laughed and waved.

Stan put a firm hand upon Sue's shoulder. "You are really a sweetheart." He leaned over to give her a kiss. It was a kiss on the cheek, naturally, but hearty. "She was once kind of my girl," he added teasingly, his eyes dancing, almost as if he had said, "and still just might be."

Monty was too sure of himself to care; he chuckled. "Not for you, my boy—" But Stan had already started across the wide lounge, swinging along, stopping to speak to somebody as he went.

From the terrace they could look out at the lights on the water; there were few of them now. Almost all of the small sailing boats had come in at sunset and were anchored out in the quiet water of the shallow cove near the Club. Even the ferry, sturdily thumping from Long Island and back, had returned to home port.

As they were being seated in the dining room, several people there smiled and nodded; everybody liked Monty. Many, too, had spoken to Sue. Although it was warm and friendly, yet in its way, dignified.

"To tell you the truth," Monty said after he'd ordered

lobster for them both, "I'm glad Stan is going with us. Fact is, I've only had the *Felice* out for very short trips. Nothing as far as Eleuthera. I'm not sure I'd have been able to cope with Cape Hatteras on my own. I hear you never can tell exactly what the Cape will cook up. However, I have the weather reports. Should be accurate. If the guys that make them looked out the right window," he added sourly but then laughed and ordered champagne.

The lobster was excellent; the champagne was excellent; the dinner was excellent. Sue listened to Monty, who liked to talk and really not always of himself, she thought sternly. She enjoyed her dinner and the one glass of champagne she permitted herself. The hard grind of nurses' training, and the harder grind following it when she had undertaken nursing itself, had rather discouraged her about drinking. Yet she hadn't had any alcoholics to nurse, if one excluded dear Addie, her father's sister. Addie had cared for an orphaned Sue as if Sue had been her own daughter. The money, of course, had vanished somehow, but then there hadn't been that much to vanish in the first place.

"I expect Aunt Addie will be on the yacht by now," she told Monty as he negotiated his salad. "I phoned her before I took the train out from New York."

"Good. Want dessert? I do."

Rather to her disapproval, Monty ordered a large helping of ice cream with chocolate sauce and a huge piece of cake. Monty was a big man, only slightly beginning to show flesh, which he fought with riding and tennis. He caught her dubious glance and sighed. "Now, Sue, don't start to tell me what to eat. Not just yet."

She ignored the implication. "Never. I promise." It was impossible to disagree with Monty when he laughed and his eyelids wrinkled up so charmingly over his blue eyes.

They had finished dinner and were crossing the big lounge when Monty snapped his fingers. "Forgot. I must phone to the man on Eleuthera. Only a few minutes—" He disappeared.

She went to the entrance and sat down; from there she could see the parking lot and the cars and had just a glimpse of the *Felice*. Portholes were lighted; she wondered what it was like inside. She had known a few small boats; she had never been on a big luxurious yacht.

Monty liked luxury. She knew that about him. Indeed, she knew many things about him, for he had been around the Club on occasions for some time. Yet she had known him intimately for only a few months. Not even that long, she reminded herself. He had broken an ankle skating at Rockefeller Plaza only the past March. He had happened to be sent to the hospital where by then she was working full time, a graduate nurse. She had happened to be assigned to the wing where he lay, fretted, read books, read the *Wall Street Journal,* and disagreed, but in a friendly way, with the doctors, even Dr. Smith, who all but ruled the entire hospital.

He had recognized Sue at once as she had recognized him. They had become rather friendly even while he was in the hospital (anything beyond a polite degree of friendliness was sternly discouraged there). But then he had been dismissed and immediately had gone south on business, he told her later. When he returned he got her address and telephone number from Aunt Addie, and, Sue thought, the rest is history.

Or about to be history.

She was intensely aware of the possibility that this cruise was intended to signal a big change in their relationship. She couldn't have missed Monty's few, yet pointed, hints. Indeed, it was time for her to face it: she felt in her bones that he was about to ask her to marry him. And if he did—why, if he did, there was just one answer, and she intended to give it.

During the recent weekend she had spent with Addie in the charming cottage her aunt had bought near Stratford, Addie had made it clear. "This cruise settles it," Addie had said happily. "Another sherry, dear?"

She shook her head at the sherry and eyed Addie's pretty face, only a little flushed, rather worriedly. Addie really must not indulge so frequently and so generously in drinking—any kind of alcoholic drinking, Sue thought rather grimly.

Addie's pansy-brown eyes were dreamy. "It's a real Cinderella story. Rags to riches."

Addie was very likely to burst into quotations, songs or platitudes, unfortunately many of them a bit muddled or not quite accurate, when she had had a drop or two too many.

Sue had looked down at herself and the suit she had recently bought with her newly acquired earnings. "Not rags, Addie dear, I do hope. If so, I've been cheated."

"Looks Chanel," said Addie over the rim of her glass. Not sherry this time, but Sue couldn't be sure just what it was and listened as the dog, Toughy, burst into uproarious barking. "Never mind, it *looks* Chanel," repeated Addie, reading Sue's negative reaction. "Now, if that's your taxi, he'll wait a minute. That train is usually late on Sunday nights anyway. Now, my dear, don't try to evade. You know perfectly well why Monty has invited you and me on a lovely, lovely cruise in his beautiful, beautiful new yacht—"

"Not new," Sue had mumbled, reaching for handbag and gloves.

"Never mind. A cruise. And he's going to ask you, and you are going to say yes and—" Not unexpectedly, she began to carol. " 'Happy the bride the sun shines on today.' Or any day if it's you." She sobered and in high time, too. "My dear, I'd never tell you to marry for money. But . . ." Addie sighed and pushed one rosily manicured hand through her softly waved hair, once a golden brown and now lightly frosted. She settled her dress, a long black-velvet hostess gown, grown rather shabby and napworn. She wore pearls, too, but Sue had reason to know she had long ago sold the real pearls that had come from her mother, Sue's grandmother, and replaced them with an almost palpably false string. But she was still dear, charming Addie, who was much smarter than she pretended to be. Women, Addie had told her, must never try to be intelligent; hide any grain of sense you have— that is, if you ever want to marry.

Having smoothed down her dress as she rose, she went on, "I was about to say money simply always is a help. Not, Sue, that I would ever advise you—"

"I know. I know. Thank you, darling. I must go. See you—"

Addie's pretty face beamed. "At the yacht."

"And Addie . . . that is . . ." Sue's glance went to the cupboard where Addie kept sundry but sometimes rather a number of bottles.

Addie guessed what she wanted to say. "My dear child, I never, never do."

Sue swallowed an unkind reply; she said mildly, "Be sure the fire is out at night. It's very nice these chilly nights but . . . and be sure the doors are locked."

"Yes, yes, I'll see you. Be sure to bring some sport clothes. Oh, yes, and tennis shoes. Sue—he's going to ask you, I just know he is. Otherwise why would he have invited me? And Lalie, too? I don't know all the guests, but it really does seem a formal kind of affair. I mean, almost like an announcement in itself."

"I don't know . . . I'm not sure. . . ."

Addie's face showed everything. It almost crumpled now with fear. "Sue, you can't miss such an opportunity! What have you got against Monty? He's wonderful—"

"And rich," Sue said and then wished she hadn't. "Never mind, Aunt Addie. I'll be sensible."

Addie took that for agreement. Sue added, "But perhaps I'll not have a chance. I really haven't the least idea—"

"Come on now," Addie put her hands on Sue's and

lifted her pink cheek for her niece's kiss. "You do know. In your heart. He must have given all sorts of indications."

Sue had said good night as the ancient Airedale's bark reached a crescendo and she heard the wheezing taxi stop with a squeal of brakes. She ran out to the picket fence, stopped at the gate to wave back to the little, if rather plump, figure in the lighted doorway, and went on her way. Back to New York, back to her rather Spartan room near the hospital, back to the hospital, and there she began to look forward to the cruise.

Would he—or wouldn't he? And if he did, what about her answer? Sometime in that stretch of the past three weeks, during which she saw Monty frequently, was wined and dined, and taken to the theater and dancing, and sent flowers by him, she had decided what her answer would be. That is, if he really meant to ask her to marry him. Don't count your chickens, she told herself crossly, as Monty appeared again. He was in high good humor.

"Finally got him. Everything is fixed. You'll like my little shack on the island."

They went down the steps to the circular driveway. At one side, below them, tied up, was the *Felice*; Sue had a glimpse of people in the salon. So, some of the guests had arrived.

Actually, the yacht rode so high that they could have taken a long step from the pier directly to the *Felice*'s deck. Juan, however, had put down a small teak gangway and stood by, grinning; all his teeth glistened as brightly white as his coat. As they came into the lighted salon, a little dog ran up and nudged Monty's ankles.

Two

Monty uttered a very hard and angry word; his face flushed red as he stopped and snatched up the dog. "Cut it out!"

The dog gave him one liquid brown look and wriggled happily, wagging her tail and making small affectionate sounds. She was a miniature French poodle, not too well brushed but, now, obviously, very happy.

A woman said, "Sorry, Monty. She does love you."

"Fine way of showing it," Monty growled. He seemed to be extremely annoyed. Then Sue realized that he was trying not to show real anger. She looked at the woman who was strolling toward them.

"Juan made me welcome. He did say that I wasn't on his list, but he knew you'd make me welcome, too," the woman said lightly and looked at Sue.

Sue suddenly felt very youthful, gauche and badly dressed in her simple blue cotton frock with its neat collar, for the woman advancing was slim, beautiful, with wide dark eyes and thick dark hair done up smoothly. She was dressed perfectly—white slacks and shirt, and neither could have spoken the name of a famous designer more explicitly.

"Aren't you going to introduce me, Monty?" she asked in a rather deep voice.

Monty flushed redder. Then he said, awkwardly for Monty, "Mrs. Hadley—"

The lovely woman interrupted charmingly. "But I know: Why, it's little Sue Gates! I remember you: Don't you know me? Celia Hadley? My dear." She put out a hand, which had a surprisingly strong grip. Sue took it.

"Yes, of course. It's just that I haven't seen you for so long."

14

Celia Hadley laughed lightly. "Not since I married and moved away. You were in your teens then."

Sue did vaguely remember Celia Hadley, who wasn't Celia Hadley before her marriage, but she couldn't remember her husband. Monty broke in, "Come along, Sue; here is your Aunt Addie. And Mr. Wiley."

They were seated in the salon. Addie was smiling. Mr. Wiley was looking rather glum and twisting one end of a small gray mustache, which had of all things, stiffly waxed ends zooming up toward his cheekbones and suggesting a dandy of, say, the nineties.

Mrs. Hadley used a lovely scent; it floated out gently but pervasively. "I really didn't know that Monty had planned such a party." She turned to Monty. "I do hope I'm not intruding. Juan seemed so certain that I would be welcome."

"Surely," Monty said in his throat, "surely," and advanced toward Addie. "My dear . . ."

Addie put down a glass (a gesture that gave Sue a little tweak of apprehension) and extended a hand toward Monty, who wasn't satisfied with the hand but bent and kissed her. Addie said vaguely, "I don't know who this gentleman is. He says he sold you the yacht."

"Of course! How are you, Wiley?" Monty was recovering from his moment of anger. "Glad your doctor let you come."

The uninvited guest looked at Sue; her eyes were not friendly. They were hard as steel and measured Sue as if she knew the exact fabric in the blue dress, the exact tint of her lipstick, and how much each had cost.

The little poodle sat down and scratched behind one ear. Celia Hadley said, "Sissy's quite accustomed to the yacht, of course. I don't know why she should jump at Monty like that. Just high spirits."

Monty, talking to Wiley, heard the comment and said shortly over his shoulder, "She jumped at me because she doesn't like sailing. She gets seasick."

So, Sue thought, it couldn't be clearer that both the dog and her owner had made at least a few trips on the *Felice*.

Addie rose, surging with a little difficulty out of her chair and walking only a little unsteadily across to the glass shelves of the bar. "I think I'll just have a nightcap...."

She was slightly vague, yet quite in command of herself, a little plump, perhaps, sagging a little at the chin, but displaying indestructible charm. Oh, dear, Sue thought! I do hope she's not off to the races. What will the night, what will the cruise hold?

Sue went to her. "Darling, I'm very tired. Let's go to bed. We'll see about our cabins."

"Of course ... yes, to be sure ... bed ..."

Addie, wavering only the slightest bit but clutching a newly filled glass in one dimpled hand, came with Sue. The glass joggled and splashed a little on Addie's pale-pink sports dress. She giggled softly.

Outside the salon, Juan's head was bent as he scrutinized the tags on a stack of suitcases and garment bags. He looked puzzled, Sue thought, as he looked at a list in his hand, clearly trying to coordinate each guest's baggage with each guest's name. His large dark eyes lifted as she spoke to him and the shade of perplexity deepened. He said, however, "Yes, Señorita—oh, your cabins? This way."

Celia's little dog came and sniffed at Sue's ankles. Monty came up beside them and said, "More guests may be arriving, Juan."

Behind her Juan said, "Yes, Señor Captain. Everything all right, Señor Captain?" He smoothed down his white jacket.

Monty frowned. "I don't like the look of Mr. Wiley. It's lucky his doctor is coming, too. I think the doctor ought to go in my big cabin, C, with Mr. Wiley."

"Yes, Señor Captain."

"Another guest will be joining us in the morning. Lieutenant Brooke. And then—well, perhaps another guest with him. That would make us pretty full. I may have to take your cabin, Juan.''

Juan made the gesture of an agreeable bow, which wasn't really a bow. ''I can take the hammock. This way, please, Miss—I mean, Señorita.''

Sue had had time for only a quick impression of much gleaming mahogany in the salon, deeply cushioned chairs, the glittering bar, and Addie. Clearly the first thing for Sue to do was to get Addie to her bed. She was a darling, even if she had succumbed to one sad comfort for lonely women. She was never boisterous, she was never quarrelsome or unpleasant; she merely, smilingly, drank. It had begun so quietly that Sue had only now and then noticed that Addie was increasingly vague. But as her nursing education went on, she was forced to accept the plain fact that Addie had become a home drunk—not secretly, really, just too often addressing herself to any kind of alcoholic nourishment that her dimpled, still very white and lovely hands could grasp.

It was, Sue knew by then, not unusual. All the same, after her marriage (if indeed there was to be a marriage to Monty) she could certainly look after Addie more effectively than she had been able to do so far.

Monty was at her elbow. ''Juan will show you the way, Sue. Come back when—come back later.''

Yes, Monty knew, too. But everyone liked Addie, who now waved her glass and said vaguely, ''You can't be seasick on a boat this size, can you? At least not where we're going. Oh—'' Her velvety brown eyes were wide and troubled. ''Where are we going, Monty?''

He smiled good-naturedly. ''I'll tell you all about it in the morning. Now, good night, my dear.''

Juan said, ''This way, Señorita. This way.''

Even though Sue had never been on the *Felice* before, she had been prepared for elegance, but not quite on the scale that was revealed as she and Addie, who was clinging to her arm with one hand and to the glass with the other, followed Juan. There were glimpses of some small cabins, rather like old-fashioned Pullman bedrooms but equipped with shining chromium plumbing and mahogany wherever there could be mahogany. Everywhere, too, were colors: a soft green along what she was to learn to call the bulkheads; chairs and curtains showing floral but shiny— probably waterproof nylon—material that looked like chintz in the tiny niche of a cabin into which Juan ushered Addie. Again he consulted the list in one swarthy hand. "This for Miss Gates. Cabin B." He knew which Miss Gates was intended, for his black eyes singled out Addie and he carried in Addie's small dressing case and large garment bag, putting them down on a luggage rack with the loving care he might have given a baby. "Your stateroom, A, is farther along, Miss," he said, this time definitely to Sue.

There was barely room in Addie's cabin for one small but comfortable-looking chair. Addie sank down into it and lifted her pretty face and large eyes to Juan. "You are so kind. Thank you so much."

The charm and feminine appeal in her soft voice and flattering gaze did not warm Juan's dark face. "If there is anything you wish, only press that button. I'll come at once."

There was a tiny button beside the door. All the luxuries, Sue thought, rather amused. Addie smiled and dimpled and murmured vaguely, and Sue herself contrived to murmur in Juan's ear as he turned away, "Please, Juan, nothing!" She lifted her hand slightly toward her mouth, and she was sure that he understood, although he only said, "Your cabin is this way, Miss Gates. Oh! There's that dog."

There was the dog frisking happily along ahead of them. Juan muttered something under his breath and brushed past Sue to reach for the dog, but Sissy escaped him, scampering through an open door at the end of the passage. Juan was angry. "That little—I'll get her—"

He ran after the dog. She followed and looked into the cabin. "Mine? It's beautiful!"

Juan's white teeth glittered. He had grasped Sissy and was holding her tightly as she uttered a small sound of remonstrance and wriggled.

"Señor Captain wanted you to have this cabin. He thought you would wish to be alone."

"But it's so big!" Sue looked around. The cabin was all soft yellow and gray, with two narrow but real beds bolted solidly to the floor, a tiny bedside table, a dressing table with drawers and, also bolted down, a chair and a short chaise longue.

Juan clutched Sissy. "There is nothing like it on board. Usually the Señor Captain uses that one next door, Cabin C. Tonight Mr. Wiley will use it. Now I'll sort out your bags, Miss Gates, and bring them to you."

"Thank you—" But Juan was sliding away swiftly; a disgusted whine from Sissy floated back.

She would wait a few moments and make sure that Addie was quiet. She sat down in the deep chair. The bolted furniture didn't really bother her with its suggestion of rough seas. She could only observe the extreme luxury and after a while think what a lucky girl anyone would be if she had in fact taken the fancy—no, no, the love—of a man like Monty.

Lights had been turned on above the built-in dressing table and drawers. One bed, she observed with disbelief, had already been neatly turned down; the sheet and pale-yellow blanket cover had a monogram, however, that certainly wasn't Monty's. She deciphered a W, intertwined with some other letters. So when he bought the yacht, Monty had also taken over not only Juan but all the furnishings, including the linens. Mr. Wiley had offered it; Monty had paid for it—just like that, she supposed. When Monty liked anything, he acted at once.

She wondered briefly how old the yacht could be. There was an odd but definite impression of outdated but well-preserved elegance in the mahogany and teak woodwork and panels. And something about the style of chairs and dressing table, the chintz patterns of the upholstery, belied the undoubtedly new chromium that glittered from a tiny adjoining bathroom, a shower neatly wedged in an unbelievably small space.

The diesel engines Monty had spoken of with pride must have been new. But there was something about the entire atmosphere that suggested huge, lavish cruises, extravagant days when people owned and used elaborately decorated yachts. The bar itself was an anachronism; she remembered her quick glimpse of it—a huge, built-in, mahogany cupboard with glass doors and many glasses and bottles. Probably, she hoped, it was kept locked when not in use.

There were sounds from the salon; voices, but far away. Some late boat, arriving cautiously along the Sound, gave a warning toot. Sue paused at the mirror to give her hair attention and then went out to Addie's cabin and peeked in. Her aunt was already asleep, long eyelashes on her pink cheeks, and making very light, almost musical little sounds that couldn't precisely be called snores. She tiptoed in, took a light eiderdown from its rack, and put it cautiously over Addie's feet. But the slight motion roused her aunt; her pansy-brown eyes opened and she gave Sue a hazy yet sensible look and said, "Monty's mistress."

"What—"

"She invited herself."

"Addie! What on earth—"

"Didn't you see how surprised Monty was and how angry? Really, Sue!"

"No. That is . . . Addie, you did say—"

Her aunt propped herself up on one elbow. "Of course. Celia Hadley. I invet-invet—that is—" She couldn't pronounce "investigation," so she substituted, "I asked around about him. Soon as I began to see what was on his mind. Oh, yes, she was his mistress. Has been for years. Now I'm going to sleep."

"No. Wait. Do you know what you said?"

The velvety eyes opened wider. "Certainly I know. She didn't like your coming. Didn't you see that? I expect she knows all about you and Monty."

"There's nothing yet to—" She stopped. Addie had shut her eyes.

Sue took a breath and said shortly, "Look at me! How did she know—I mean how did she happen to come to the yacht? Aunt Addie, please answer me."

Addie opened one eye and yawned. "Lalie told me. That is, I knew about Celia and Monty, so when Lalie and Celia arrived at the same time I did—here at the yacht, I mean—I got Lalie aside. She—Celia—had been staying with Lalie. At Monty's house in the Weston hills. So when Celia heard that Lalie was going on a trip on the yacht, she—" Addie blinked the open eye. "I suppose she just decided to come, too. I'm perfectly sure of her reasons. She's scared. She's heard about you. She wants to stop your marriage to Monty."

"But Aunt Addie, listen. There may not be a marriage."

Both her aunt's eyes flew open. She sat up with a jerk. "You can't mean you refused him!"

"I mean he hasn't asked me!"

"If he hasn't asked you, it's all your fault. Really, Sue! How can you be so—so—" she took a deep breath—"so chilly. I could have wrangled—I mean gotten—something definite out of him long ago."

"You should talk, you never married," Sue said.

But Addie had the best of her. "That's my business. Now you listen to me! You're not to let that Celia come between you and Monty. I think I'll go to sleep now."

This time she fell back, plump and pretty, snuggled her face into the pillow.

Sue stood looking down at her. *In vino veritas?* But that old saying did not always hold true with Addie. There was usually some basis of fact in Addie's account of any situation; however, she did add dramatics if she felt like it. Clearly Addie had felt that Celia had been, until that night, nothing that need concern Sue. Yes, that was the way Addie would reason. She was kind, innocent in a way, guileful in other ways.

Suddenly Addie opened one eye again. "Don't you care?"

"I—I don't really know. Are you sure, Addie?"

"Certainly. I told you." The other eye opened, and Addie hoisted herself up on one elbow again. "I think you should have Monty get rid of her. Get her off the boat. The idea! Coming here like that! You act as if you don't care at all." This was reproachful; Sue's was not at all a romantic reaction in Addie's view and certainly not moral.

Sue sighed. "Why should I care?"

Addie blushed. "Now, Sue! Don't act so—so—well, don't," she said, making her meaning perfectly clear.

But I *don't* care, Sue thought. She said aloud, "Addie, dear, it's really none of my business."

Addie shut her eyes again and fell back. "I simple don't understand you. It's all that nurses' training! I suppose the modern girl just thinks nothing of her husband's other women."

"Darling, he's not my husband."

"He's going to be. Unless you do something stupid. Surely you don't want your later life cluttered up with former—" she checked herself for a moment, as if trying to think of an appropriate description, and finished triumphantly, "his castoff girl friends."

"Oh, Addie, honestly, I don't think anything like that would be a bother. Now do go to sleep."

Her aunt opened both eyes again to give her a reproachful glare, closed them, and at once began to utter little whistling sounds.

She turned out the bedside lamp and went back to her own cabin.

After a while, as she waited to make sure Addie would not fumble out of her cabin and make for the bar, it occurred to her that perhaps she ought to have cared, been indignant, indicating, but tactfully, to Monty that he must get rid of Celia—or anybody he might have been on, say, very affectionate terms with in the past. The fact was, however, she really didn't care. And certainly she had no right even to hint at a knowledge of Celia's past in Monty's life. Not yet, anyway.

However muddled Addie could at times become, there was a convincing indication of truth to her comments. The little dog had gone like a streak to the big choice cabin. So then, Celia had occupied that cabin, at least at times, Sue thought with a wave of half-amused, half-wry cynicism. It was no business of hers—but nevertheless she couldn't think it in good taste for Celia to accompany them on the cruise.

On the other hand, if a woman makes a determined effort to keep the attention of a good-looking (and very rich) man, who could blame her? Only natural, said Sue to herself. But she did not intend to enter into a drawn battle with Celia for Monty. She braced herself against such rivalry and went back toward the salon.

Juan was again at the entrance, scrutinizing lists and baggage, and as she passed he gave a peculiarly surprised, yet low, exclamation that sounded like "I'm right—can't be, but I'm right—"

"What's that, Juan?" she asked.

"What?" He blinked at her and then showed his white teeth. "Oh, nothing, Miss—I mean, Señorita—nothing at all."

The salon ran across the width of the yacht. It had everything: sofas, tables, deep chairs, the handsome old-fashioned bar, and more people, for there had been new arrivals. The room seemed suddenly crowded. Monty's half sister, Lalie Montgomery, sat on a sofa, idly twirling one of Sissy's long ears in her jeweled fingers. She was barely eighteen and occasionally looked a hard forty, mainly because of her excessive thinness. But she and

Monty had had the same father and shared a certain determined, fair likeness. She lifted her head toward Sue, nodded and waved one hand. Celia stood like a presiding and knowledgeable hostess beside a kind of buffet table that stood near the bar; she was holding a tray of caviar and biscuits toward a man whose back was turned to Sue.

But she knew that back. She knew the crisp, gray hair and the sturdy shoulders; she even knew the set of his tweed jacket, although she had, as a rule, seen him only in a doctor's white coat. It was her own Dr. Smith.

She quickly amended that; he was not her doctor, he was her boss. He headed the big, well-known hospital where she had taken training. Monty, officiating at the bar, called her. "Sue, my dear. Come and speak to Dr. Smith—"

The doctor turned at his name, blinked for a second and, to Sue's great pleasure, recognized her. "Why, it's—it's little, little—I mean it's—" Obviously he was fishing for her name.

She supplied it. "Sewell Gates, sir. That is, Sue Gates."

She could not have helped the "sir"; it was automatic. But Dr. Smith put out his hand. "Why, certainly. A good girl." He turned to Monty. "How very nice to see this child! Friend of yours, of course. I remember—yes, she lived near Sea Cove. I do try to keep up with our nurses and their backgrounds—don't always make it." He turned to Mr. Wiley. "You didn't tell me what a party this was to be. I expected to see only you and your—our—host. Just a short cruise, you said, time to look you over and—" The doctor shrugged. "And give me a bit of rest."

"Something you need," said Mr. Wiley.

His Christian name proved to be Sam, for Monty said, "Now, Sam, surely you told the doctor there would be a party. Just a little party because the boat's sleeping accommodations are limited. I'm delighted that you could join us, Doctor."

Sam Wiley sighed. "So am I," he said with such sincerity that his tone struck Sue. Aside from the gallant mustache, he did not look well. His pleasant, polite manner did not agree with certain signs of illness, such as his pallor and the tired lines of his face below huge bushy eyebrows that seemed to be doing their best to compensate for the scant hair on his head. Heart? Something she wasn't wise enough even to guess. But clearly Dr. Smith had come at Wiley's request and Monty's invitation.

Monty said cheerfully (and perhaps not very tactfully), "But after all, Doctor, Sam does plan to give you that new wing for your hospital."

Sam Wiley smiled. "But not until he manages to kill me off!" he said jocularly.

Dr. Smith smiled thinly at the well-worn joke. Wiley continued, "Monty helped. I'm sure I told you. He bought this yacht. I felt that my real yachting days were over. And I must say he paid a fancy price for the *Felice*." Something snapped with a crystal tinkle somewhere nearby.

Three

The sound was close enough to Sue so she looked at the table near the bar. Celia was picking up a champagne glass, its tulip shape intact but the stem broken. No one else, except perhaps Lalie, had heard or noted the tiny sharp clink. At the mention of the probable price Monty had paid for the yacht?

I'm imagining this, Sue thought, and wished that Addie had kept her pretty mouth shut, at least on the subject of Celia.

Lalie stirred; her firm chin and her blue-gray, determined eyes were startlingly like Monty's. "What's next on your schedule, Monty, now that you've got a yacht? Marriage, maybe? Are you thinking of marriage, Monty?"

Are you indeed? Sue thought and looked down into her glass.

No one seemed to show the slightest interest in Lalie's observation. Only Sue felt her pulse quicken a little, but she thought, That's only Lalie trying to tease Monty. But he ignored it, too. Lalie giggled. "You don't have to tell me—"

Monty broke in. "I do wish you would dress properly."

Lalie surged up angrily. "I'm fully clothed!" She was not precisely factual, for she wore a ruffled chiffon blouse with nothing underneath, which lack was abundantly evident, above very tight jeans. "It's high time you married, Monty. Get some of the starch out of you. I'm going to marry—soon as I meet somebody with the right idea. I'm getting old!"

Monty laughed. "You are eighteen—"

"Well, then," said Lalie. "Time I married."

"Not any of those good-for-nothing, jeaned, long-haired specimens you take riding. And drinking!"

Lalie shrugged and changed the subject. "I'm going to bed. I don't see why you have to leave so early in the morning."

Monty had conquered his little flare of temper. He said good-naturedly, "Because we want to get to Montauk. And then—we'll see." He turned to Sam Wiley. "You assured me this is an ocean-going yacht. I'm counting on it."

Sam Wiley nodded. "Oh, yes. I've taken her up and down the coast—the Keys, Miami, Fort Lauderdale, back to Palm Beach. I had a two-man crew for those trips, though. And, of course, Juan."

"We're going to have a crew," Monty said, pleased. "He's to come aboard in the morning, early."

Lalie, in the doorway, checked herself. "Good-looking?"

Monty returned to his brotherly or, more precisely, avuncular manner. "You'd say anything in pants is good-looking. But . . ." He hesitated. "Yes. I think he might be called good-looking. You think so, Sue?"

"Who? Oh, Stan! Why, yes. Very much so."

Dr. Smith yawned without bothering to disguise it. "I think I'll recommend that Wiley and I go to bed, if you please, Monty."

Monty sprang to his duties as host. "Of course. Yes. You two are to share my own stateroom. Juan will show you. But first how about some champagne, everybody? Just a nightcap."

"Not for me," Wiley said, tweaked a corner of his mustache, and gave a sour look at Dr. Smith.

Lalie, in the passage talking to Juan, heard the word "champagne" and came back instantly. Dr. Smith said good night briskly to Monty and Sue, made a kind of bow to Celia, and held a steadying hand at Wiley's elbow as they moved toward Juan. For the first time Sue felt the slightest, smallest unsteadiness, which betokened the fact that the *Felice* was a yacht and moving a little, like a breath, upon the placid water near the Club. Monty got out more glasses and took a bottle of champagne from Celia, who had known exactly where to find it. He opened it dexterously, but the pop sounded like a gunshot. Sissy didn't like that and gave a sharp bark.

Monty poured the champagne—which was exactly the right temperature, cold and sparkling—and Sue let him fill her glass a second time as Lalie and Monty discussed the cruise, the facilities of the yacht, the arrival of Dr. Smith.

"He is Wiley's doctor. In fact, I sent him to Dr. Smith. I had heard of him and his distinguished career and then met him while I was in the hospital. He promised to go on this cruise, not for a rest for himself," Monty said, "and not for that new wing Wiley appears to have promised him sometime either. Simply out of friendship. And, of course, his concern for a patient."

"And concern for that man Wiley's money," Lalie said, red lips at her glass.

Celia had quietly retreated to a sofa, where she sat, saying nothing, yet, Sue felt, missing nothing.

Monty refilled her glass almost before she realized it was empty. Lalie began to chatter about Monty's country house; Monty told her of the change of plans for the cruise. Lalie was delighted. "Eleuthera! Oh, Monty! Great! You'll love it, Sue, Celia."

Celia smiled smugly, it seemed to Sue. Quite as if she already knew Eleuthera. Lalie continued to question Monty about his place there. Monty replied rather shortly.

Sue herself began to feel the effect of a big dinner and more champagne than probably she had ever had at one time in her life. She did have the strength of mind to refuse a fourth glass, to say good night to Celia—extra politely, so it sounded frozen—then to Lalie, who grinned to her and raised her glass toward Monty; she went out, toward her cabin. She almost ran into Juan, who was leaning against the bulkhead in deep thought. "Oh, sorry, Señorita." He righted himself and also, Sue was rather shocked to find, righted her. She—or the yacht—was really a little unsteady. Juan said, "Take my arm, Miss Gates. There's a rail. Seems the tide is coming in."

Once in her cabin, with its reassuring bolted-down chair, she turned to thank Juan.

"Not at all," Juan said absently.

Sue clasped the back of a chair. "Juan, you don't sound like . . . like . . ."

Juan's dark eyes gleamed. "No. Not Chicano. Merely part Spanish. From San Francisco I was attracted to Florida. Palm Beach. Mr. Wiley suited me. I've been with him four years."

"You do seem Spanish or . . . or . . ." she said awkwardly.

He showed white teeth. "I know. I throw in a few 'Señors' and 'Señoritas' and gesture with my hands and—oh, anything that occurs to me. People seem to like it."

Sue laughed, amused. "Stage dressing?"

"Precisely. Is there anything I can get for you?"

"Oh, no. To tell you the truth, Juan, I think I've had too much already."

"Not at all, Miss. Thank you." He started away, then turned back briefly. "*Vaya con Dios.* Do you understand that?"

It was an odd thing to say, she felt, but didn't try to analyze it. Instead, she drew upon her slight stock of Spanish phrases and said, "*Muchas gracias. Buenas noches,* Juan," and closed the door.

The murmur of voices from the large salon seemed very far away. She found that Juan had unpacked for her, laying out a nightdress, a dressing gown and slippers.

It was a good thing she was going to bed without that fourth glass of champagne. She supposed she ought to do some serious thinking about Celia Hadley. But if Sue ever married Monty it must be a marriage entered into with sincerity and respect. It must have nothing to do with the fact that he was rich. In her heart, she knew that for some years her aunt had been learning the importance of money; probably Addie was thinking ahead of her own imminent old age and Sue's doubtful power to earn.

However, there was no use in crossing bridges or counting chickens. Monty had never definitely mentioned marriage and might never mention it.

But if he did, she wouldn't let Celia stand in her way!

That settled in her mind, rather hazily, perhaps, she crawled into bed.

Her cabin was on the right—the starboard side, she told herself, feeling obscurely pleased because she managed to remember that. Once in bed, she drew open the curtain beside her and opened the delicately shuttered shade. She could see part of the Club; there still seemed to be a handful of cars in the parking lot.

A tall, swiftly moving figure that looked like Monty vanished into the Club. She closed the curtains.

She was asleep when there was a low knock on the

door; she roused slightly as Monty opened the door and quickly came in, closing the door behind him.

"Awake?" he said in a very low voice.

"Yes. That is, I guess so."

He sat down on the edge of the bed. "You didn't turn out your bedlight. I thought you'd be awake."

"I'm not. Not really, Monty. I had too much champagne."

"Won't hurt you. Now then, are you sensible enough to understand me?"

She nodded and pushed back her hair. He leaned over, quite near. "Sue, I'd just like to say one thing. I don't want Celia here. I didn't invite her. Lalie shouldn't have brought her. I'll get rid of her."

He was waiting for her reply, so she said, rather inadequately, "Oh."

"You do understand me."

"Oh, yes. That is—" She must be polite and friendly. "It is a lovely party. It's going to be a lovely cruise."

He did smile then. "All right. Go back to sleep." He leaned over, kissed her hard but swiftly, snapped out the bedside light and left. She heard the door close softly through the darkness and went to sleep again, after resolving not to duel with Celia and never, never to drink so much champagne again. She didn't intend to become another Addie. She must keep a strict eye on her tomorrow, for the entire cruise. The lovely cruise, she thought cozily, and slept.

It was not a lovely cruise.

In the first place, a heavy fog had crept in during the night and blanketed the Club, the Sound, everything, with an almost impenetrable gray veil and must have given the weather forecasters, who had predicted fair and clear weather, an unpleasant surprise.

There had also been a more than slight altercation between Stan Brooke and Monty about leaving, but Sue knew nothing of that at the time. In spite of this, however, when Sue struggled out of sleep, she became aware of the motion of the boat and the remote, steady throb of engines. So they had started.

The champagne she'd had the previous night hadn't affected her as much as she had believed. Her head was perfectly clear, her eyes bright in the mirror over the dressing table. She had been, simply and completely, very tired.

A flicker of uneasiness touched her at the thought of Addie. It might have been better to leave her at home; but, no, propriety, in Monty's eyes, demanded Addie's presence. Besides, Monty was truly fond of Addie.

Celia's presence might put a kind of damper on the cruise. But Monty had told Sue the night before that he intended to get Celia off the yacht before they sailed. Hadn't he said that? She had been half asleep, but she was sure of that.

It was a small shock when she came into the freshly straightened, neat salon to find Celia still there, holding a magazine and looking out one of the windows (portholes, Sue reminded herself) into the thick grayness beyond.

Celia turned. "Oh, it's you. Breakfast is over there." She nodded toward the buffet table. There was an appetizing scent of bacon, or ham, muffins and coffee in the air. Two small tables had been set up with linens and dishes and silver.

Celia noted her look and said, "Juan is a good cook. Besides his other gifts. You might as well eat, you know. That is—I promise you I'm not going to make any scenes. But—" said Celia abruptly, putting down her magazine, "if you think you can get Monty away from me, you can think again."

Sue thought back to Celia's wedding. Celia must be in her early thirties now, for that was at least ten years ago. She could see herself wearing a suitable dress-up dress, seated with Addie. Celia had looked stunningly beautiful in her white lace gown and veil. Sue still could not remember her husband; somewhere, somehow he seemed to have disappeared—death, divorce, she couldn't recall. Celia hadn't been a part of the life Sue had known as she grew up, discovered the dangerous state of Gates finances and determined upon training to be a nurse because her practical mind suggested that there was always a need for nurses. Nurses and dentists.

Celia sounded faintly exasperated, as if she were talking to a child. "Didn't you hear me?"

"What? Oh, yes. Yes . . ."

"Aren't you going to say something?"

Sue considered it. "No."

Celia blinked. Sue filled a plate and sat down at one of the little tables. Celia said presently, "I can't understand you."

"By the way, where are we?"

"Out in the Sound," Celia replied after a moment. "I saw a very good-looking young man come aboard early. Shirt and jeans, but Monty told me that he is real navy."

Sue drank her coffee. "Oh, he is. On leave."

"You know him?"

"Certainly. Why, you ought to know him, too, Celia. But then you've been away so long."

"What's his name?"

"Stan Brooke."

"Where does he live?" Celia sounded very snappish.

"In Stratford." She wished that Celia would relax into at least reasonably polite speech. Luckily the dog, Sissy, came dancing in, and Celia scooped her up under one arm. "All right—all right. I'll take you on deck in a minute."

Sue looked up. "Are you landing?"

"Landing? In the middle of the Sound! What are you talking about? I'm going on this cruise all the way, of course."

I don't think you are, Sue thought but prudently did not say so and went to the buffet, where she supplied herself with more ham and crisp muffins. As she was loading her plate and thinking of her appetite rather smugly—for if it was any indication, she really couldn't have got into a state of intoxication the previous night— Monty and a man in a gray business suit, wearing eyeglasses and carrying a brief case, appeared. Monty smiled and waved good morning in Sue's direction. The other man gave her a searching look through glittering spectacles. Then both went on, it developed, toward the cabin Monty was using. Juan was following them.

Celia said sharply, "Who was that man carrying a brief case?"

"I haven't the faintest idea."

"He came aboard this morning with that young Stan Brooke."

"Monty must know him."

"Obviously. And Juan was carrying a typewriter! Well..." Celia caught up a light pink raincoat from the back of her chair and took herself and Sissy out. Sue finished her coffee, brooded for a second about necessary arrangements for a dog on the yacht, and then guiltily about Addie, who would probably be having a real hangover.

The low throb of the engines and the very slight motion of the yacht kept steadily on. Sue went to see Addie.

Juan trudged along just ahead of her down what Sue's landlubber mind wished to think of as a hall, one, however, with rails on both sides. She felt that there must be a nautical term. A passage? A corridor? And stairs were ladders, weren't they? It would be wiser for her to stick to "corridor" and "stairs."

Juan was carrying what looked like a large tool bag; he went on, his white shoulders and heavily bushy black head clear in the tiny light along the passage, down to her own cabin—no, not to her cabin, the one beside it. He knocked lightly. As he did, he turned, saw her, and said, "Good morning, Miss. Breakfast all right?"

"Good morning. Yes, a fine breakfast." Oddly, she wondered why she felt a little, only a tinge, of discomfort around Juan. No apparent reason. He hitched up the heavy bag he carried and, unexpectedly, explained it. "Oxygen. The doctor says Mr. Wiley must have it. Fog, you see, makes it hard for him to breathe." Surely there was a flash of something cold in his dark eyes. "Me, I have always taken care of Mr. Wiley. Now it's the doctor—"

"But Juan, he's a fine doctor. A great cardiologist. Mr. Wiley's friend, too."

Juan's eyes seemed to gleam in the hall dusk, but he nodded agreeably—too agreeably? He knocked again, louder this time, and at the sound of a voice from inside, opened the door. Sue had a glimpse of Wiley on one bed, propped up on pillows and looking rather gray, his mustache, however, perky and dandyish. Dr. Smith was sitting on the edge of the other bed. He held out something toward Sam Wiley. "Now breathe slowly. Oh, here's oxygen." Juan ducked into the cabin with the oxygen container and closed the door with a kick.

It was sensible and kind and like Monty to give up his cabin to Wiley and the doctor. Sometime that day she would find her way to Stan. But just now check on Addie.

She knocked on the cabin door, and Addie called out musically, "Come in." Not really to Sue's surprise, Addie was in perfect health, if rather disheveled. A breakfast tray was on the floor beside her, and Addie, too, had got hold of a magazine.

"Everything all right?"

"Yes."

Sue couldn't help feeling something close to admiration. Addie could really put it away, she thought, resorting to one of the expressive phrases that had accompanied her teen-age years and nurses' breezy give-and-take.

If she ever became Mrs. Montgomery, there would be no more nursing. But at the moment that was an extremely uncertain hypothesis.

Addie said cozily that she thought she'd just remain in her cabin that day since it was so foggy; no sun and nothing to see and probably nothing to do.

It developed that Addie was right when she said there was nothing to do; no sitting in the sun on the wide space of the afterdeck, no strolling along the narrow side decks around the salon and cabins. Celia and Lalie eventually began an interminable two-handed game of cards. The doctor did not appear; Wiley did not appear; Monty and the man with the brief case remained in the small cabin whence came the spasmodic tapping of a typewriter. Juan took them a tray of something for lunch, covered neatly with a handsome napkin that showed Sam Wiley's initials, beautifully embroidered, and another one like it for Addie. Stan apparently remained at the wheel. Juan took another tray from the galley through the salon; Sue, listening idly to the flip of cards and the murmurs from Lalie and Celia, guessed that this tray was for Stan. It seemed very long for Stan or anybody to stay at the wheel, where she assumed he was guiding the yacht.

Juan did not return for some time, and she remembered Mr. Wiley's statement that Juan had helped when he had taken the boat to sea. So the steward was indeed very capable.

When at last Juan returned, he provided a simple lunch for the three women, served with pristine neatness. "No drinks?" Lalie said crossly, eying the buffet. "Oh, well! Monty thinks he's a great sailor. I suppose he believes the sun is not over the yardarm."

Or he intends to keep Addie from drinking as long as he can, Sue thought with gratitude. Lalie filled a plate, went back to the card table and sat down. "What's he having such a long talk with Lawson about?"

Celia's lovely head jerked up. "Randolph Lawson?"

Lalie nodded but eyed Celia. "Sure," she said. "Monty's lawyer. You know him, Celia?"

Celia came to the buffet and selected some salad. "No. I've never seen him. But I've heard of him."

Lalie laughed shortly. "Well, they are in the cabin

Monty is using. Talking and talking. But don't ask me what about.''

Celia said pleasantly, "Didn't you try to listen?"

Lalie became very sweet. "Of course I tried to listen. I couldn't make out anything, but I did hear a typewriter going now and then. My guess is—" she took another helping of salad—"Monty is making a new will. Can't think of any other reason Monty would get Lawson aboard at practically dawn. Along with your friend—" She looked at Sue. "What did you say his name is?"

"You mean Stan Brooke."

"Right." Lalie munched as contentedly as a cat munches on a mouse.

Celia, however, was no mouse. "And why should Monty be making a will?"

Lalie almost purred. "In view of his approaching nuptials."

Four

Celia didn't even blink. "Oh, now, Lalie! What nuptials?"

"Your guess is as good as mine." But Lalie flickered her heavily beaded eyelashes mischievously at Sue.

Celia said coolly, "Monty must have a dozen affairs he wants to discuss with his lawyer."

Lalie had the best of her. She rose. "I can think of one affair Monty might want to dispose of. I'm tired of cards. See you. Well, I'll have to see you, since we share a cabin."

Chewing on a celery stalk she held in one hand, Lalie vanished with a triumphant wriggle of her extremely well outlined hips.

Celia poured herself a cup of coffee and, still very

coolly, sliced from the cake that stood on a silver platter. "Juan must have got this at that wonderful baker's in Guilford. Want some, Sue?" she asked.

"Yes. No. That is, yes, please." Sue took the cake, which she recognized as one of the specialties of the well-loved baker's. During her days of training, Addie had occasionally sent her such a cake, and Sue had shared it, to everybody's satisfaction.

Celia took her coffee and cake to a chair, but this time a chair that faced the corridor by which Monty and the lawyer would have to leave the cabin. Sue found herself some magazines, which, however, all proved to concern yachting. She tried to improve her knowledge, but only in snatches, for she was distracted by the dismal sounds of foghorns not only from the *Felice* but from other boats. Sometimes, way off, large lighted areas loomed up through the grayness. She knew that they should have passed New Haven. It seemed to her they must have veered out into the Sound, for the motion of the yacht increased slightly and the glasses on the bar tinkled.

There were small lights nearer—green, red, white—through which Stan must be steering a cautious way. The foghorns made a constant cacophony around them.

Celia eventually finished her coffee and disappeared. The day went on with increasing gloom; an early dusk came on. It was certainly not the gala cruise that had been expected.

Sue was alone in the salon when Sissy turned up, trotted down the passage to a cabin, and gave a beseeching but also determined little yelp. Celia opened the door, said something to the little dog, and closed the door sharply. But Sissy had all the assurance of a catered-to pet, so she scratched at the door again vigorously, and Sue rose.

"Lend me your raincoat," she called through the door to Celia. "I'll take her out."

"Well, all right. Here." Celia, her lovely hair for once a

little ruffled, opened the door, shoved out her pink raincoat. "Juan keeps a sandbox out there."

"A sandbox! But she's not a cat!"

"She's a poodle. They can learn anything. But watch the little monkey. Juan likes a spotless desk. Here, you'd better take her leash."

Sissy didn't much care for the leash, but Sue managed to hold her still while she snapped on the leather strap. She threw the pink raincoat over her shoulders; it had a special, pleasant perfume. Lilac? Lily? Something very fragrant.

Sissy was delighted to get out on the narrow side deck and into the space aft, a deck that lay across the width of the boat. Here, the party had been intended to lie back in deck chairs and enjoy the early summer sun. After some frolicking about, Sissy was pulling at the leash when Celia, a man's raincoat thrown over her shoulders, came up. "I'll take her now. Thanks."

"I should think a dog on a cruise would be a bit of a problem," Sue said. "Sandbox or not."

"Not for Sissy. I trained her. It was simple. But so far, we've had only short trips. Plenty of stops along the way." Celia eyed Sue and said briefly, "Monty knows perfectly well that the dog seldom gets seasick."

The seasickness possibility was just an excuse, Sue thought. What he really objected to was the abrupt announcement of Celia's presence. Sue didn't say so; there was no sense in bickering; anyway Celia had strolled away, keeping a firm hand on Sissy's leash.

Sue thought briefly but fondly of the elderly Airedale, Toughy, who lived in and zealously guarded Addie's small cottage, a pleasant place but so different from the big house on the hill where Addie had lived for many years and Sue had spent her childhood days.

Sue ventured forward around the side deck and discovered a glassed-in wheelhouse where Stan stood leaning over a chart desk, his hands on the wheel. This must be the bridge. Lalie stood near Stan, but he seemed to pay attention only to the wheel. As Sue came up behind him, she heard him shout, "Get off my tail, you damn scow."

Naturally, whatever the damn scow was, it did not reply. There was a hoarse warning hoot from somewhere in the growing gloom. Lalie giggled. "I believe there is a loud-hailer here somewhere. Of course, it may not work."

"Don't bother me." Stan bent over a chart, which was fastened to the desk. A rather dim light fell upon it, and he carefully marked a special buoy. He said, straightening, "We can't possibly make Montauk—twenty hours at least at this speed." He leaned forward to peer ahead. "*Never* should have gone out this morning," he said as if to himself. "But Monty would have it! And actually, we don't often have such a heavy and prolonged fog. Never have known one that didn't lift at least in patches."

Neither Sue nor Lalie replied. He was clearly not aware of Sue's presence or, for that matter, of Lalie's; he was concentrating on guiding the big yacht. Small red or green lights loomed up, as if in admonition, on either side, red on the left, green on the right. These signals Sue recognized. Sheer off, they seemed to say; danger. When a white light came up, it meant straight ahead, mid-channel. Sue watched Stan. Lalie grew bored and retreated.

After a very long time, it seemed to Sue, the surrounding fog turned darker, which did not seem possible but happened. Stan mopped his forehead with his sleeve, shoved back a cap, checked (Sue supposed) his position on the chart and compass, and took a long breath. At the same time he became aware of her. "Didn't know you were here."

"I didn't know how dangerous this is. Stan, are we going to make it?"

"Oh, sure. Only I have to be on the alert every minute. Can't even see the markers. You're not afraid, are you?"

"Well, I—yes, I think I am a little."

"Don't be. Actually, the traffic is not as heavy as usual.

Most pleasure boats had sense enough to stay in. Trouble is, I can't possibly go into Montauk in this weather.''

"Montauk?"

"To land this lawyer Monty had come aboard." Something attracted his attention, and he swiftly bent over the charts, looked, listened, and carefully marked another spot on the chart.

There was a slight clatter of china as Juan appeared, grasping a tray. "Señor Captain said to bring this," he said to Stan. "Also he said he couldn't get to the wheel just now. Busy with the lawyer. He said, hang in. Not much longer."

"Oh, all right." Stan spoke over one shoulder, squinting his eyes in an effort to see something ahead in the gloom. "All right. But tell Señor Captain I'm getting a little tired." He snapped on a small switch, which mysteriously lighted a dim red light over the chart and another over the compass. He snapped off the brighter lights.

"What's the red for?" Sue asked.

"Night blindness. I mean, a bright light dims your vision of anything ahead. It's a little better," he said with an edge in his voice, "to see ahead. If you can," he added morosely. "Tell you the truth, I've encountered this kind of fog very few times along the Sound. I thought it would clear this morning. Otherwise I'd never have let Monty coax me to go out."

"I'll speak to Mr. Montgomery. I mean, Señor Captain." Juan vanished.

Sue said, "Can I help?"

"No," Stan said shortly. "Oh, yes, you can. Pour me a cup of that tea, will you?"

She poured the tea, blew on it, and sipped some herself before she held it at Stan's lips. He sipped, too, gulped largely, gave her a swift nod, and bent over the desk again. After a moment, he shook his head. "You're not going to like this. The lawyer is not going to like it much either. And I'm sure Juan intended to pick up some foodstuffs in

Montauk. He didn't realize how long it would take us—especially at about five knots. He's got the galley packed with frozen things, but eggs and milk are difficult. Although I think I saw some milk powder—Hey! What do you think you're doing! Can't you see?" He shouted angrily at what was apparently a searchlight, haloed in fog, off at their right, and punched a button near the wheel. Instantly a foghorn bellowed from the yacht. The searchlight veered away. Stan ate two sandwiches absently, gulped another cup of tea, and Sue took the tray and started for the salon.

Most of the portholes were now lighted, which was a help, for the motion of the boat had increased and it was a little difficult to keep her balance. The light from a nearby porthole cast a misty path across the deck and outlined two men standing at the rail. Neither of them heard her rubber-soled sneakers. Their voices had an eerie quality, as if they were disembodied, simply arriving from the darkness and the fog. One of them said, " . . . necessary. Not a lot for you—"

The other said, "Oh, now, no need to get excited. We'll see to—"

She recognized Dr. Smith's voice and as she did so the boat gave a slight lurch and the dishes on the tray clattered. Both men whirled around from the railing, so she could see their faces. Both looked startled.

She said, feeling rather foolish, "We must be getting the swell from the ocean."

Juan merely nodded. Dr. Smith tossed a lighted cigarette rather guiltily over the rail and said something about fresh air.

The doctor had at least one human weakness: although he did not permit his patients to smoke cigarettes, he himself clung to the habit. Never in public, of course, but whenever he could, out came a cigarette case and a very fancy lighter some grateful patient who had discovered his vice had given him.

Sue went on, carrying the tray through the salon down some steps to the small galley. She looked appreciatively at the compact arrangement of range, refrigerator, cupboards. It was all shining with cleanliness, although the range and refrigerator looked a little elderly.

"One must learn special shopping," Monty had told her once jovially. "The moment we disconnect the electricity from whatever pier we are tied up at, we depend entirely upon our own power. Our batteries are charged by a small diesel generator. It stops when we stop. So when we leave the yacht for a few days or—oh, however long—we have to remove all the perishable food. Rather a bore, but otherwise it would spoil and be a real mess. Canned things are all right, sure. Juan takes out anything left over in baskets he has for that purpose."

They did indeed depend upon electricity, she thought absently. She went back to the salon, where there was no one, drifted to her own cabin, tried to read but then just lay there listening to the lessening noise of fog whistles from afar and from the yacht and the confident and reassuring throb of the engines.

No, it wasn't the gala day she had expected. If Monty was in fact making a new will, she gave it merely a dismissive thought; he must have many business affairs to talk over with his lawyer.

All at once it was time for cocktails and dinner. There had been an occasional bell now and then, but she hadn't yet learned the significance of ships' bells. Now there was a kind of stir about the boat—doors opening, voices—so she looked at her watch; she showered in the tiny, handsomely decorated bathroom off her room, then put on an ankle-length white silk dress with a red sash, the ends of which dropped to the hemline. She brushed her hair, added lipstick, and looked at herself rather approvingly in the small but extremely good mirror. When she walked into the salon, she was instantly pleased with herself for dressing up. Lalie was in the chiffon blouse again but wearing, quite evidently, an adequate kind of slip and, of all things, a long green chiffon skirt and gold-colored sandals.

Addie, she suspected, had been in the deep chair very close to the bar for some time, for she was a pretty pink-and-white bundle of content. Her curls had been brushed, however, and she had got the zipper closing of her pink dress fastened neatly.

Wiley was not there; the doctor was not there; Monty was not there. But Stan came in at once. He looked a little tired but had certainly changed clothes (a clean T-shirt, clean jeans and even a jacket). Monty, he explained, had taken over the wheel. He introduced the lawyer who had followed him in, a thin, fortyish, sharp-featured, too-meticulously tailored man with a slightly disapproving air who sat down near Addie and said shortly, "When do we stop at Montauk? I really must make a train back in the morning. I am sure Gurney's Inn will take me in for the night. I'm an old customer of theirs."

Stan frowned. "Mr. Lawson, we can't possibly make it to Montauk. It's quite a trip in the best of weather. We've had to creep along. And at about five knots." Stan filled a plate.

"But what are we supposed to do?" the lawyer said testily. "Just sit here?"

Stan grinned a little. "Not exactly. Just keep going. But very slowly."

"But—but—"

"Oh, we'll see to things." Stan was wolfing his food hastily.

The lawyer spluttered. Nobody paid any attention except Addie, who looked over the glass in her hand, smiled happily at him, and murmured, "We who go down to the sea in ships—"

"Oh, Addie, darling!" She checked herself and Stan said abruptly, "Sorry. I've got to sack out for a while. I promised to relieve Monty." He disappeared. The lawyer took off his spectacles, cleaned them with a snowy handkerchief, and said in a matter-of-fact, philosophic tone, "I think Monty's pajamas might do for me. But where am I going to sleep?"

Juan materialized with more ice. "We shall arrange a cabin, sir."

Addie held an empty glass toward Juan, who flashed one swift look at Sue, seemed to read negation in her eyes, and pretended he didn't see Addie. Addie then held the glass toward Lalie, who refused to look up from a delicious lobster casserole. Celia, however, took the glass and filled it generously at the bar without even glancing at Sue.

Naturally, quite soon after dinner, Addie had to be helped to bed by Sue. Almost at once, it seemed, everyone disappeared.

A slumberous kind of haze settled over the yacht and its occupants. The ship continued to move, but very cautiously and slowly, just as she had all day. The slower beat of the engines was comforting and hypnotic. Sue latched open the door to her cabin.

She didn't really expect Monty to come in to speak to her, but she lay back in the bolted-down chaise longue and put a sweater over her feet. She could barely feel the throb of the engines now, but they must be fairly far out at sea because an occasional wave surged upon the boat, quite as if, she thought drowsily, the ocean were saying, "Just look what I could do if I wanted to."

It was a rather unnerving thought.

Presently she got up and went to the door, took off the latch, closed the door, but then went back again only to the chaise longue. She felt sure that Monty was with Stan in the wheelhouse; perhaps Juan, too. The increasingly definite motion of the boat was soothing.

She was asleep when she heard a scream, a shout: "Man overboard!"

Five

Probably the two most dreadful things anyone can hear at sea are "Man overboard" and "Fire."

The cry came again, a man's voice shouting, "Man overboard! Help—help—man overboard!"

Sue heard it as she snatched up her sweater and ran. The whole yacht roused with voices, a blaze of lights and, everywhere, running feet, more voices. As she flung into the corridor she had a glimpse of Wiley, sitting against pillows, staring through the doorway. "What is it?" he called to her. "Who is it?"

"I don't know. I'll see. Stay there now! Don't move." That was the nurse speaking. She ran on.

Already there was a little white-faced, frenzied group at the rail of the deck. Celia clutched Sue's arm. Lalie leaned over the rail and shoved out her hands. "Here you are, Stan! Here."

The yacht was still moving but at a swiftly diminishing speed. Slowing though it was, the yacht was already ahead of the sound of splashes in the water and the dimly seen circles of life preservers. The white splashes of men swimming came nearer out of the darkness; the white circles of life preservers took clearer shape. Out of the tumult, white faces surged in the black and foggy water.

Then suddenly Juan and Lalie dragged Monty up a kind of ladder and over the rail, and thrust him down on the deck; Juan rolled him over on his face and began to pump his ribs up and down. Lalie leaned over the rail. "All right. Here I am—here's the ladder—now hold on."

Sue pushed past Juan and Celia to help Lalie. Together they pulled in Dr. Smith, and then Stan dragged himself up and over the rail, where he lay flat, panting, on the deck. Juan was still working over Monty.

Lalie cried, "Here, Stan! I'll get something—" She flashed around a side deck, a thin figure clad in a bright-green caftan.

Celia knelt beside Monty, who struggled over on his back, opened his eyes, shook his head, and said hoarsely, "For God's sake, stop punching me, Juan." He coughed up water.

Dr. Smith lay flat, sputtering and drenched, but vigorous enough to shout, "Did you get him out?"

Stan, water streaming from his black hair and his white shirt, gasped and shouted, "Sure!"

The doctor struggled to sit up. Sue felt she ought to be of some help and couldn't for the life of her think of anything to do but get towels and—yes, brandy or—

Lalie flashed back with a bottle of brandy. Sue resumed the powers of locomotion, took the bottle, tipped back Monty's head and poured some into his mouth. He gulped, sputtered; she turned to Dr. Smith. "Here, Doctor, take this."

He obeyed—probably a new experience for him.

Behind him Stan gave a kind of laugh. "Me, too."

A hurried but subdued kind of tumult followed. Juan rushed off in the direction of the bridge. Nobody actually led the way, but somehow they were all creeping along the side deck and into the salon when Addie appeared, groggily holding blankets. "Wrap up quickly! Then get into hot showers. Who was overboard?"

Monty yelled, "Me."

Addie merely draped a pale-pink blanket around Monty, who glared out above it and shouted, "I was pushed!"

Nobody seemed to listen. Mr. Lawson came quietly into the salon, looked around him with surprise, fiddled in a pajama pocket for his spectacles. Monty shouted again, "I tell you I was pushed! Damn it, who did it?"

Mr. Lawson polished his spectacles and hooked them over his nose. "Now really, Monty," he began soothingly.

"Don't talk to me! Somebody pushed me into the water. Right over the rail. And somebody—" He put his hands to his head, where, in fact, there was a gash and a trickle of blood coming afresh. "Somebody hit me first. Knocked me out. The next thing I knew there I was in the water. Trying to swim and dizzy and not a bit sure—all right, *who pushed me*?"

There wasn't much reaction to his quite savage question. Celia poured more brandy and brought it to him. Stan got a towel from somewhere and was mopping his head and face. The doctor did show a flicker of interest and went rather unsteadily to look at Monty's head.

"H'm," said the doctor. His thick grayish hair was in tight wet curls. His usually ruddy face was pale.

Monty glared. "Who pushed me?"

"Well, now, Monty," the doctor said. "You might be polite enough to ask who pulled you out."

"Oh, I know that. You and—I guess, Stan. And Juan. I was kind of dazed. But I knew it when you yelled 'Man overboard' and got your hands under my armpits." He shook his head as if to shake off the water—and the blood. "Fix me up, will you? There's a kind of cut—"

The doctor glanced around and spoke to Sue as he would to any nurse. "My bag is in the big cabin. Get it for me. Now then, Monty—" He leaned over but clutched at a table to steady himself. "Have to take a stitch or two, Monty. I promise you it won't hurt."

Monty was still savage. "I don't care if it hurts. All I want to know is who did it."

His angry voice boomed out as Sue sped down the corridor to the big cabin next to her own. Wiley was sitting up in bed, his lips altogether too blue, his dandyish mustache turning down at the points. "What is it? What happened?"

"It's all right now," she said hurriedly. "It was an accident."

He leaned back but said sternly, "I heard the call 'Man overboard.' Who?"

"It's all right now. They got him out. I don't know how it happened. They are all in the salon. The doctor sent me for his bag."

"Why? Who's been hurt?"

"Monty." She saw the black bag and grasped it. "But I tell you—"

"Why does the doctor want his bag?"

"Monty has a cut on his head. The doctor is going to stitch it up. Please, Mr. Wiley."

He smiled a little. "Must have been quite a cut if he's got to be stitched. Well, run along. But wait—give me one of those pills before you go. And water, there in a glass."

She shook one pill from a small envelope, took the glass of water and held them toward Mr. Wiley, who put the pill in his mouth, sipped from the glass, swallowed, and said, "I'm all right. Seems it was a damn good thing we were barely moving." He cocked his head, listened, and added, "Engines were reversed and then shut off. Going again now. Good. But I hope Monty has got the right lights. Nobody seems to know exactly where we are."

"Stan knows, I think. He's regular navy, you know. He was at the wheel. This is, he must have been—he jumped into the water to help get Monty out. So did Dr. Smith."

Wiley's lips twitched briefly. "Must have been quite a lot of rescue work. When you find out just what happened, come back and tell me."

"Yes. Yes, I will." She hurried back to the salon, where things were more confused instead of less.

Everybody was talking at once. Celia had heard the cry; she'd been asleep, Lalie had screamed and run out. Celia had followed her. Stan had been at the bridge, heard the shout for help, reversed, lashed the wheel and then shut off the engines and ran to help. The doctor had gone out to the big deck to get a little air (Sue translated this to "get a discreet cigarette"), heard Monty's cries for help, and flung himself across to the rail; he saw Monty thrashing in the water. "At least," the doctor said amid the relieved but rather confused chatter, "I saw a man's face, white—so I yelled 'Man overboard' and jumped in."

Stan secured a moment's silence by thumping on a table. "Monty was sleeping in Juan's hammock. He left me at the wheel, but he said he didn't want to leave me alone to cope on such a foggy night. And anyway Mr. Lawson was using his cabin. So he told Juan to rig up the hammock."

Monty had a glass of something that steamed in his hand. "I was sound asleep when I got this—" He shook his head and the doctor said, "Look here, Monty! If you won't hold still it is going to hurt."

Monty held still. The doctor worked swiftly. Addie watched and said softly, "Why, it's just like sewing."

Dr. Smith gave her an amused, sharp glance. "It is sewing," he said shortly. "Now just another minute or two, Monty."

"Somebody hit me," Monty mumbled stubbornly.

Stan put down the towel he was still mopping himself with, which, however, proved not to be a towel; rather, it was a beautifully monogrammed small tablecloth.

"Didn't you hear anything, Stan?" Monty demanded.

Stan shook his head. "Nope. I knew you were there in the hammock but no, I didn't hear or see anything at all until I heard the doctor yell 'man overboard.'"

"Somebody hit me," Monty mumbled again.

"Oh, do shut up about that!" Lalie cried sharply. "You probably just rolled out of that hammock."

The doctor gestured to Sue, who knew he intended to sterilize the gash he had stitched and bandage it. She reached into his open bag. Monty gave a howl at the touch of the alcohol, and the doctor said briskly, "Monty, don't you think it likely that your sister is right? You just fell out of the hammock and knocked yourself out against the rail—''

"No! I do *not* think so!" Monty shouted.

"And then probably rolled toward the rail. I suppose you could have been so dazed that somehow you got yourself into the water. This is quite a gash, you know."

"I didn't!" Monty huddled the pink blanket closer around him.

The doctor took charge. "All right. Excitement's over. Get back to bed all of you. You—" he looked at Stan— "get a hot shower and into some dry clothes. I take it you'll be responsible for the boat tonight. If you and Juan can't manage, Lawson and I could spell you, if you'll tell us what to do."

The lawyer looked reluctant but nodded.

"It's a damn good thing we were barely moving," Stan said thoughtfully. "It'd have been bad if we had had to turn around and try to find anybody in this fog. I was scared to reverse too much. I was afraid of running down whoever was overboard. Oh, all right, Doctor." His jeans were so wet they stuck to him like a dark-blue skin. Lalie said, "I'll bring you some hot coffee, Stan."

Naturally, Addie had stationed herself near the bar and was helping herself rather lavishly. Sue thought, Oh, well, let her. "This has been upsetting for everybody," she said to the doctor, who nodded briefly.

"Me, too. Did you see Wiley?"

"Yes, sir. I gave him one of the pills. He told me—"

"Right. I'll go and get into dry clothes myself."

Monty looked up at him. "Well, thanks for getting me out."

"I had help. But sure—" The doctor opened his bag again. "We've all had a bit of a shock. You'd better take one of these—each of you." He drew out a bottle and looked carefully at the label, shook out some small capsules, and followed the rule of three that Sue had been taught: look at the label before you measure medicine; close the container, then look at the label again; when you replace the container on the shelf look at the label a third time—be sure— The doctor's directions were checked by a hearty sneeze. "All right. Now then . . ."

Addie started to take one of the pills from his hand, but after a quick glance at the glass she held, the doctor told her sharply, "Not now," and went on to Celia. Everyone but Addie and Stan took the dose.

Stan refused. "Have to stay at the wheel. Juan and I will handle it tonight. I'll not need you, Doctor. Or you, Mr. Lawson. Thanks."

"All right. Call us if you do need us." The doctor snapped his bag shut. "Monty, get into a hot shower. Don't get water on your head just now. Then into bed quick. I'm going—" He sneezed again, waved his hand, and thudded down the corridor, water dripping from his clothes.

Monty said stubbornly, "But I tell you—it wasn't an accident!"

Celia went to him and put her hand on his shoulder. "Whatever it was, you'd better do as the doctor says. You don't want trouble from that gash on your head, do you? Or pneumonia?"

Monty gave in. He looked at Stan. "Think you can manage?"

"Sure. Juan and I will cope."

"All right." Monty heaved himself up and, the pink blanket trailing dismally after him, followed the doctor.

Lalie said in a rather disappointed voice, "I thought there were going to be fireworks. Do you suppose somebody really did knock him out? And then push him? Oh, I can't believe it."

The lawyer inserted himself with a judicial manner into the conversation. "Certainly, you can't believe it. None of us can. Doesn't make sense at all. Now then, may I suggest we all go back to bed." He nodded at somebody, the room, all of them, and made a cool and quiet departure.

Addie steathily secured a bottle from the bar and hid it in the voluminous folds of her coquettishly ruffled pink dressing gown, but Sue saw it and followed her to her cabin, where she simply took the bottle from Addie, who this time really made very little protest. Probably, Sue thought tartly, because she had put away several swift drinks during the confusion in the salon.

Then Sue went to her own cabin. The door to Wiley's room was closed now, but she thought she heard the shower running vigorously.

After a moment of very serious thought, she got out of her wrinkled, water-stained white dinner dress and into newly purchased jeans, a shirt and a heavy sweater. Then looked along the passage, listening and hearing no voices, she let herself quietly out to one of the two narrow side decks that ran on either side of the yacht; the big sun deck (Sun? she thought dismally) ran across the width of the boat aft. There was a sim reddish light, haloed by the fog, coming from the bridge deck. At her left something dangled and touched her rather ghostily, so she started back before she realized that it was only Juan's hammock dangling there. She had an odd impulse to rub off the dank touch of its fibers. It might be splendid for rest and sleep during warm weather but not in a chilly damp fog. She held to the rail, avoiding the scuppers, and looked dimly below at the black water where Monty had fallen. White circles of life preservers hung neatly in place again.

Six

She went on very carefully, for the deck felt slippery in spite of her rubber-soled loafers, and stopped at the bridge.

Stan was again bending over charts, his face rosy from the tiny red light. A huge compass glinted dimly on a standard. The glass windows were as black as if they had been painted. He heard her and looked up. "Oh, it's you. You ought to be in bed." Stan rubbed his eyes, opened a window and stared out. After a moment he closed it. "Only way to see on a night like this," he explained and sighed. "Juan and I did get the engines going all right. But I wish to God I knew more about this glorious yacht. Is Wiley in any shape so I can talk to him?"

"I don't know. I don't think so. Doesn't Juan know— whatever it is you aren't sure about?"

"No," Stan said shortly. "He knows damn little about her. It's as black as ink out there, and I'm not even sure we are on the right course. I think so. But there are about a million little islands around. The buoy lights help. I'm not sure of anything except I must keep out of traffic. A big tug, towing a barge, could smash us to kindling wood, if I got across the tow rope."

"But Stan, you are a navy man. You ought to know all this better than anybody." She waved at an array of instruments.

He didn't quite glare at her, but the effect was the same. "Listen, Sue, the navy is different. We have every kind of equipment and all of it works. Matter of fact, most ships have two of everything electrical, so if one breaks down there is a quick replacement." He rubbed his eyes again ruefully. "That's a kind of problem, really. There are so many new instruments that when one breaks down we *have* to have a quick replacement. Not," he said with disgust, "that this thing has much that is new! I mean—look at this confounded rich man's hobby. It's supposed to have everything, sure. Everything but the proper equipment for going to sea."

"But Monty said—"

Stan laughed shortly. "I had a great mix-up with Monty this morning. Soon as I got a better look at this elegant, ancient old lady! I think the truth is that her newish engines and a fine overhaul of such things as plumbing and decoration and paintwork, all that must have bedazzled Monty. When I got on board, and he ushered me up here this morning, I took one look at the instruments and the fog and said, no, we don't go out this morning."

"Then why—"

"Monty said I'd promised. I replied that I hadn't known he'd been sold a lemon. He said we were going to go. I said we were not; I wouldn't. Finally he yelled at me, really lost his temper, you know. Well, so did I. About that time Lalie came along and said she thought we ought not to go out in the fog. That settled it for Monty. He told me to get back to shore if I was afraid and he and Juan would manage." Stan shrugged. "So I gave in. He meant it. I knew it would be dangerous. But I didn't realize then how many of the gadgets he had wouldn't work. Remember how he said the yacht had everything?"

Sue nodded.

"Practically everything, except the engines, dates back to when the ship was built and most of what is here is not working properly. Only the wheel, the compass, the barometer, the foghorn, those blessed engines. Even the radio is a little feeble." Stan hit the wheel with the palm of his hand. "We'll be fortunate if any ship gets near enough to see us and sheer off. I was a great fool to let myself be trapped by Monty. But there were you and your aunt and Lalie and—Good God, Sue, I had to do my best. Now a man overboard and all that fuss Monty is making. Not," Stan added seriously, "that I blame him."

"No—"

Stan went on, squinting his eyes as if to pierce the blackness outside. "I wish I were back on the *Lancaster*," he said. "Then I'd know what to do. Although—" His angry, accusatory manner relaxed, so he suddenly grinned at her. "Fact is, I do what the exec tells me to do. But here and now—why, Sue, I think we are at sea—sure, I mean I know we are at sea. But either everything but the engines has gone wrong in this nutty, elegant yacht, or I can't find anything, or—'' He rubbed his head and then his eyes again.

"You've been working too long."

"Had to, didn't I? Who else would? Your Monty, shut up talking to his lawyer all day? Juan, who does know a little but not very much, and is kept busy seeing to meals and making beds? Oh, yes, I am tired. That dive into the sea didn't help. But I'll tell you this. If we'd been going at even a normal speed we'd never have got Monty out. Or the doctor either. The yacht had enough weigh as it was to leave them much too far behind. Very, very lucky to get them out at all.''

"Stan, where are we, then?"

Stan rubbed his eyes again, picked up binoculars, stared through them, put them down and glared at the compass. "Glasses don't help on a night like this—I'm not really sure exactly where we are. We made only five knots or so today. I told Monty we'd have to tie up at Groton, that's nearer, or New London—anywhere. He wouldn't listen. I hope to God I can make it through the major shipping lanes. Didn't Monty have an expert go over this yacht before he bought her?''

"I don't know."

"He said he had taken her out a few times. Along the Sound in daylight. He didn't tell me how many things in his beautiful toy wouldn't work. And how many instruments it simply doesn't have. Modern aids—sonar, loran. Ship-to-shore phone—it's there but—She's a handsome old lady but not practical any more. Must have actually been built during the fabulously rich days of the twenties. The famous Elco yacht came along then, too. Damn, I really thought the fog would clear before this.''

"It should clear by morning."

"Maybe," Stan said dourly. "I wouldn't count on anything. Wait a minute—'' Some faint glow of light off to the left (port, Sue told herself) attracted his attention. He tried the glasses again, put them down and bent over the chart once more. After some thought he made a tiny mark and sighed. "I think that's right. I'm just not sure of anything. Even what caused Monty's dip in the sea."

"What—do you—can you possibly mean—"

"Sure, I mean it. I can't imagine who'd push him. On the other hand, anybody who believes Monty's dive in the drink was an accident ought to have his head examined."

"Stan!"

"Look at it sensibly. Who on board could tip Monty out of that hammock and shove him over the rail?"

"Juan?" she said doubtfully.

"Or me? I know I didn't do it. Too busy, for one thing." There was the faintest shade of a smile on his lips. "Might have been tempted, in a way. But didn't. That leaves the doctor and the former owner. What's his name?"

"Wiley. But he's sick, Stan. Really sick. I think it is his heart."

"I can't see why he would crawl out of his bed, evade the doctor, slide up here, hit Monty over the head, and drag him to the rail and dump him."

"It's just not possible."

"It was possible that Monty found himself overboard with a gash in his head."

"Yes. But Wiley—"

"All right, then, the doctor. He was prowling around on deck. Smoking, as a matter of fact. I saw his cigarette. Of course, he did hear Monty yell for help. So did I. I shoved that thing"—he pointed—"to reverse and then full stop, but if we'd been going at anything like a normal speed we'd have had to circle around and try to pick up Monty. He can swim all right, but maybe not for long. A person can panic—even a good swimmer. And with such a bump on the head—no, we'd not have been likely to pick him up. We'd have tried, but—"

"Stan, you do realize what you are saying!"

"Of course I do. So do you. That's why you came up here to talk to me. What about the women on board?"

"Not possible!" It came out in a husky whisper.

"Lalie swims, plays golf, rides. Good set of muscles. Monty is her older brother—"

"Half brother."

"And he does exercise a sort of parental discipline. Did you see how flimsy that blouse was she was wearing tonight, even with some kind of garment underneath? Monty told her off about that, I'll bet."

So you noticed that, Sue thought with the barest flicker of amusement. She said soberly, "But to push him overboard—"

"After taking a whack at his head? I don't say she did. I say she'd be able to. She could certainly have a motive. Close to Monty. Couldn't have always liked his authority. Besides—" Stan leaned out to peer ahead, his profile rosy in the wall light, and shook his head. "Like ink out there! Well, Monty made a new will today. That's why he and the lawyer were in such close conference all day."

"How do you know?"

"Signed it as one of the witnesses. Doctor was the other one."

"But when you sign anything like that don't you see—"

"No. Not the will itself. The lawyer held a paper over it. You want to know why Monty did that today? My guess is it had something to do with Celia Hadley's being on this cruise. I gather she invited herself. So Monty must have felt he had to make a—make some definite kind of move. Maybe indicating that he had no more interest in Celia."

She thought for a moment. "But Monty is not like that. It sounds so malicious."

"No," Stan said after considering it. "Sounds more to me as if Monty is having a rough time getting rid of her. She might make some claims at any time. Might be perfectly justified, as a matter of fact. You knew about Celia and Monty. Or—" He shot a swift glance at her. "Did you?"

"Well, no. That is, yes, but not until Addie told me."

"So she knew."

"Yes."

"I expect a lot of people knew. My mother told me. By the way, we shouldn't forget Mr. Lawson. He seemed to me pretty cool and collected when he strolled out and found us all in hysterics. Or almost hysterics."

"But what reason could Mr. Lawson—"

"Oh, go back to bed. If you want to say that some evil spirit came down from the night and hauled Monty over the rail after first hitting him hard on the head, it's all right with me. Honestly, I've got to watch what I'm doing. As well as I can."

But he looked away from the wheel. She knew he was looking at her. She had no notion of his intent until he took both hands off the wheel, put his arms tight around her, drew her to him, and kissed her.

As abruptly he released her and went back to the wheel. But in the faintly reddish light she thought she saw a very slight smile on his lips.

"Stan!" His arms had all but squeezed the breath out of her.

"Sure," he said, "I've wanted to do that for a long time. Go back to bed. I told you I've got to think about my job."

She thought, This is absurd. Her heart was pounding. She tried to think of something to say, but as Stan only bent closely over the desk, she turned around and went out, along the same side deck, cautiously clinging to the rail, back toward the salon. When she passed the porthole of the galley, which was lighted, she turned absently to look.

Then she froze for a second or two, for Juan was at a shining table, polishing something that looked like an undersized but deadly hatchet.

It gleamed in the light. It looked quite capable of giving Monty—giving anybody—a really lethal blow. Juan's bent face was dark and implacable.

Seven

She felt that someone—herself?—would have to see about this. It was a quick but positive impulse.

She went quietly on her rubber-soled shoes through the salon and into the narrow galley. But quiet though she was, Juan was instantly aware of her and as instantly moved his thickset body to shield the hatchet.

She said, evenly she hoped, but at the same time heard a kind of unevenness in her voice, "What is that, Juan?"

"I beg your pardon?" Juan's face was perfectly still; his eyes, though, gleamed. She thought (deliriously, she told herself later) of a rattlesnake about to strike. But indeed he didn't rattle; there was only a kind of small clash of cooking utensils.

"That—that thing. On the table. What is it, Juan?"

He waited a second, then moved aside and said innocently (too innocently?), "Do you mean the meat cleaver?"

Sue nodded.

Juan made a facial motion that was probably intended to be an indulgent smile. "Oh, you do mean the meat cleaver. A most useful tool."

"What for?"

"Why, for cutting meat. Steaks, chops, anything. Goes right through bone," Juan added, smiling almost in a secretly confidential way at the meat cleaver.

"But—on a yacht?"

"Mr. Wiley liked to hold barbecues sometimes when we tied up somewhere."

"But we are not about to give a barbecue." It was feeble.

"Probably not," Juan said smoothly. "I only like to keep my galley and all my tools in good shape."

"Well," Sue said. "Well—" She rallied a little under Juan's dark gaze. "I think you'll be needed at the wheel, Juan. You seem to know more about this yacht than anyone."

Juan acknowledged this with another imitation of a smile. "I think I do. Even more than Mr. Wiley perhaps. At least he always requested my aid when sometimes he needed it. And occasionally we took on a crew—that is, no more than two men. We did that when we brought *Felice* up from Palm Beach. I'll just get another sweater before I go to the bridge. Good night," he said firmly.

There was nothing to do but retreat, and Sue did. When she reached her own cabin, she shoved off her damp clothing and huddled thankfully under blankets for a moment before she rose again—not really intending to—found a key inside the narrow door, and turned it.

She knew she would never sleep. Her fancy hurtled off into strange and surely impossible realms of conjecture, but Juan wouldn't have struck Monty with the blunt side of that cleaver and tugged and pulled him over the rail. Why should he?

Why should anyone, if it came to that?

But Stan was sure, he was positive, he said, it was not an accident. So that meant a deliberate attempt at murder.

She sat up. Murder.

That was not a word one ever associated with one's self or anyone known. It was a word for news and police. She checked herself sternly. Go back to sleep.

But I haven't been asleep, she thought drearily, not since that shout, "man overboard."

Gradually, though, sheer weariness and the faraway, slow throb of the engines did act as a lullaby. Once she half roused, remembering the warmth and vigor of Stan's arms as well as his kiss.

That was a fine way to act, she told herself crossly,

when she was thinking so seriously of marriage to Monty. Provided, of course, he had the same idea. Stan's kiss was only a friendly little gesture.

She dozed a bit at last in spite of the yacht's engaging in a most determined kind of roll. Her bedside light was very dim, giving feeble and unnerving flickers. With a notion, probably foolish, that they must conserve what power was working, she snapped out the light. The yacht took a sudden upward slant and after a long pause came down again and then began to rock from side to side as she drifted off to sleep.

She awoke to find gray daylight and gray fog still at the portholes. She had forgotten to wind her watch, but it was certainly morning. Cautiously circumventing the chair, she managed to get clothed and out into the corridor. Wiley's door was open and he shouted at her, "Nurse! Find Juan! Send him to me!"

She wondered momentarily how a sick man could get so much force and volume into his voice.

She was not obliged to look for Juan, for he came out of the gloom of the passage. "Thought you'd be wanting me, Mr. Wiley. I'm doing everything I can. But that young navy officer has certainly got us into some problems."

"We have no power at all. What in hell is wrong?"

"The engines. Fuel line, perhaps." There was an odd trace of doubt in Juan's voice.

Wiley shouted again, "But those are good engines! We took on plenty of fuel. I told Mr. Montgomery—"

"Yes, sir. We had plenty of fuel. Can't seem to get the engines going, though. Just sputtered and started and sputtered. And stopped," said Juan.

Wiley must have scrambled out of bed, for he stood in the doorway, a startling figure in loudly striped pajamas. "But there shouldn't be anything the matter with the fuel lines."

"No, sir," said Juan.

There was a long pause. Finally Juan said, "I'll see what I can do, Mr. Wiley."

"All right. Get busy. I don't want to lie here while this ship wallows like an old scow. I'm a sick man."

"Yes, sir." Juan spoke respectfully enough, but added, "Lucky you've got a doctor and"—he nodded at Sue—"I hear, a nurse to stay with you. Might not have all that attention even in a hospital." Mr. Wiley snarled so viciously that he dislodged a fine set of upper teeth, which came close to tangling with his waxed mustache. He shoved at both furiously. "Get busy!" he yelled at Juan, who turned away; but Sue thought there was a fleeting smile on his dark face. However, he turned back at the door, all respect. "I'll do everything I can, sir. I think some of the women—I mean ladies—are trying to fix up breakfast."

"Breakfast," Wiley snorted. "What time is it?"

"Just eight o'clock, sir." With an effect of bowing and backing away, Juan disappeared.

Wiley sighed. "This ancient—I mean this beautiful yacht did originally have a fine ship's bell. But they tell me very few people nowadays actually use bells to tell the time, at least on boats like this. Fact is that the original bell was removed. Your friend Monty was disappointed and installed another one, not very satisfactory, really. He does like being a sailor, adopts every word he hears." Wiley chuckled. "Next thing you know he'll begin to greet everybody with 'Welcome aboard.' I thought he'd say that yesterday morning when your navy friend and Lawson arrived, but I expect he never thought of it. A fine fellow, Monty, nevertheless. Fine! Lots of money, too." His white teeth gleamed below his mustache. "Now then, I'd like to know what that young navy smarty has been up to."

"He's not been up to fooling around with any—any fuel lines."

Wiley looked hard at her. "What's the matter with you? Mad at something?"

"He is not a young navy smarty. He is a—a two-striper. On a destroyer," she added triumphantly.

Wiley was not impressed. "Didn't learn much," he said and retreated to bed, perhaps fortunately, for Sue was boiling with a sudden wave of fury.

Dr. Smith came heavily along the corridor just as the boat gave a sideways roll. The doctor executed a nimble stagger into the cabin, clutched a chair, righted himself, and as the boat rolled the other way, he sat down, probably harder than he intended, on the other bed. Sue braced herself on the handrail. Wiley glared at the doctor. "What's gone wrong?"

"Too much, I understand."

"Juan says it's the engines."

"Everything. Engines. Radio."

"What did that young navy—" he glanced at Sue and said, "man do?"

"Nothing. In fact," Dr. Smith said, "only the compass seems to be in its usual working order. And fortunately, the wheel. At least we can steer for—wherever the lieutenant has decided to steer for until—"

"Better make sure no steel puts the compass wrong," Wiley muttered and added, "Until what?"

"It seems your man, Juan, has a working knowledge of electricity. He may be able to do something helpful about the radio. Find the antenna wire. Stan says that may have worn through. Eroded. Or," the doctor said morosely, "been broken. Intentionally. Unintentionally. Doesn't matter, since the radio won't work. He has been trying it, sending out messages, but can't get a reply. He is mainly occupied with trying to avoid major shipping lanes as best he can. But there's still the fog."

"I can see that. Feel it, too." Wiley coughed, but not very convincingly. "At least, as Juan says, I have a doctor and a nurse to see to me." He gave Sue a commanding, do-as-you-are-told-my-girl look, which she refused to permit herself to resent.

Dr. Smith knew it. "All right, Nurse. You go and help the women in the galley. We really ought to have some food, and it may be a rather bothersome day."

Sue didn't run, but she got out of the cabin, away from the sour gaze of Wiley, and made her way to the salon.

There was a welcome fragrance of coffee, bacon, eggs; she went on down the steps to the alley and found Addie presiding at the range. Celia was talking. "I can't make this bread cut very neatly. I don't see why Juan insists on ordering whole loaves instead of precut bread." She looked up from a cutting board. "Oh, hello, Sue."

Lalie was exploring drawers. "I can't find anything better in the way of a knife, Celia."

A meat cleaver wouldn't be of much help in slicing bread, Sue thought vaguely, and went to get cups.

There ought to have been a kind of picnic atmosphere to the meal; there wasn't. However, it was breakfast of a sort. Lalie cut her hand opening cans of frozen juice; Sue was called upon to bandage it and was thankful it was not a big cut, because as it was, Lalie grumbled, not to herself but to everyone within hearing distance, until Celia told her to shut up. "It's no worse for you than for anybody! No, Miss Addie, the bar is not open yet."

Addie sighed and sat down, choosing the most comfortable sofa. The *Felice* gave another and rather apropos roll, for it did suggest drunkenness. Lalie sat down abruptly and scowled.

As the roll continued, Mr. Lawson appeared in the doorway; he was neatly dressed, shaven, prim in a chilly way. Celia had poured coffee for the men at the wheel and was starting for the deck with it when the roll reversed itself so suddenly that the lawyer grasped at Celia, and the tray in Celia's hands went down, scattering cups and splashing hot coffee everywhere. Mr. Lawson used some colorful language and got his balance by hanging onto Celia's shoulder.

"We are a smug little gathering," Lalie said and chuckled. "Here, I'll help you, Celia."

"Let me—" Sue ran or, rather, staggered toward the galley for towels, grasped some, and staggered back again, to find that at this unpropitious moment Sissy decided to prove the truth of Monty's accusations about seasickness.

"Right in the middle of the carpet," said Addie in what actually seemed a merely polite observation. The lawyer mopped his beautiful gray coat and trousers, Celia mopped the rug, Lalie took Sissy under one arm and made for the deck, and Sue cleared up broken china.

"Dear, dear," said Addie cozily. "Come on in, Mr. Lowery. I think there's more coffee. If not, I can make some."

"Name is Lawson," said the lawyer crossly, but he followed Addie, who managed to heave herself up from the sofa and billow into the galley.

Order was not entirely restored. Celia and Sue were gathering up crockery and mopping up when Dr. Smith came in, looked around disapprovingly, stepped over the varied debris, and said his patient needed breakfast.

Celia looked up from her vigorous scrubbing. "In the galley. Miss Addie and the lawyer are there now."

"Thank you," the doctor said as if he meant to say "thank you for nothing," but he stepped carefully over Celia and the dark patches on the rug and went down into the galley.

Lalie came back with Sissy, still subdued, every curl drooping. "Can't find her sandbox. Must have gone overboard in all the hoopla last night. I mopped with face tissues but Juan will kill me. He wants a spotless deck." Lalie put down the dog, which gave a kind of moan. "Honestly, Celia, a yacht is simply no place for a dog. Why on earth did you bring her?"

Celia didn't bother to reply.

It was the beginning of a nightmarish day. The yacht lay in the waves, wallowing from side to side. The waves were not high; luckily there was little wind, but the force of the sea made itself felt at every moment, its force sometimes threatening.

There was some other shipping. Occasionally ships came fairly near, but obviously no radio messages were received. It was depressing in the extreme to note the casual way other ships went quietly on, very soon disappearing in the heavy fog. Once Stan got Monty to hunt out flares and tried them; but Sue could tell from the attitudes of the two men that something was wrong, and Stan stopped his attempts with a certain vehemence. It developed that all the flares had gone stale, gotten too damp. Whatever the reason, there was only a dull little pop of flame that went out at once. By that time both men were in a state of helpless fury, and watching and listening, Sue thought it was probably a good thing for Wiley that he remained in his bunk all day.

Almost all of them began to feel some disagreeable effects of the constant pitching and rolling. Addie probably was the only one who escaped that certain queasiness. Like seasickness? It was seasickness, Sue realized dismally and, being on the big deck, made it to the rail barely in time.

But perhaps Addie's remedy was an effective one; Sue didn't know where she had gotten the bottle of whiskey that stood on her bedside table but suspected that Lalie had contrived to procure it and passed it stealthily to Addie. Sue didn't care. Addie slept peacefully, relaxed, giving to the motion of the boat, quite unaware of any discomfort.

A truly nightmarish day, with the fog continuing, low and menacing, with Juan, Stan and now Monty working in mysterious ways and means to get the engines going again. The lawyer—under pressure, Sue supposed—turned up in jeans at the wheel. The doctor simply sat in a deck chair he had hauled out from somewhere, apparently determined not to yield to any qualms of sickness and insisting, when Sue asked, that fresh air was the best cure for seasickness. He didn't look cured; his usually ruddy face looked rather pale and his jaws were set firmly as if to forbid the infringement of anything such as nausea upon his authority. Eventually, however, the lawyer spotted his idleness and demanded help at the wheel. The doctor gave Sue a defiant glance, threw a cigarette over the rail and went to the bridge.

She huddled in a coat and tried the doctor's remedy in his deck chair; but it was cold and damp, and she decided, prudently, that a bad head cold would be of no help whatever and retired to her own cabin. She met only Sissy on the way, and the poodle was in no mood for fun and games; she huddled in a corner and moaned slightly, her eyes beseeching, as Sue spoke to her.

Sue glanced in at Addie again, but Addie didn't even open her eyes. There was no doubt of her treatment; a strong smell of whiskey pervaded the little cabin. Once in her own cabin, Sue got under the blanket and simply lay there, trying to hang on to the bed as the boat rolled back and forth sickly, and wished Monty had not insisted upon starting the cruise in spite of Stan's objections.

Stan ought to have been firm about refusing to take the boat out in such weather!

She wished she could forget Juan and his ominous meat cleaver.

She wished Stan had not been so sure that somebody had tried to murder Monty. She wished she could dismiss his statement; she wished she didn't have to admit the truth of it. She permitted herself to amend that: the possible truth.

Lalie was the hardiest of the passengers, for she came to Sue's cabin as it grew dark. "Time for dinner. If Juan is in the mood. He's not too pleased about things. Nobody mentioned lunch," Lalie said and giggled. "I'm afraid I put even the doctor off that. I met him and started to tell the story about the Frenchman crossing the Channel who was asked if he had had lunch—''

"Yes, I know."

But Lalie was merciless. "He said, *'Au contraire.'* Look here, Sue, you're not going to be squeamish, are you?"

"I already am. Have been. What's happened?"

Lalie looked rather sober. She was bundled up in jeans and a man's heavy sea jacket. "Monty's," she said, following Sue's gaze. "He got all sort of things when he bought this damn boat. He always does everything full tilt. Doesn't stop sometimes, though, to consider the practical side of it. This yacht, for instance," she explained. "He took it, almost sight unseen, it seems. Didn't have it checked, looked at by an expert. Just trusted that Wiley. And believe me, dear, invalid Wiley is no slouch when it comes to money. Otherwise how could he have made so much! This wallowing ark! The new wing he's promised to build for that hospital! Probably only in his will at that. Oh, I forgot, it's your hospital!"

"That's all right." Sue swung herself upright rather cautiously and began to feel, cautiously, too, that food just might be acceptable.

"I must look a sight." She ran her fingers through her hair.

"A little green around the edges," Lalie said frankly. "Want something to drink?"

Sue shuddered. "No, thank you. I'll do well if I can manage a cup of tea."

"Oh, come on. Take a lesson from your aunt. She's slept like a lamb all this ghastly day. Sissy," she added (callously, Sue felt just then), "has been sick again. Luckily I had her on deck. Juan is too busy to be scolding about his clean decks. Your friend Stan is one doll of a man, isn't he?"

"Sure," Sue said groggily. And thought, My friend Stan thinks there's a murderer on this boat. Or, more accurately, someone who attempted a murder.

Lalie said nonchalantly. "Sea's making up a bit. Not a storm, according to Stan. I don't know how he knows. Barometer. Or maybe has a nose for weather. Say, how long have you known him?"

"Always." Sue clung to the rim of the wash basin and waited for the *Felice* to check her roll.

"Always? You mean really since you were little kids?"

"Just about. I think I ought to get Aunt Addie up."

"Don't you even try it. I just hooked a bottle of rum from a cupboard Juan keeps in the galley. Left it at your aunt's bedside table. My advice is leave her alone. Come on, if you're ready."

Stan knocked at the open door and came in. Lalie smiled. "Hello, Stan. How are things coming? Any chance of starting to sail the high seas?"

Stan caught himself at the door casing as the yacht began her usual reverse roll and said, "The high seas are getting up a little. Don't get upset—"

"I'm not upset," Lalie said. "I only hope nothing collides with us."

"So do I. Lalie, can you by any chance tell me why your brother actually paid money for this tub? After Noah left it when the water receded, of course," he added sourly.

Lalie flashed a grin. "Because the boat is pretty. Ever see such luxury? Mahogany everywhere. Teak. Fittings superb. And don't forget the diesel engines. Noah never heard of diesel engines."

"Don't be too sure," Stan said darkly. "Take a look at this thing. But, all right, I'll waive Noah and the ark. I think it very likely that General Washington used this elegant number to travel between Washington and Mount Vernon."

Lalie said, more soberly, "I do admit that Monty ought to have checked out the yacht. On the other hand, you have to admit it's a lovely boat to look at."

"That's where it belongs. Right in some museum."

"But there's a ship-to-shore phone," Lalie said. "I'll bet Honest George never had that."

"When it works." Stan was thoroughly grim. "If I'd had the sense God gave a goose, I'd have taken a longer and better look around before I set out on this cruise. Cruise!" He gave a short and angry laugh. "Here we sit until something or other comes along and—well, there. My fault in a way. I gave in to Monty mainly because he was so determined to set out on this cruise that he'd have gone on without me. So here we are. You all right, Sue?"

"Oh, yes," Sue lied.

"You don't look it!" Stan was as unduly frank as Lalie. He looked at Lalie. "Get out, kid, will you? I want to talk to Sue."

"Well!" said Lalie haughtily but then grinned mischievously. "Sure, I'll get out. You two dear, dear friends go ahead and talk. But don't forget dinner, Sue! Anytime!"

She gave a flip to her hand and disappeared. Stan shut the door after her.

"Are you really all right, Sue?"

"No. What are you going to do?"

"See that you are safe."

"But Stan, I *am* safe."

"That thing last night was deliberate. And it looks as if somebody wants to keep us out at sea until—" He rubbed his face wearily. "Until something he wants to accomplish has been accomplished." He looked apologetic and very tired. "Don't ask me what. I do know that simply nothing works. I can't even count on the compass. Whirls around now and then. We have probably gotten way off course. May wind up anywhere."

"I hope not at the bottom of the sea."

"So do I. This blasted fog has got to clear sometime. If only the engines were all right. The only new and efficient things about this tub! But there could be something in the fuel tanks—"

"What?"

"Oh, sugar. Sand. Water would be worse. Sand would go to the bottom but not immediately."

"But how could—"

"Never mind. I'll show you the fuel tanks if you—"

"I don't."

"Well, then, listen. There's a kind of plug to each filter. Two tanks. Anybody with half a knowledge of engines could get the plug out and dump in water—or, I think, from the way the engines sputtered, probably sugar. Or sand. It's the same as with the fuel line of a car. But I don't think Juan would have that much sugar in the galley. And sand on a yacht—"

Sue stared at him. "There was sand! A sandbox for the dog. Not that I think she likes it much. But anyway—oh, Stan!—the sandbox has disappeared."

After a moment, he said slowly. "That could prove it. If it needed proof. Somebody tried to kill Monty. And somebody wants us to remain right here until he gets whatever it is he wants. Probably from Monty."

Eight

Sue stood, thinking. Stan leaned against the door, thinking. "Well," he said at last, "what does he want from Monty? That's the point."

"But then Monty would know who had attacked him, wouldn't he?"

"He keeps saying he doesn't."

"Isn't anything working? I mean any of all those instruments—"

Stan shook his head. "The compass ought to tell me which way we are going. But even it is erratic. But," he added cryptically, "there may be reasons for that. The fact is, I didn't suspect anything right away. I just followed what I took to be our course until—oh, never mind. Now I simply don't have the slightest notion where we are, and that's a fact. Just out here in the fog, groping along. Hoping we'll not hit anything. Or for God's sake, get hit by anything. A freighter, for instance. Say, one carrying oil to New Jersey. Or anywhere. Ever seen a fire at sea? Of course you haven't. Neither have I, as a matter of fact, and I don't want to. We can't swim to shore. I don't know where shore is! There's a rubber dinghy we could inflate and two of us try to find help, but I don't care for setting out myself in this kind of weather or seeing anybody else set off in a rubber raft. We are simply stuck here. Until—'' He stopped, kicking at the carpet with one foot, staring down, hands in his reefer pockets.

Sue cast about in her mind for possible assistance. ''You have talked to Mr. Wiley?''

''Oh, sure. He didn't want to talk. Very grumpy. Said nothing like that had ever happened while he was the owner. It was a fine boat, emphasis on the new engines. Seemed to blame Monty.'' Stan lifted his eyes to meet Sue's gaze. ''Lalie came in while I was talking to him, and I must say she's quite a girl.'' The barest flicker of a laugh touched his tired mouth. ''Sat on the edge of the bed and positively flirted with that old duck. When I left she had him smiling. I'm not sure he wasn't holding her hand. She sort of put it close enough—felt his chest and his pulse and said he was fine. Accused him of scaring everybody by just pretending to be sick. The doctor was there, too, and took a dim view of it, but there wasn't much he could do without making a scene. How come she's Monty's sister? Not much like him.''

''Half sister,'' Sue said absently. ''Much younger—oh, you know that.''

''No, I don't, really. I was away when Monty began to make so much money and started coming to Sea Cove and Weston. That is, he really isn't an old-timer here but he has a gift for making friends. And he bought that place in the hills. Sounds very grand.''

''It isn't all that grand,'' Sue said slowly. ''But it's nice.''

''Of course you've seen it many times.'' Stan looked steadily at the blankly gray porthole.

''Not so many. Once or twice. He's thinking of selling it.''

''If he's thinking of selling it, he will. Monty is a man who gets things done. I wish,'' Stan said unexpectedly, ''that I didn't like him.''

''Why on earth?''

''Reasons. By the way, that former girl friend of his—'' Stan's eyes were riveted to the fog behind the glass—''is certainly a beauty. You aren't bad-looking yourself.''

''Why, Stan, you never gave me anything like a compliment in your life!''

''Time I changed, then. Besides, it wasn't really a compliment. Just a quiet statement of fact. Ever look at yourself in the mirror?'' He eyed her judicially. ''Fact is, I like your style of beauty more than Celia's. More . . . more . . . well, I like it better.''

Sue opened her mouth, reconsidered, and shut it again. Stan said, ''Monty likes you. Probably thinking of marriage. It surprises me that you haven't had a run-in with Celia. Asserting her position, you know.''

''Oh, yes. She did that. She doesn't like the idea of my''—she hesitated—''friendship with Monty.''

Stan lifted an eyebrow. ''What did you expect? No objections from her?''

''I didn't expect her to come on this cruise, certainly. No, I didn't like it but mainly because—oh, I didn't like it.''

''Or don't like her? Who could blame you!''

''No, Stan. It's not jealousy. In fact—'' Sue made the discovery with a certain surprise—''I rather like her. But I'm not going to change me—'' (resolve? intention?) she hurriedly said, "any friendship with Monty because she wants me to."

"You like Monty?"

"Of course I do."

"Intend to marry him?"

"Why not?" If he asks me, she thought hastily.

"Reasons," Stan said remotely.

"That's my business!"

"Nursing too hard for you?" Stan asked with an edge to his voice.

She was growing angry. "I'm not afraid of hard work. But my job does sometimes seem to me a kind of dead end."

"Good salary, though."

"Now. Yes. But later—"

"Prudent girl," Stan said shortly.

"Monty hasn't even talked of marriage!"

"But you think he will."

"I don't know. But I do like him!"

At this, Stan gave a rather lopsided but entirely skeptical smile. "Oh, sure. Anybody with all that money is a great guy. Everybody loves him. Honestly, I like him, too. Not that I want to—"

It seemed mandatory to change the subject. She said, "All right, Stan. Now we've covered my possible matrimonial hopes, what are we going to do to protect Monty? Juan has a vicious-looking meat cleaver. It could have been used to knock out Monty."

"Oh, that. I asked Juan what he had in the way of a club. He showed me the cleaver, which, by the way, he seems to carry around with him stuffed under that long white coat he insists upon wearing. Every time he passes the compass it jiggles around this way, that way. Now I know a reason for some of its gyrations, I told him not to bring the cleaver near the wheel. I'd like to search everybody for steel. Or a battery—flashlight, anything. I don't want us to go on and on like a modern—that is, not too modern—Flying Dutchman because somebody is doing tricks with the compass. I must get back there. Monty is on the job, sore head and all. I really do like him, and I don't like attempted murder.''

"But who could possibly—"

"If you think that Monty knocked himself out and then leaped overboard with damn near a skull fracture, you're really a donkey. See you," he said and abruptly went away.

Next thing I know, I'll be listening for the stealthy creeping of a homicidal maniac, Sue told herself severely, but she closed the door and locked it fast.

She was beginning, however, to feel rather empty and to wonder just what stores Juan had left aboard besides alcoholic nourishment when Monty himself knocked and called her name, so she unlocked the door again. The door being narrow and Monty big, he had to sidle in. He looked around, sank down in the chair, and adjusted the bandage on his head, which had slipped to a rather rakish angle over one ear. "Everything all right?"

"How's your head?"

"Hurts," Monty said. A gleam of wrath again lighted his eyes. "I'll find out who did it and make mincemeat of him."

"Why did he do it?"

"For God's sake, Sue, how do I know? Somebody just doesn't like me and prefers to see me drown, that's why! What a question to ask, Sue."

"I know. But, Monty, I can't think of anybody at all who would do that."

"If I knew who did it, he'd find himself floundering around in the sea and fog, but this time there'd be no stopping, no aid, no life preservers. We'd just go on—at least, no, right now we can't seem to go anywhere."

"Can't Mr. Wiley help?"

"That man!" Monty leaned his chin on one hand and

glowered. "That man doesn't know as much as I do about this boat. Not that I know anything myself."

It was like Monty to admit his own fault. He said, brooding, "Your young navy man—"

"Your navy man," Sue corrected him. "You asked him to come along, Monty."

"Yes. Yes, I did." He shot her a rather baleful glance. "But I expected him to know more than he seems to know. Oh, never mind. You needn't defend him. He can't use equipment that is either not on the boat or, if here, doesn't work. I know he's an old friend of yours. I've known him since he was a teen-ager myself. That is—no, I haven't really known him. I've just seen him around now and then. But I thought he could handle this boat. After all, a man who can handle a destroyer—"

"He says on a destroyer he does what the exec tells him to do. I'm not sure what an exec is, but he must be the commanding officer."

"Great thinking," Monty said with one of his rare moments of sarcasm. He relented. "Sorry, Sue, of course, that's right. Executive officer. And *he* does what the commanding officer tells him to do. However, I did expect more of Stan. Otherwise, I wouldn't have suggested going by sea to Eleuthera. But frankly—foolishly, I expected more of this boat." He added gloomily, "At this rate we aren't going anywhere. Unless some tanker hits us. Or a cargo ship. We'd go down like a stone."

She swallowed rather hard. She said, but weakly, "Don't let Aunt Addie hear that."

"No. Brings me to something I want to tell you. That man Lawson, my lawyer. I've made a new will. Last night shows you! Somebody tried to kill me. Somebody—"

"*Who*, Monty, *who?*"

"I tell you, I only wish I knew." His pleasant face darkened. His eyes shot angry gleams. In a moment, though, he sighed. "About my will—I want to tell you. I have the original. Lawson has a copy. It was made in anticipation of our marriage. If whoever it was that shot me into the sea last night had succeeded in killing me, you'd have been a rich woman—and also your Aunt Addie would have been taken care of for the rest of her life. How's that?''

Sue was suddenly more or less paralyzed. ''In anticipation of our marriage,'' Monty had said.

Finally it had come. It was as if a whole Christmas tree loaded with glittering gifts had dropped into her lap. She had no aversion of any kind. Not the slightest hesitation. Had she? Certainly not!

So she was appalled to hear herself say, ''Oh, Monty. Not—not just now.''

He mistook her hesitancy. She ought to have leaped at the fulfillment of her hopes. Monty ruffled up his fair hair, adjusted the bandage again, and said, rather boyishly, half-embarrassed, ''Oh, I know this is not the time or the place. But surely it's no surprise to you? I mean this to be a sort of—I guess, a sort of family meeting. Your aunt. My sister. Getting acquainted and getting used to the idea of our marriage. I'm older than you. But—''

''That doesn't matter. I'm only . . . I don't know . . . that is, I'm not putting you off or pretending or . . . but . . .'' She sat down, for her knees refused to hold her. ''Dear Monty, you are just great. I don't think any girl, ever, anywhere, could wait a second before . . . why, just leaping at you. I only . . . I mean, just now . . . with everything—''

''Oh, things will be settled. You and I will be settled. You and your aunt will be taken care of if anything should happen to me. We can make our plans later. No hurry. Only if anything should happen to me—''

''*Monty, don't talk like that!*''

He smiled. ''Like me, huh?''

''Of course I do.''

He rose, winced, and put his hand to his head. ''I do get a little dizzy. No—not that much. I'm really all right.''

He waved aside her hand, put out to help him. ''Now

then. I'm getting back to that damn wheel and what your navy man calls the bridge. Whatever we call it we just sit here, wallowing like a—a pig!" he said angrily. "If Wiley wasn't a sick man I'd—oh, I don't know what I'd do. But this blasted boat isn't what I thought she'd be."

"No, wait a minute, Monty. You haven't told me exactly what you knew about your head and—I mean, how it all happened."

"I tell you, I don't know. But this is the way it was." He held up one hand and counted on the fingers of the other. "First, I gave Wiley my own cabin, the big one beside yours. He is a sick man. And honestly, I thought it a little—oh, something—anyway, I thought it better not to use the cabin so close to yours." He coughed in an embarrassed way.

"I see." She almost giggled but checked herself in time: Monty had a strong regard for propriety; yet there was Celia.

Monty was going on, "Then Lawson came. So I gave him the cabin I had taken and told Juan I would use his cabin and he could use the hammock. Clear so far?"

Sue nodded.

"Then the night being so unexpectedly foggy. Stan says a fog like this happens only once in a blue moon."

"But then, anything can happen. I mean, when the moon is blue. That is—" She faltered as Monty merely looked at her, a little bothered at her totally unintended and certainly, to him, inappropriate, murmur. "Never mind. Do go on."

"Yes, well, anyway. I thought I'd stay on deck, near Stan. In the hammock. But then I drifted off to sleep, dead to the world. Damn near dead in the sea, come to think of it. First thing I knew was a kind of flash—oh, light and pain and then nothing till there I was in the water. I did come to a little, at least enough to know I was about to drown and began to swim as well as I could, and—oh, I yelled. Yes, I was conscious enough for that. The doctor had sense enough to jump in after me and try to get me out. He yelled, too—''

"I heard that."

"Stan heard him, reversed a little, then stopped the engines. The yacht couldn't stop on a dime but went on, and Stan jumped in, too. The yacht was getting farther away. All I could do was hang on to the doctor and try to swim. Then Stan was there, splashing around and grabbing me by the arm, and then Juan began throwing out life preservers and ropes, and I knew I was being hauled aboard the yacht—and I don't mind telling you I was damn grateful. Whew! Not an experience anybody would like."

"No! But Monty, couldn't it have been an accident?"

He gave her a look of amazement. "If I didn't know you, Sue, I'd think you were the dumbest girl that ever lived."

"You may be right," she said ruefully, thinking of her failure to leap at his talk of marriage. "But who could have tried to—kill you? That's what it was, you say."

"That's what it was, I know. I just don't know who. Juan doesn't like me, but he did help get me out of the sea."

This diverted her. "Why doesn't Juan like you?"

He shrugged, winced again, as if the slightest motion hurt his head. "I don't know. No reason. Perhaps because he likes Wiley and I bought the Wiley yacht and—but that's not much of a reason for trying to stun me first and then pushing me overboard." He brooded for a moment. "But then, I never know what people are thinking, only what they are doing. That sounds pretty dumb. And I guess I am, somebody trying to kill me and I don't know why. Stan might want to get rid of me—''

"Stan! Why on earth would Stan—''

"He likes you," Monty said flatly. "Oh, I can see that. Childhood sweetheart—''

"He was not! There are other able-bodied men on board."

"Able-bodied women, too, if it comes to that." His face darkened. "Well, see you—" He staggered a little going out the door, but then went on toward the salon.

And I *am* the dumbest girl in the world; Stan had told her of a new will. She might have surmised its provisions. Surely in her heart she had expected a proposal of marriage! She was amazed at her own utter, complete stupidity. She ought to have been clearheaded and accepted him at once. She must have believed it was coming; yet she had just stared at him and mumbled, and she was a fool.

Next time she'd act, she'd make everything definite, she'd say, yes, yes, I want to be your wife. If, of course, there was to be a next time.

It was possible, in her abject frame of mind she thought it only too likely, that Monty would think over her blank reception of what amounted to a firm proposal of marriage and tell himself, prudently, to think it over; perhaps she wasn't the woman he wanted for a wife after all.

In fact, she thought dismally, I'm just back where I started with Monty; no, worse. He had every right to expect some kind of enthusiasm and—oh, forget it.

She'd do better. She'd watch her every word, every movement, every thought! She would be very, very sensible. Meanwhile, she must see to Addie.

Addie had managed very well on her own. She was cozily seated on the sofa nearest the bar again. Where does she put it? Sue thought in amazement. Addie showed not the slightest sign of having slept a drunken sleep almost all day. She was pretty, as always; her hair was neatly brushed; she wore a suitable, nicely tailored sports dress and clasped a glass in one fond hand.

Celia was officiating calmly at the bar. Lalie, still in a T-shirt and jeans, was draped very pleasantly over the arm of a chair, listening with what seemed the most concentrated interest to something the lawyer was saying. Sissy gave a slight moan as the boat started a long roll, and Sue clutched the nearest shoulder, which proved to belong to the doctor, who had legs firmly braced and seemed to be obstinately refusing to yield to anything, let alone a wayward yacht. The lawyer was taken unaware by the roll and fell forward, sprawling in a most undignified way. Addie lifted her prettily arched eyebrows. "Dear me, Mr. Lawson! Have another."

He gathered himself together, gave her a furious look, and scrambled back into his chair just as Celia started forward to help him, but Lalie was first, her hands firm but her lips twitching.

"No, no. I'm quite all right. Never touch the stuff." He clearly referred to the array of bottles on the bar and to Addie's not very subtle suggestion.

"Do you good," Lalie said, shoving the lawyer more securely into his chair.

" 'Oh, it's life on the ocean wa-ave . . .' " Addie sang to the tune of "For he's a jolly good fellow," and Celia turned to Sue. "We'd better get some food into—" She glanced at Addie but said, "Into everybody. Come on."

So Sue staggered after her into the galley. Juan was not there; neither was the wicked-looking meat cleaver. There was, however, a refrigerator well stocked with food.

"Does she always do that?" Celia asked coolly.

"She?"

Celia gave her a scornful but also a tolerant look. "Your aunt, of course. Tank up. Frankly, I don't see how she does it."

Sue sighed. "Neither do I. But she's so dear and sweet and—How can I stop her?"

Celia arranged a dish. "I'd stop her," she said trenchantly, and Sue believed her.

"How?"

"I'd think of some way. Just keep her off the sauce, that's all."

"I can't. I'm not at home enough."

"Everybody knows about it. At least that's what I gather. I haven't been around that neck of the woods much for a long time." Sue wanted to know what had happened to Mr. Hadley but didn't quite have the courage to ask. Celia went on, though, after giving her one thoughtful glance. "I see you want to know why. To put it briefly, mine wasn't a happy marriage. A divorce was imminent when my husband got into a car crash. A fatal car crash," she added. "That's why I see the evidence in your aunt. He was a real drunk. Wouldn't have driven so fast otherwise. But you were at my wedding! You must remember him."

"I remember how beautiful you were."

Celia's finely marked face sharpened a little. Her eyelashes lay gently, however, on her lovely cheeks. "I was, wasn't I? I'm still not bad to look at, am I?"

"No!" Sue was beginning to like Celia more and more and obscurely felt that she shouldn't. Certainly Celia was a rival for Monty's affections. Or at least, had been. Celia was behaving now more like a wife than a castoff mistress. Also, she knew exactly where everything was—saucepans, cups, plates, silver, everything.

Sissy came in, flung herself down in a miserable curly heap at Celia's feet and uttered a whine.

"Oh, God," said Celia. "She's going to be sick again. Juan will have a fit. His immaculate galley—"

"I'll take her," Sue offered.

"All right, I'll manage the food. Send that lazy Lalie to help me."

Sissy perversely seemed better out in the fresh but foggy air. On the bridge, there was a faintly rosy glow, haloed by fog.

Sue made her way to the bridge, where Monty and Stan stood, both leaning over the tiny red binnacle light.

"Seems a little dim," Monty said.

"It is dim," Stan said sharply. "Some of the fuses must have given up. But even through the fog any other boat should be able to see us."

Sue, followed by a friskier Sissy, returned to the salon, where plates were balanced on everybody's knee but

Addie's, who clung to a glass, newly filled. The lights here were rather dim, too.

Celia said imperatively, "Better eat before we have to resort to candles."

"'How far that little candle throws its beam,'" Addie sang, this time to the drawled-out tune of "It's three o'clock in the morning," which somewhat but not altogether disguised the words.

Celia glanced at her, then at Sue, rose, and politely but briskly whisked the glass from Addie's pretty white hand. "Now eat your dinner."

Addie was not at all disconcerted. "Makes sense. You always made sense, Celia. Even when you were a girl. So long ago. But I do remember you."

She wan't so fuddled that she couldn't throw a dart, or attempt to, for Celia only looked amused.

"Go on, now. Eat," she said, pleasantly but very firmly, and Addie, looking rather startled, picked up a fork.

The lawyer, holding a plate uneasily on his knees, muttered, as if to himself, "Depends on evidence that someone knew that Monty borrowed Juan's hammock. Who heard him?"

Lalie gave a quick, startled jerk of her pretty blond hair. Everybody stared at the lawyer, who said, "Evidence. That's what we need. Now whoever tried to murder Monty—if someone actually did—had to know that he had taken over Juan's hammock."

It was the first time the word had been uttered flatly. Every one of them, Sue felt, was either truly shocked or gave a good performance of shock.

Yet probably not a single one of them had failed to arrive at that unwelcome conclusion.

After a moment Lalie said, with a fairly obvious air of nonchalance, "By the way, where is Juan?"

The doctor replied, "Trying to help the navy probably. Any coffee?"

"I'll get it." Celia rose. Sue hadn't seen her prepare coffee, but she reappeared, holding another tray, just as the boat gave another skittish, short roll, and the coffee slopped.

"Take it and like it," Celia said shortly and set the tray down on the bar. "There's fresh fruit in the galley. Get it, will you, Lalie?"

Nobody cared much for the meal, but at least they were not to suffer from hunger.

Juan did not appear. Lalie arranged trays and said she would take them to Monty and Stan.

Addie tried to rise, couldn't, and Celia and Sue between them pulled her to her little feet. " 'Home is the sailor,' " Addie caroled. They got her to her cabin.

"Thank you," Sue told Celia. "I'll take care of her."

Addie didn't need care. She collapsed in a pink-frilled heap and fell asleep.

The door to Wiley's cabin was firmly closed. Juan was not to be seen. Foghorns near and far wailed eerily all night.

In the morning Juan was not anywhere on board.

The meat cleaver had vanished also. There was, however, an ominous red trail leading to splotches from the galley to the deck.

Nine

Nobody had heard anything unusual or at least did not admit it.

The night had passed slowly, yet had passed. Nobody had heard a scream, a shout, anything but foghorns and the little clatter of china and glasses and the creaks of the yacht, which seemed, in the night, to take on a personality and sentience of its own and to protest the helpless battering and rolling to which it was subjected.

Occasionally, vaguely in her heavy and tired sleep, Sue thought she had heard ships, but certainly none of them could have come near. A more vigorous wave finally threw her out on the carpet; she pulled herself up, worried about her aunt, remembered that Addie was the least troubled person on board, and crawled back under the blankets again. It had become dismally and certainly dampishly cold.

The next morning Lalie came bouncing in with Sissy to tell her that nobody could find Juan. "He's been murdered, Sue! There's blood—whole spots of it. Leading across the salon and the deck and—so what do you suppose, Sue?"

"Juan!"

"Sure!" Lalie was only pretending to be brave. Sue saw the white line around her mouth. There was lipstick on her lips but applied so hastily that it was only a bright-pink smear.

"I can't believe it," Sue whispered, heard her own whisper, and repeated it aloud.

Lalie merely dumped Sissy on the bed. "I told you. It's got to be murder. Somebody killed him and dragged him to the deck and just—just tossed him overboard. Miles away by now probably. And even if he—it—were near, nobody could see it—him—on account of the fog. Oh, yes"—as Sue glanced at a porthole—"it's heavier than ever, I do believe. Stan says it's not possible but can happen. Makes no sense, but I understand him. Listen, Sue. Don't you see that Juan was around the night Monty was knocked senseless and dragged overboard and left to drown? Except he didn't and—but Juan must have seen who did that. So Juan had to be killed. That's the way of it. Your teeth are chattering."

Sue tried to control what really was an odd feeling in her teeth. "I'm not, I mean they are not. I mean—oh, Lalie! What does Monty say?"

"What I told you. We've really got a murderer on board with us. Sounds horrible."

"It is horrible! Get off the bed. I want to get up."

"Much better just stay right here and pull the covers over your head." Lalie pushed herself up and into the chair, nevertheless. Sissy grunted and stretched.

"Getting over her seasickness," Lalie said, absently eyeing Sissy's little brown figure. "Wish I could get over the horrors. Honestly, Sue, it's got to be the doctor or the lawyer." She attempted a feeble grin. "Rich man, poor man, beggarman, thief—"

"Oh, shut up, Lalie." Sue reeled to the infinitesimal bathroom and turned on the shower, but she could hear Lalie chant, "Doctor, lawyer, merchant, chief." Apparently Lalie thought that over exhaustively, for when Sue emerged from the bathroom, clutching for clothes, Lalie was frowning. "Monty's a rich man; so's that Wiley. No beggarmen or—at least I think—no thief. Can't be sure about that, can you? Merchant! In a way that's Monty, too, but Monty wouldn't hit himself over the head and take a dive into the sea. Chief—I don't know that Stan can exactly be called a chief. But anyway, there you are. Unless, of course—" Lalie looked at her with Monty's own speculative glance—"unless we have a stowaway on the boat."

"We can't have!" Sue stared at her.

"Why not? Just because we haven't seen a stowaway doesn't prove there isn't one."

"In this yacht? There isn't room. Besides, somebody would have known."

"Maybe somebody does know," Lalie said ghoulishly, yet obviously, beneath the airy front she was putting up, she was terrified. Who wouldn't be? Sue thought; I am.

"Lalie, has anybody seen Juan's meat cleaver?"

"His—good heavens, what do you mean?" Lalie sat up with a jerk.

"He had a meat cleaver. He was polishing it. I saw him and spoke to him and he said he—" Suddenly Sue had to swallow hard. "He said he liked to keep his tools clean."

Lalie stared at her blankly for a moment. "Then if it was a meat cleaver—it just could have been that! I left Celia cleaning up the—the splotches with a scrubbing brush and—and things. I must say she doesn't try to get out of unpleasant work," Lalie finished.

"As you do," Sue said. "And as I do. Celia is certainly not afraid of work."

"Not afraid of anything, if you ask me." Lalie had a swift reversion to her more natural manner. "It beats me how she ever let Monty get away."

Sue began to brush her hair. Lalie said, "Aren't you going to put on any pants? Here—" she tossed the discarded jeans toward Sue. They were clammy to the touch; everything was clammy.

Lalie said, "So now you know. They are all talking about it. Except your aunt. She's probably having a real hangover. But the rest of them are talking all the time and not much of it means anything as far as I can tell. Except murder!" Lalie closed her smeared lips firmly, scooped up Sissy, and departed, the door swinging behind her.

There was no stowaway. There was no meat cleaver. And there was still no comforting murmur of engines.

Monty met her as she entered the salon. He was drawn and pale; his face, usually so confident, seemed to have sagged. He said, half mumbling, "Something has happened. Now, take it easy—"

"I know. Lalie told me."

"That little—oh, of course she would. Doctor, does Wiley know?"

"No," replied Dr. Smith firmly. "And I'm not going to let any of you tell him. He's my patient."

Celia asked softly, "How can you keep it from him?"

"I intend to. And unless you want another—I mean a dead man, this time right here on the boat, you'll not tell him. Understand me?"

"Where's Stan?" Sue asked.

Monty replied; there was now a neat plaster instead of a

white kind of turban on his head. "On the bridge. We were there together when it must have happened."

The lawyer was drinking coffee; Celia had apparently prepared coffee and toast and fruit. He said glumly, "All the time, Monty? Every minute? It wouldn't have taken long, you know. Whack Juan with something and drop him overboard. This time," the lawyer said judicially, "it was successful. Failed that time when it proved to be you in the hammock. Succeeded this time though." He lifted his coffee cup as if he had said all there was to say.

Sue said, surprised by her unsteady voice, "Juan had a meat cleaver."

"It's not in the galley now," Celia said. "I saw him with it yesterday. When I heard a few minutes ago and saw—" She hesitated, looking at the damp spots on the carpet where she had been scrubbing. "When I saw all that—I went to the galley for a scrubbing brush and a pail, and I remembered his meat cleaver and looked, and it's not there." She finished so definitely that no one questioned her statement.

"There's no chance of recovering Juan?" Dr. Smith asked.

Monty shook his head. He was beginning to show sheer fatigue and, not remarkably, considerable nervous strain. "Not an earthly," he said rather weakly. "Stan thinks so, too. My God, we don't even know where we are. We've tried to signal for help, but no answer anywhere. Obviously the radio antenna is not working. We'll just have to stick it out till somebody comes near enough to see our distress signals. Oh, yes," he replied to the lawyer's lifted and very keen gaze, "we found a few signal flags. One of them, Stan says, is a distress signal. Something or other, upside down. Call for help."

Lalie came staggering in as the boat gave another roll. Sissy followed at her heels. "No fun being out there alone," said Lalie and looked around her and added, needlessly, "I can't say it's much fun being with all of you either. Any one of you—"

Celia broke in. "Come on, now, Lalie. Don't make things worse."

"Is that coffee?" Lalie streaked across to the buffet and reached for a cup.

Addie, entering the salon, almost fell as the boat started its return roll, luckily not a bad one, but Addie had to clutch a chair to keep her balance. "What is the matter with all of you?" she asked. "You look like death warmed over!"

It was an unfortunate observation.

"Oh, my God," Monty muttered and fled, presumably for the wheel. Or even, Sue thought wildly, for the nearest rail.

Celia seized Addie with force and deposited her in the chair. "Just be quiet. I'll get some coffee for you."

"How good you are!" Addie said. "Really, more like Monty's wife than his mistress. Oh, dear!" Her face turned bright pink; she clapped one hand over her mouth and mumbled apologetically in Celia's direction. "I didn't mean—What a thing to say!"

"Here's your coffee," Celia said. "Now hang on to it. I've scrubbed this carpet once already this morning."

Addie took the coffee; she said very politely, "Really, why?"

Lalie grasped the nettle. "Never mind, Miss Addie. Just—never mind—"

"But I do want to know why somebody had to help Juan up on deck last night," said Addie, cuddling her coffee.

This produced a completely stunned silence except for the dismal wail of some faraway foghorn, the tinkly clatter of glasses and china and the stubborn little creaks and groans of the yacht, to which, by then, they were all growing accustomed. Then everybody spoke at once.

"You saw—"

"When?"

"Addie!" This was Monty, back at the doorway, thundering, "What did you see?"

"Somebody helping Juan. At least I thought so. The poor man must have been sick, or drunk; at least he acted that way. But I don't suppose—"

"Aunt Addie!" Sue pounced upon her, almost losing her balance as she moved. "Aunt Addie, *who* was helping Juan?"

Addie sipped her coffee and smiled. "Perhaps they were both a little under the weather. In their cups, shall I say? Ouch!"

A roll caught her coffee cup and the hot liquid splashed along Addie's dressing gown.

It struck Sue, but remotely then, that the waves were becoming more purposeful in an odd way; rather as if they meant business. If a storm caught them—she broke off her own unpleasant speculations.

Lalie, instead of a storm, caught Sue's arm. "Make her tell! Make her tell!"

"Dear me, tell what?" Addie said with, it appeared to Sue, just too wide-eyed innocence. "Look what I've done to this pretty robe you gave me, Sue. But I couldn't help it. It does seem to be the motion of the boat is stronger. We can't be getting into a storm, can we?" She appealed to Monty. "I've heard of the Gulf Stream. Are we crossing that? Surely we can't be that far—"

"Aunt Addie," Sue cut in sternly, "who was helping Juan last night?"

Addie had always had a certain amount of luck that she had come to count on. This time it was an enormous wave that sent Monty leaping for the bridge, his athletic body moving with complete control in spite of his size, and everyone else in the salon clutching for support. Addie dropped her coffee, put both hands to her pretty mouth and mumbled behind them, "Oh, dear, oh, dear. I've got to—"

Celia sprang into action; she took one of Addie's arms,

Sue took the other. They managed to get her to her cabin, but barely. "A waste of coffee," Celia said, wielding towels a few moments later. Addie lay back in her bed, looking very pale.

Sue said, "All right now, Aunt Addie, you *must* tell us who it was you saw with Juan. Come on, now. You can speak."

But Addie only moaned, hands on her throat.

Celia said, "I'll get out. Maybe she'll talk then. But make her tell, Sue."

Of course Celia didn't know that if Addie made up her mind not to do anything she could have given lessons to a Missouri mule. And she did not know that Addie had a lively imagination. Celia, however, paused at the door. "One thing that seems to be working on this blasted, elegant scow is the barometer. And, it signals—" She didn't say what; she only pointed her thumb downward.

Storm, Sue thought; that's all we need. A fine storm and we'll be at the bottom of the sea. Or perhaps the wreck of the *Felice* could go down in history like the *Mary Deare*. No: there were no bodies on the *Mary Deare*; the *Felice* would have a plethora of bodies. She took a firm grip upon her galloping imagination as Addie moaned again.

"Now listen, Aunt Addie. I've got to talk to Stan. You are to stay right here." Too late Sue had a wave of dreadful caution. "But don't let anybody—*anybody*—in. I mean it, Aunt Addie. You get up now—"

"I can't," Addie moaned.

"Yes, you can, if you don't want to be murdered yourself."

At that or Sue's forceful voice, Addie's eyelids opened. "What do you mean?"

"I mean that Juan has disappeared and we found blood on the deck. He may have been murdered last night. All of us heard you say just now that you had seen Juan being helped out of the salon. I'll not ask what you were doing last night, prowling into the salon, but I can guess. Now don't cry—'' Addie's pretty face had wrinkled up. ''Just lock your door, there's a key, see it? And mind me. I mean it, Aunt Addie.''

''Nobody's going to hurt me.'' Addie lifted herself defiantly on one elbow. ''I only saw Juan's white jacket. The corridor was dark, and maybe I didn't really see who helped him—if anybody did.''

''Oh, Aunt Addie, don't make up—I mean, stick to facts. Everybody heard you as good as say that you can identify Juan's murderer—if he was murdered and—but everybody was in the salon and—''

''Not Stan,'' said Addie triumphantly. ''Nor that Wiley. Oh—'' She clutched at her throat.

Sue all but yelled as the boat took a delirious leap. ''Please, do as I say. Lock your door. I'll be back.''

Her aunt seemed to nod. Sue crushed any humane impulse to help Addie and made her way, clinging to one of the rails, along the corridor out into the fresh if foggy air.

Stan was at the wheel. He and Monty were both leaning over the compass. Stan said, ''Oh, Sue! You've heard.''

''She's heard some of it,'' Monty said. ''Not all. Not about the dinghy—or did Lalie tell you that?''

Stan said, ''Lalie didn't know it. Only you and I know about that.''

''We had a collapsible rubber dinghy. All you have to do is pull something and it inflates. In a matter of seconds. It's gone. Probably,'' Monty continued grimly, ''with Juan's body in it.''

Sue considered. ''But he could have taken it himself.''

Stan said nothing, but his silence spoke emphatically for itself.

Monty said, ''Setting himself adrift in this fog?''

Monty grasped the binoculars, squinted, and shook his head. ''Can't see a thing through these.''

Stan broke in. ''Have you asked Wiley about it?''

''The doctor won't let me see him yet.''

"Usually that kind of raft has a certain amount of stores—food, water, a compass, even sometimes—By God, sometimes a battery radio!" It was a very brief flare of hope. Stan's face fell. "But if it was like everything else around here, the batteries would have run down. And we don't know where the raft is. We don't know who got it out and inflated it. We don't know whether or not Juan is alive. That blood on the deck and the missing ax—"

"Meat cleaver," said Monty. "Stan, the compass is going mad again. Look!"

Sue peered over, between their shoulders. By the binnacle light she could see the needle of the compass dancing around, until Stan asked sharply. "What in hell have you got on, Sue?"

"Me? Why—nothing."

Suddenly Monty shoved a hand in his pocket and drew out a revolver.

Stan glared at him. "A fine thing to be carrying around!"

"On a boat where somebody tried to kill me? Don't be an ass."

"But how did it get on board with you? Do you always carry a gun around?"

"No." Monty brushed his forehead and slightly displaced the bandage. "That is, sometimes. That is—oh, hell, Stan, I'm a rather rich man. Not a rich, rich man but—"

"Afraid of being abducted? Or just robbed?" Stan's words were sarcastic, his manner interested in almost an objective way—so objective that Sue looked at him with suspicion.

But Monty took it coolly. "Nope. I simply keep a gun around—lots of people do. Here on the yacht I put it in a drawer in my cabin."

"The cabin Wiley and the doctor are now using?"

"Yes, of course. But I got it out as soon as I saw the shape Wiley was in. Put it in Juan's cabin that I've been using. But after that attack upon me—well, naturally, I took it and—there you are."

"Get it away. Keep it away. Give it to Sue. It's affecting the compass. Anything with steel. We are already off course. You know that!"

"I wasn't thinking! Take it, Sue. Hide it somewhere in your cabin, and, by the way, just don't forget that it's loaded."

She took the revolver and moved back but looked up as Stan gave a shout. "Look! It's clearing over there. Clouds. Wind. Way off there toward the—I think toward the south!"

At least the barometer might be right. Gradually the compass needle swung around as Sue backed hurriedly away from it.

"You mean it's going to storm?" Monty shouted as angrily as if it were Stan's fault.

"How do I know? We've had some biggish swells. I'd guess a storm. Not bad, I hope. But it's coming up fast. Anyway, it's driving the fog off. Now maybe somebody will see us."

As he spoke, Sue became aware of a drone in the fog, in the air, somewhere above them and at one side.

Stan heard it, too, and as Monty started to speak, said, "Shut up, Monty! Listen! It's the Coast Guard. I'm sure! It's a helicopter."

Monty seized the binoculars again. "I can't see it. Go on, Stan! S.O.S. Hurry! Try the radio. I'll work the hooter."

Nothing at all happened. Beyond the yacht's foghorn they could hear the helicopter roar over their heads, on and on and gradually distant, and then out of hearing.

Monty heaved a long sigh. "Didn't see us."

"Get the revolver out of the wheelhouse, Sue. Isn't there a safe of some kind on this boat, Monty?"

Monty shook his head and said, disarmingly, "I seem to have bought it with eyes blindfolded. Sorry, Stan."

"Oh, well." Stan never held a grudge; for that matter, neither did Monty. Sue felt a wave of complete fury.

"Why don't you do something—anything? Isn't there such a thing as an anchor? A sea anchor? Surely I've heard of—"

Stan silenced her with the kind of look he might have given an unusually backward child. "On this boat?"

"There was one," Monty said feebly. "Once. I understand something happened to it or the chain and—anyway there isn't one now."

"Oh. Well"—she looked at the array of signals—"what are all those flags for?"

Stan gave her a wry grin. "They say, distress, fire, smallpox, mutiny—yellow fever, for all I know. You have quite a collection, Monty."

"Not mine," Monty said shortly. "Wiley's. How would I have any idea of what all those damn flags mean? Anyway if it does clear before the storm, somebody will see us. The Coast Guard copter just might come back," he said, with the first gleam of hope Sue had seen in him for what seemed a year or two, not only two days and nearly two nights.

"Stan, how far from land are we?" she asked.

"Too far," Stan said glumly, eying the compass, which was still performing a dance. "Get that gun out of the way!"

"I'm going!" Sue cried. "I'll put the revolver somewhere safe." Safe, I hope, she added silently to herself. "But I was thinking that perhaps Juan got himself into the dinghy and is trying to row to land and get help for us."

Both men looked at her as if she'd taken leave of her senses. As perhaps I have, she reflected, or at least am about to.

"He wouldn't know where he was going," Monty said after a moment. She thought the faintest gleam of hope had leaped again into his eyes, but if so, it faded quickly.

"However," Stan said thoughtfully, "I told you. That raft ought to have a compass." He hit his forehead with one hand. "If only you'd told me about that gun yesterday when the compass began to jump around—"

Monty said sharply, "Was I here at that time? That very moment?"

"No . . ." Stan, too, looked very tired, unshaven, dirty, his face smeared with some kind of dark grease, his heavy blue jacket wrinkled and damp. "I don't remember. All right, call me a fool. Wait a minute—yes, I believe the doctor was here. And I think Celia had come to ask if I wanted coffee or anything. And—yes, somebody—maybe it was you—came up as I was bending over the compass and I just said 'Get out' over my shoulder—"

"If the compass was already whirling around, it wasn't because whoever that was had been carrying something that would cause it," Monty said obscurely yet logically.

Stan's hard-held temper snapped. "All right! I'm a first-class idiot. Get yourself out of this mess. I've had it."

"Oh, come on, Stan, you can't just leave things like this. We've got nobody but you," Monty said with desperate truth. He caught Stan's arms. "Believe me!"

"Oh, I know! But the plain fact is there isn't anything I can do."

Sue said glumly, "I'll put this thing away."

Stan felt sorry for her. "Take it easy, Sue."

Monty put his arm around her. "If it storms, we'll weather it. See if we don't."

We'll see all right, she thought bitterly as she went down to the salon where Lalie sat watching Sissy, who was sniffing at the damp spots on the carpet in a ghoulishly interested way. Lalie lifted horrified eyes. "She's been doing that, over and over, and she won't stop except once in a while she lifts up her nose and gives a weird sound like a howl. Juan was murdered right there! I'm sure of it, and Sissy is sure of it."

"Sissy is sure of nothing." Sue had almost to shout, for the boat gave an unnerving lurch, ominously different from the former steady roll. She bumped her head on the sofa as she leaned over to take Sissy up in her arms. The little dog wriggled. Sue dropped the revolver, but she scooped it up again. Lalie began to cry. And then Addie screamed.

Ten

It was Addie's scream. No mistake about it. Sue clutched the revolver, held Sissy tightly with one arm, ran, staggering, between those very practical rails and fell against Addie's door. "Addie—"

Addie merely screamed again.

"Addie—"

Celia suddenly appeared behind her. "What's she screaming about?"

"I don't know. I told her to lock this door and she did and—"

"Let me try. Miss Addie! Hey! Open the door!" Celia added quietly, "She's just had a spot of d.t.'s, Sue. Don't get upset."

"No, she never drinks that much. Besides, she had nothing to drink this morning and—"

"She's had enough over the years," Celia said shortly. "Reminds me of my late husband—"

The narrow door flung open and Addie, screaming, fell against them, squeezing Sissy, who gave a yelp of indignation and squirmed furiously out of Sue's clasp. Celia caught Addie. Sue, aware of the gun in her hand, put it down quickly to assist Celia. They drew Addie back into the cabin and put her on the bed. Celia said sternly, "Now what were you screaming about?"

"That man," Addie said. "That horrible man! He was here."

Celia eyed Addie closely and speculatively; she said, as if to herself, "Not pink elephants or snakes. Not even spiders or—'' She turned to Sue. ''Might be merely the shakes, so to speak. Not d.t.'s at all.''

Sue, more accustomed to Addie, said crisply. ''What man?''

''The one with the heart,'' Addie cried breathlessly.

Again more accustomed to Addie than Celia, Sue leaped to the conclusion. ''You mean the patient, Wiley?''

''Oh, that's his name! Of course. Yes, I remember. But I didn't when he came in here and just stood there breathing at me—''

''Gasping for breath,'' Sue translated for Celia.

Addie went on, ''and stood and stood. All in white—''

''Pajamas, probably, and blanket,'' Sue translated again.

''And then he grabbed at the table and disappeared. Oh—'' Addie wailed. ''He took it away.''

''What did he take?'' Celia asked shortly.

But Sue put a hand upon Celia's arm. ''He's gone now, Aunt Addie. Try and settle down.''

Addie lifted pleading eyes to Sue. ''But he is not supposed to walk at all. Is he?''

Celia had recovered. ''No,'' she said. ''And certainly the doctor wouldn't want him to come into your room scaring you half to death. Look here! How did he get in your cabin? Wasn't the door locked?''

''He had a key,'' Addie said simply. She ran her pretty fingers through tousled curls. ''He said he had keys to everything on the yacht.''

''And forgot to give them to Monty, I suppose,'' Celia said icily.

''I don't know. Oh, I don't know, but I don't want him coming in here again—''

Addie was about to sob. Sue put her firmly back upon pillows. ''Now stay there. Don't move. I'll get you something—''

''I will,'' Celia said and flashed away at once.

The light from the porthole in the cabin was grayish and dim.

Addie said, "Sue dear, did she mean—"

"Yes, I think so." Celia, Sue decided, not for the first time, was a very practical and realistic woman.

Addie adjusted pillows behind her head, and the yacht shuddered. There was the crash of glass from the table nearby and the faint odor of whiskey drifting up from the carpet. Addie moaned and stretched over to survey the damage (and the lost whiskey, Sue noted) and was in that dangerous position when the yacht seemed to heave up in the middle like a cat arching its back. Addie screamed, but softly, and the yacht lowered itself, quivering.

"Oh, Sue," Addie wailed. "I'm not fit to die—"

Sue shoved her back onto pillows. "You're not going to die. Celia will bring some more whiskey or something. Here she is now."

The door had flung back, but it wasn't Celia. It was Dr. Smith who stormed in. A fitting entrance, Sue thought deliriously.

The doctor was very angry. "What's all this? What about my patient? Why did you let him walk around?"

Addie put both hands over her mouth and stared, terrified, at the doctor. And indeed, he was terrifying: even Sue, who had seen him in such moods and ought to have been inured to the sight of the enraged sparks in his eyes, the bloom of red color in his square jowls, the thrusting set of his always rather formidable chin, was intimidated. She braced herself. "She had nothing to do with Mr. Wiley—"

Dr. Smith shot her one look. "I'm not talking to you, Nurse."

"You're talking to my aunt!" Only another unnerving pitch of the yacht gave Sue the courage to shout back at the doctor. "She didn't invite that—that wandering patient of yours. He came in here, scared her, grabbed a bottle and—"

"A bottle! Oh, no! He's not supposed to drink. My God, he shouldn't walk—"

Dr. Smith clutched at the door to keep his balance and then disappeared toward the big cabin and his patient.

Addie gasped, lifted her head, and whispered piercingly, "Sue! If that man can walk, then maybe he did all those terrible things to Monty and Juan!"

Sue had also leaped to that surmise. She shook her head, although she rather welcomed the conjecture. "But he's not strong. I don't think he could possibly have attacked Monty and then dragged him into the sea and— Listen! What do you know about Juan?"

Addie waited a moment. Then she spoke with a chilling matter-of-fact, if hushed, voice. "I'm not sure. I think he was struck with something, probably from the galley. Then he was put out to sea in a rubber thing, a float, and now he's lost forever in this horrible fog and sea. And storm!" Addie sighed, again with no dramatics whatever, merely a horribly convincing pragmatic acceptance.

Sue sat down, harder than she had intended, for the yacht gave symptoms of engaging in another Nijinsky leap. "Tell me everything."

"I've told you what I know. Don't you think I have ears? I listened. This morning. You were all talking about it and Celia was mopping up—" Addie turned slightly green.

"But when you came in you acted as if you knew nothing at all—"

"I *don't* know anything about it. Only what everybody was saying. I thought I'd feel better about it if I had just a small drink. But then—"

"You didn't hear about the rubber dinghy?"

"Oh, that!" Addie sighed. "Don't ask me that."

"I do ask you. Come on now."

"Well . . . all right. But you're not to tell anybody. I saw it."

"You saw—"

"Of course. I told you I saw a man helping Juan; that's what I said, helping—"

Sue was slightly diverted. "Why did you say help?"

"My dear, I'm no fool. Not really. I'm not sure whether or not I saw anybody with him. But did I intend to say to everybody that I thought Juan was dead? It was something about the way his head lolled back. You know, in the movies they seem always to forget that heads loll. They lift up people and say isn't it too bad, So-and-so is dead, but then So-and-so is holding his head upright, perfectly normal—"

"Aunt Addie!" Sue had a sense of being cast adrift, a feeling that was not improved by the boat's leaping in the air again and then shivering as it came down. "Now wait, Aunt Addie. You didn't want to say that you knew who murdered him—"

"You told me I mustn't tell—that is, identify anybody. You told me to lock that door and—"

"You didn't tell me everything—oh, never mind. The same danger exists. Aunt Addie, it's real. Now then, what do you know about the dinghy?"

Addie blinked, clutched the bed, but said quite calmly. "I saw something out there on that narrow deck that goes around part of my cabin. It was like a—like a mattress, sort of."

"When was that? After, you say, that you saw Juan being helped out of the salon?"

"I didn't say exactly that! But I did see Juan's white coat, and he was sort of staggering along, so—perhaps I didn't really see anybody helping him. But I was frightened. Why not? I hurried back here and was just in time to look out that window."

"But you couldn't see—"

"Yes, I could. Not clearly, but I saw enough—" She stopped dead still and set her lips.

Oh, now she's turning mulish again, Sue thought. Unfairly, as it developed, for Addie twisted her hands together suddenly and said, in a voice barely loud enough to be heard over the increasing creaks of the boat. "I saw the mattress lifted over the rail, like a big blot of shadow. It went over. I thought there was a body in it. Juan's, I'm sure. I tell you I could see his white jacket. Oh, Sue, it was really dreadful.''

She moistened her lips. Addie's words were far too graphic. "But then, why did you take such a chance telling everybody you had seen someone, as you said, helping Juan?''

"Because I wanted to find out who did it, of course. I felt it must be whoever it was that put him in the mattress—''

"Dinghy," Sue said.

Addie paid no attention. "But then you made me hustle back here, and I knew it was no use talking to you then.''

It did make sense, Addie's kind of sense, Sue told herself. "Then you may as well tell me who—who you think it may have been.''

Addie had closed her eyes; she opened one eye, and suddenly an older, wiser, far more realistic Addie peered out. "And put you in danger? No.''

It was Addie's reasoning, and in a way it was sensible: she had been trying to protect Sue and in her addled way had succeeded. Addled for Addie, Sue thought wearily, and the yacht gave another heave as Celia appeared in the doorway, clutching a bottle. Only a quarter full, Sue noted, relieved; Addie was fully capable of doing away with that and yet keeping some kind of equilibrium.

Celia gasped. "That was rather a big one! Who was it she saw?''

Addie set her lips in an almost childish grimace of determination.

"She won't tell," Sue said wearily. "She's not sure she saw anybody.''

"I'll give her some of this. What happened to that glass on the carpet?''

"The storm," Addie said clearly.

"I'll get another." Celia knew exactly where to go; she moved across the tiny room easily, also gracefully, Sue thought, eying her with an admiration she could not possibly have denied. In the gray light in the cabin, Celia's white face looked whiter, her fine features, nose, chin and the beautifully defined cheekbones, which left charming little hollows below them, her dark eyes and the sleek curve of her black eyebrows, were still lovely. Celia was a beauty. No denying that. Monty had picked well, and apparently he had been faithful to Celia for some time. Celia turned back, poured a drink for Addie with perfectly controlled hands, adorned with oval pale-pink fingernails, and thrust it at Addie, who said, "Thank you, Celia. How very kind of you!"

This ought to be a fantastic situation, Sue thought vaguely; instead it is quiet, not at all dramatic, only curiously normal and everyday. But just the same, things seemed to have gone quite awry in the world. The yacht shot up again. Celia said, "I'm afraid we are in for a little rough weather. That barometer was telling the truth. Not quite like everybody on this boat, but at least we can credit the barometer."

Addie lifted pansylike eyes above the rim of her glass. "I tell the truth, always. Just perhaps not if it is not interesting." She took a gentle and quite small sip from the glass.

Celia brooded for a moment, hanging onto the foot of the bed and still graceful and controlled. Finally she said, "The point just now is that that man, Wiley, is fully capable of running around the place. If we happened to talk of alibis, his would have been that he couldn't leave his bed. I think we'll have to tell Monty about this, Sue. Don't you?"

"Yes. And Stan and—oh, dear me—" She pitched with the boat and the arm of her chair struck her amidships. Suitable word, she thought on the very edge of her mind as she lay on the edge of the chair. "He's pretty busy right now, though. I didn't tell you. There was a helicopter over us. Coast Guard. But they didn't see us."

Celia's lovely dark eyes narrowed. "Still, it's just possible that somebody along the Sound reported us missing. But I don't see how anybody can do anything for us just now."

Addie had got away with half the liquor in the glass, very swiftly, very smoothly before Sue looked at her again. She said then, very pleasantly, "'And in the graves are coral made—'"

"Oh, Aunt Addie, not now, please—"

But Addie couldn't be stopped. "'Fear at my heart, as at a cup, my lifeblood seemed to sip.'"

"Aunt Addie, didn't you ever read anything but Coleridge?"

"The coral was Shakespeare, dear." Addie raised a rather lofty eyebrow and sipped again.

"Besides," Celia said neatly, "it isn't your lifeblood you seem to sip, it's whiskey-and-water."

Addie said comfortably, "An old lady does read a great deal. No money left for bridge or—oh, yes, one reads."

Sue, knowing on whom the remaining Gates money had been spent, said, "But, darling, I'll make it up to you."

Celia said dryly, "Why don't you read Browning? 'Grow old along with me, the best is yet to be—'"

"That's simply not true," Addie said. "Just you wait. Browning!" She took a rather large gulp and finished, "Damn fool! Pompous ass!"

"That should settle Mr. Browning," Sue began.

The doctor thundered from the doorway, "I've given my patient strict orders to stay in his cabin. He shouldn't walk around at all and he knows it! Here, is this yours?" He held out a bottle to Addie, who smiled happily and reached out her hands.

But the doctor withdrew it sternly. "Looks to me as if you have had quite enough. Now then," he addressed Celia. "Have you ever been on this ridiculous boat in a storm?"

Celia lifted her beautifully arched black eyebrows. "No."

"Wiley says he has. He says this is not a real storm and everything will be fine. I'd like to know whether he's right—"

A lurch sent him staggering against the table.

"We'll soon find out," Celia said, rather ominously. "Meantime, did your patient kill Juan? And try to kill Monty?"

The doctor pulled himself erect and rubbed an undoubtedly bruised thigh. "*No*, of course not!"

"Don't shout," Addie murmured into her drink, eying the bottle still in the doctor's hands.

"I wish to be heard," Dr. Smith said nastily. "Certainly my patient is in no condition to do anything that requires physical strength. Just don't give him anything to drink."

"I suppose you don't mean water?" Celia said.

This, rather unfortunately, set Addie off again. " 'Water, water, everywhere, and not a drop to drink—' "

"Oh, my God!" The doctor pushed himself around, still holding the bottle, and reeled off toward the salon.

"Looks as if he'd had a drop too much himself," Addie said pleasantly. "I'll bet he did, too. Perhaps in his younger days. Look at the color of his face. Red. That is, not now." She considered it gravely and nodded, "Looks green. Or gray. Or both."

Sue felt as if hysteria might seize upon her; there was something fantastically out of place in many conversations with her aunt, but never had she and Addie been in just such a situation before. Involving murder.

"Aunt Addie," Sue said desperately, "we'll talk to Monty and to Stan. Now just once more, will you tell us who—"

She stopped, for Addie was shaking her curls and reaching for the bottle on the bedside table. "Silly of him to take that other bottle away. I had a hard time getting in the salon when none of you could see me. Now don't look at me like that, Sue. Celia, you are a witness. Sue knows nothing at all about the person I saw with Juan last night.''

Celia eyed her thoughtfully. "All right. But you are in a—"

"Dangerous position? I don't think so," said Addie.

There was nothing to do but leave Addie to her solace. Sue whispered to Celia as they left and as Addie cheerfully waved at them with the hand that didn't hold a glass, "She'll be all right, I think. It's the storm and everything. She's really upset and doesn't want to show it."

"I hope," Celia said dryly, "that she doesn't get upset often."

"There was something—" The force of the sea, like an invisible hand, pushed Sue against the bulkhead; oddly, Celia was shoved in the opposite direction.

"Wow," Celia said, "that was a big one. However, I don't think coral grows in the Atlantic—not right here, anyway."

"Oh, don't!" Sue had got herself upright again. "I wish Aunt Addie wouldn't quote such—Celia! What did I do with that gun?"

Celia checked herself, bracing her lithe body against the rail. "What gun? Monty's?"

"Yes! He had it in his pocket. It was making the compass whirl around. Stan and Monty told me to put it away. I don't know what I did with it."

Celia swayed and clutched the rail and swayed again, but her dark eyes were very steady. "I didn't see it at all." She shut her eyes. "Let me think. There was your aunt and the bedside table and a broken glass and the smell of whiskey, but—no, I cannot remember seeing a gun. You must have dropped it when she screamed. We'd better look."

They looked, but there was no gun anywhere. From Aunt Addie's cabin there came a wavering chant that resolved itself into " 'Fifteen men on a dead man's chest—yo, ho, ho—' "

Celia's lovely mouth twitched. "It wasn't rum I gave her. Do you think that's what she wants?"

"She won't get it. Honestly, Celia, she's not like this as a rule. That is, she does tipple a little. I mean, probably quite a lot. I mean, yes, she does. But not as much as this. She's frightened."

"I'd be frightened, too, if I had seen whoever it was killed poor little Juan and shoved him overboard. What's that?"

That was a yell from the deck. Another yell. The doctor thudded out of the salon. The lawyer strode toward them as rapidly as his dignity would allow. "Sounds like something or other—" He disappeared toward the bridge deck. Lalie darted up and shot between them. Celia glanced at Sue. "I'm going, too."

Sue didn't even answer. They both crawled outside and along the slippery, still too foggy side deck. There were gusts of wind, so strong a scarf whipped off Sue's throat. On deck an enormous bright halo surrounded the yacht and everybody.

Not one light, but lights. Floodlights coming from somewhere, outlining sharply the figures of Monty and Stan, both leaning over the rail and shouting. "Want a tow?" were the first clear words Sue heard, coming from beyond the bright glow.

Sue and Celia ran to the rail slipping and sliding. Monty was shouting and waving the binoculars. Stan was shouting at a strong-looking, sturdy boat that lay near, washing up and down with the waves.

Stan yelled into cupped hands. "Sure, thanks!" He turned and saw Sue, "It's the Coast Guard. They'll give us a tow. We are just off Groton."

"Groton?" Celia cried shrilly. "How did we get here? I thought we were going south."

Stan replied tersely, "Winds drove us a little north. Twenty miles or so from Montauk. Compass kept getting us off course. Coast Guard found us."

Monty shouted above the tumult, "How did they know where we were?"

Stan again replied. "They can do anything."

Celia persisted. "But how did they find us?"

A young voice shouted from below, "Ready for us?"

"Oh, my God, yes," Monty shouted. "How did you find us?"

The young man replied proudly, "We can find anything. We've got all the latest equipment. If a sub hiccups in—" A wave appeared to threaten his balance. He gulped and finished, " . . . in the Caspian Sea we know it! Any women with you?"

"Four." Monty was clinging hard to the rail.

The floodlights were now bright and clear, sharply outlining everybody on deck. The doctor was there, hanging over the rail, too. Lalie was huddled in a blanket, peering over Sue's shoulders, her pretty face pallid in the strong, yellow lights.

A more decisive, authoritative voice came this time by way of a loud-hailer, so it resounded in their ears. "We'll get the towlines rigged. Hang in."

Monty leaned over. "We've lost power! Everything! Did the copter see us?"

"Sure. And then some little guy was washed up. On a life raft. Damn near done in, too. Said the yacht had drifted out here in distress. Seems you had a bit of a blow. If you have women, better get them below. It's turning kind of cold."

Stan said in Sue's ear, "The little guy must be Juan."

Eleven

Celia took Sue's arm. "Come on. You, too, Lalie. That's good advice. Let's get below. My teeth are chattering, I'm so cold and wet."

If the storm had blown away the fog, it had stealthily crept in again as if determined not to let up on its prey. And instead of drifting helplessly south, they had drifted as helplessly out to sea but in a northern direction. Only twenty miles from Montauk! But with a peculiarly erratic compass, who knew where they were or had been! The important, the astounding fact was that Juan must be alive. He must have floated off in the rubber dinghy. So Addie simply had not seen two figures. Addie had been befuddled.

The boat was still heaving up and down in an unnerving way. Sue would have liked to watch the procedure of attaching the lines for a tow but she was urgently interested just then in getting warm; her jeans and sweater clung to her with a damp chill. Addie's door was closed. Sometime she'd try to pin her aunt down more precisely about what Addie thought she had seen in the night: Juan being assisted by somebody—she must have meant a man—and then shoved overboard in the dinghy. But the important fact was that Juan had not been killed.

Celia gave a gurgle of laughter. "You know, I was perfectly sure that I was cleaning up the remains of a murder there in the salon. As your aunt would say, 'Out, damned spot!'" She opened the door and went into the cabin she shared with Lalie, where Sissy greeted her with yelps of joy.

Lalie said dourly, "I don't see anything to laugh about. I was never so cold and miserable in my life. Suppose their tow rope, line, hawser, or whatever they call it, breaks and we drift off again?"

"They'll not let that happen," Sue told her firmly and hoped she was right.

Wiley's door was closed. Once in her own cabin, Sue shed her clammy clothes, got into everything warm she could find, and huddled under the blankets. She was aware of shouts, clattering, various sounds from above.

At last she was also aware of a stealthy, wonderfully slow motion of the yacht.

So the boat was being towed to harbor.

Eventually a wavering gleam of what actually had to be evening sunlight streamed through the cabin, and Sue went groggily to sleep, lulled by the streak of sunlight as much as by the cautious motion of the boat.

Monty woke her. He looked tired, dirty and years younger. "Everything's all right. We're tied up at the Coast Guard Station. Later they'll give us a tow to a nearby docking facility. They can't repair us, but they'll do everything they can. You okay?"

"Oh, yes. I'm so glad! I guess I'm just tired. Is Aunt Addie all right?"

Monty gave a short but pleasant laugh. "Sure. She had her cabin door locked, but I called to her. She said she's fine."

"She's got hold of something to drink."

"That's all right. Deserves it. Sue, darling, this has not been the cruise I wanted it to be."

"I'm sorry, Monty. About the yacht—"

"She's old. I didn't realize how old. But Stan says it was built sometime in the twenties. Lots of money around then. Think of that. Over fifty, fifty-five years old. Not," Monty said with dignity, "that that is old for a good boat. But"—his handsome face sagged a little—"the fact is, I just took Wiley's word for it when he said the boat was in fine shape. Told me he hadn't kept a real log but I could examine what he had and get her history. I didn't bother. I bought too hastily. Took a fancy to the old girl, I guess. Wiley certainly sold me a pup."

"But a very handsome and luxurious pup," Sue said comfortingly. "We'll take more cruises—"

"Nope." Monty shook his head. "I'm leaving her here. She can be sold for what anybody will pay. I've had it with this antique!"

"Monty, I just remembered, what happened to the fuel?"

"I don't know. But I'm going to find out. Meantime, I

must say the Coast Guard is doing us proud. They act as if Stan were an admiral at least, so glad to find a real sailor on board. Although they are a little puzzled, too, how a navy man managed to get off course and lose power! But at least the storm has blown itself out. I'm going ashore now, Sue. Oh! Give me my gun."

Her throat tightened a little. "I'm sorry, Monty. But I can't find it anywhere. I looked and—"

"But you must remember where you left it."

"No, I don't. I think I must have put it down in—or near—Aunt Addie's cabin. Celia and I looked, but we couldn't find it."

"Sue, a gun is nothing to leave lying around casually! It's loaded, too."

"Surely somebody just picked it up. Put it away. I'll ask Lalie."

Monty's face darkened. "I wouldn't put it past Lawson. He's been damn disagreeable about all this. Sissy bit him just now. Don't blame her. He kicked her. She got in the way and—oh, he said he had stumbled and didn't see the dog. Tell that to Sissy." There was a fleeting smile on his handsome face. He leaned over, kissed her lightly, and started for the door.

"Wait, Monty. How did you happen to know Mr. Wiley?"

He turned back. "Met him in Palm Beach. He has a huge kind of castle there—must have been built about the same time as this boat. Or even earlier. He's trying to sell the house now. Five million or so, and I'll bet he gets it. That," Monty said crossly, "is how he got his clutches on so much money. I think he's probably sold everything he felt like selling, no matter what condition it was in. I'll bet that house of his is full of rats and spiders and falling plaster and falling ceilings."

"Oh, you've seen it?"

"Only from the outside. He lives in an apartment near Celia's—" Monty stopped and looked faintly embarrassed.

"That's where you met him? At Celia's?"

"Sue, all that is in the past! You said it didn't matter—"

"How did Mr. Wiley find Dr. Smith?"

"Oh, I suggested Dr. Smith. Wiley had decided to come to New York when he found he was having trouble. Dr. Smith is a good man. I met him in your hospital. Remember? Now I suppose you'll want to go to your aunt's house when we get back."

"Oh, yes." Sue had a sudden nostalgic vision of the airy, sunny cottage, vine-draped and hedged with trees and flowers. "Then we're going back?"

"Yes. I guess so. By plane, if I can charter one. Actually, though, I'd like to take the yacht back by Long Island Sound. Then hire somebody to take her to Florida. Better chance there for a good sale."

"Monty, have you talked to Juan? What does he say?"

Monty's face darkened again. "Says only he doesn't want to leave Sam Wiley. Says he took the dinghy hoping to find help. Thought he could get to the coast and obviously did. He's got a gash across his head. Juan says he doesn't know what hit him but thinks he stumbled on a cleaver he happened to have in his hand."

"But how could he!"

"That's what he says."

"Then what about the dinghy?"

"I told you. He says he got it out and inflated and overboard. We needed help. Sam Wiley needed help. He didn't tell me because he was afraid I'd stop him. Makes himself out quite a hero."

She said reflectively, "Somebody struck you over the head."

Monty's face turned to handsomely carved stone. "Don't think I've forgotten that. I must go and see what they are doing."

The door closed after him, and Sue lay back, listening to the sounds that were going on all over the boat. She couldn't identify any of them precisely, but they did certainly indicate activity. So now what? she thought, but calmly. Sometime later, Lalie broke into her warm comfort.

"Can I come in, Sue?"

"Of course."

"Then open the door."

"It's not locked. Come on in."

"My hands are full."

"Oh," Sue scrambled out of bed, tangling herself in the covers, and opened the door upon Lalie carrying a large and softly clinking basket.

"Courtesy of the Coast Guard." Lalie put the basket on the bedside table. "Smell it."

"What is in there?"

Lalie was happily pulling out thermos bottles, covered plates, plastic tableware. "There's New England clam chowder. Don't grab! Coffee is in the other one. Oh, all right, Sissy. Come in. But you can't have any more chowder. I fed you half of mine."

Sissy pranced in, bright eyes fixed upon the basket.

"Do you mean to say all this—"

"Certainly. Every single one of us has been supplied with a basket like this."

"Aunt Addie?"

"She's sitting up and happy as a—as a clam," said Lalie with a giggle. "Not a drop of rum or whiskey or anything in her whole cabin. Not that it's big enough to hold much more than Auntie." Lalie settled herself in a chair.

"When do we leave?"

"Leave? What do you mean?"

"Monty said he might charter a plane and leave the yacht here and sell her. But he preferred returning along the Sound and then sending her to Florida."

Lalie laughed shortly. "You may know Monty, but not as well as I do. This yacht is one of his dreams come true. You see, he was a poor boy, had goals, and he's achieved most of them. This yacht was a sort of pinnacle, I guess you'd say. This and marriage. To you." Lalie added firmly, "Don't pretend that is not the idea. Everybody guesses it."

"It's not—that is—" Sue gave up any suitable reply and said, "Monty a poor boy! What do you mean?"

Lalie stretched out her legs and yawned. "Just that. Our father was a country lawyer without much money until after his first wife, Monty's mother, died. Then he married my mother. She had money, and later on they had me. Now my mother and father are both gone. Monty right away took over guardianship of me. He is a trustee of the money my mother left me. Besides, he's been really good and sensible and kind. Gives me hell once in a while when he's afraid I'll take on something or other—a man or drugs or—oh, anything he disapproves of. He's very straight, a born conservative, you know. Can't help it."

"But Celia?"

Lalie shrugged thin shoulders under a big loose blue jacket that she must have borrowed. "Oh, that. I thought he'd told you all about that."

"In a way, yes."

"Simple." Lalie crossed one leg over the other and yawned again. "You must have known Celia. She's often been around these parts. I don't know where she was born, but that doesn't matter. She was quite a favorite at the dances, I've heard."

"I went to her wedding. She looked so lovely."

"Must have! She's lovely still. I don't know what happened to her husband, but anyway he disappeared. Don't know when Monty met her, but he liked her and she liked him and—there you have it. For several years."

"Why—"

Lalie picked it up. "I haven't really explained Monty to you. Not sure I can, but I think Monty had a kind of inferiority complex, Mother's money, all that. Anyway, I told you, he started in to make money, and, by God, he did. Hand over fist. But then—this is only a guess—I think he began to feel he wants a family now. A good marriage, good background. Oh, he likes you, Sue." Lalie laughed, exactly as Monty laughed, in a friendly way. "But I think he likes also just—just you and your Aunt Addie and everything. Blue blood."

"My blood's as red as anybody's. And I don't have any money at all. I took nurses' training so I'd have a job."

Lalie could look shrewd; again there was a fleeting likeness to her half brother. "You can give that up for Monty, can't you?"

"I like Monty, don't forget."

Lalie pursed up her lips and said flatly, "You must like him if you are seriously thinking of marriage. Why do you suppose he arranged this cruise? Meant it to be a sort of family trip. You, your aunt, me. Wiley just happened to be included."

"And Celia," Sue said.

Lalie looked at her with a sparkle in her eyes. "Now look here, Sue. Don't make a fuss about Celia. It's my fault in a way that she's on board. She was visiting, heard me planning the cruise, and just came along. She felt it her right," Lalie said sternly. "Not sure I blame her."

"Oh, Lalie, that's no business of mine."

"I wouldn't be so sure of that. If you *are* planning marriage. I like you. I like Celia, too. Monty's my brother, but I honestly think I ought to warn you. He's been supporting Celia for several years. Bought her an apartment in Palm Beach, bought—oh, everything she wanted. She's not going to give up all that without a struggle."

"You mean she came up from Florida to see you in the hope of—"

"Sure. Monty was the reason. I don't know; they may have had—must have had—some difference of opinion, let's say. I can't see them quarreling—still . . . But whatever happened, Celia won't give up Monty easily."

The soup was too hot. Sue blew on it, thinking, and said slowly, "That's all in the past."

"So you say. So I'm sure Monty has said."

"Naturally. Sensible."

"Sensible! All right, if that's the way your generation looks at things—"

This stung Sue. "*My* generation! I'm twenty-three. Only five years older than you!"

"I know, but you've been sheltered—"

"In a big city hospital! You don't know what you're talking about! You've never had to do any real work in your life."

"Well, but—"

"I can still converse with persons even in their teens. Honestly, I can."

"Now don't fuss at me. I'd have a job, believe me, if it was necessary. I'm not very rich, but I have enough. That is, when I'm twenty-one I get part of a trust fund. The rest of it when I'm thirty. Why should I work?" She paused and added very righteously, "Take the bread out of the mouth of some girl who needs it?"

"Noble, noble you," said Sue meanly.

"Oh, well." Lalie giggled but then sobered. "All the same, you may know the world in a way, but if I were you I'd look out for Celia. If you really want Monty."

"I like Celia," Sue said stubbornly and also truthfully.

"Do you think she really likes you?" Lalie asked all too pertinently. There was a knock at the door and Stan came in.

He was full of good humor. "By morning we'll be ready to set out again. Hello, Lalie. That soup you brought me was fine."

"I cooked it myself," Lalie assured him gravely. Stan chuckled and put a friendly hand on her shoulder.

"I'll bet you did. It was great. Put a new heart into all of us. Now get out, kid. I want to talk to Sue."

Lalie frowned. "All right. But I think I ought to stay. A chaperone. Monty would prefer that."

"Out," said Stan and pushed her, but gently, out the door, which he closed.

"She's a very nice girl," Sue said.

"Sure. In a minute you'll say she's just right for me. And maybe she is." He sat in the chair Lalie had vacated. "You have to hand it to the Coast Guard. Towed us to a nearby docking facility. Greased the wheels as far as they could. Now the fuel tanks have been cleaned. Somebody managed to dig up some plugs for the filters, no more sand, thank you. New fuses where needed, which is just about everywhere. Batteries checked—everything. So here we are. Leaving tomorrow. I've got new charts. Monty's were a little antiquated. Like this yacht—"

"He told me he would charter a plane and we'd go home! Leave the yacht here or send it to Florida! Anyway, sell it!"

"Sell it! Not he! He loves it like a child. That is, a rather elderly child, but he loves it, and now he's all for starting again for Eleuthera."

"But he can't do that! This boat—"

"I think we have a reasonably good chance for a pleasant cruise. If we're careful and the weather cooperates. Wouldn't swear to it, however," Stan said seriously, "with all these people on board."

"You can't mean he has decided to take us all—"

"Oh, yes. Wiley, too. Sick or well."

"That means Dr. Smith, too."

"Sure. Says he'd like to enjoy something about this jaunt. Anyway Wiley refused to go without the doctor, and the doctor may be thinking about that new wing for his hospital, but my guess is he's thinking of a rest, which all of us need. I *never* should have let Monty start out in that fog. In this museum piece. Sue—" he leaned forward, his elbows on his still-dirty jeans, but his face sparkling with excitement and admiration—"you ought to see some of the gadgets the Coast Guard has. Everything you can think of, and a lot of things you can't think of. They've been great, too. Really turned themselves out to help us. I think they got a kind of kick out of it. The yacht may be almost a Victorian relic, but there's a certain elegance and when things work and when nobody goes berserk . . . Now don't get upset, Sue. That isn't going to happen this time."

"If we have the same people on board, who's to prevent the same things over again?"

"I am. Monty is. And we're taking one of the Coast Guard fellows along. He's due for a leave and jumped at the chance. He'll be a good, sturdy, reliable—"

Sue interrupted, "Monty can't be taking Juan, too!"

Stan frowned. "I wouldn't have taken him back. Monty, though, is determined. I don't know exactly why, unless— Oh, I'm afraid Monty is still hellbent to find out who knocked him out. But he can't believe Juan's story of hitting himself by accident and getting in the dinghy. Neither can I. Fact is, I can't see why Juan would come back in the boat unless—well, unless he wants something from somebody. I don't know what."

"Mr. Wiley? If he's thinking of putting Juan in his will."

Stan considered it. "Could be, I suppose. But that doesn't quite square with my impression of Juan. There must be a more urgent reason. But I'll be damned if I know what."

After a long pause, Sue said, "I don't like Juan."

"Nope. There's a sneaky look in those dark eyes. Yet Wiley does seem to think Juan is entirely devoted to him and the boat. Claims Juan knows more about the yacht than he does. Never mind. Monty says that once in Eleuthera he'll get over to Bahai-Mar in Fort Lauderdale and find a ship's supply, get everything he needs to outfit the yacht. That means practically restore the boat, at ghastly expense. But that won't stop Monty. As a matter of fact, he's a great guy. You'll do well to marry him," he said shortly, looking out the porthole.

"Who said—"

Stan shrugged. "Lalie, I think. But it seems to be the general idea. And a good one, I'm sure. You'll be very happy with him. Good night." The door closed rather definitely after him. She wished Lalie had not been so communicative.

She wasn't sure she liked the way Stan had shut off all discussion.

Yet, in honesty, Lalie had merely told Stan of Sue's own intentions. After some thoughtful moments, listening absently to the measured rhythm from the engine rooms, she got out of bed, dressed and went to Addie's cabin.

The door was open, and Addie was sitting cozily in her ruffled dressing gown and a blanket. Sissy frolicked after Sue and leaped into Addie's lap. Addie put down one hand to pat the dog. "Monty tells me we are off again in the morning. This time with better promises—and weather— for a lovely cruise."

"So Monty has been talking to you."

"Of course." Addie widened her pansy-brown eyes.

"Aunt Addie, I want to go home. Your house. Now."

Addie did blink. Then she said soothingly, "No, no, you have to take this cruise with Monty."

"With all these people! You must have seen one of them shoving Juan off in that dinghy."

Addie drew one of Sissy's long ears lightly through her fingers. "Oh, now, Sue! What are you talking about?"

"Aunt Addie! Look at me! You must have seen—"

"Oh, I couldn't have!" But she gave all her attention to Sissy's ear.

"And you said that you saw somebody helping Juan onto the deck. Everybody heard you say that. Then you told me about Juan and the dinghy—"

Addie was shaking her curls. "Darling, I couldn't have said all that."

Sue began to feel she was trying to push back water. And yet—and yet Addie's lively imagination did rather often affect her account of any event. Sue had to persist. "But you did! You said Juan's head was lolling, so you knew he was dead."

Addie looked up. "But he wasn't dead at all! You see, I really couldn't have said all that. That is—" She had the manner of one yielding to a need for a slight apology. "I'm sure you are telling the truth as you see it—"

"Heard it," Sue said rudely and loudly.

Addie sighed. "All right, heard it. But really . . . I'm terribly afraid that just perhaps . . . seasickness, all that . . . I may have taken a little too much of . . . something," said Addie vaguely. But then at Sue's unbelieving, stony silence, she lifted her pretty eyes. "*In vino veritas*. That's what you are about to say, isn't it? It's not true. Some of the biggest lies I've ever heard in my life were uttered in"—she did just slightly falter here and continued—"in a certain condition. But I'm very, very sorry. I didn't see anything like whatever it is you think . . . I mean, you said I said, I mean . . . I'm getting tangled up. Just understand me. That night I had only a quick glimpse of Juan's white jacket. And perhaps this rubber float. That's all. I'm glad to hear he's well enough to continue the cruise with us."

One does not say to one's loved and (usually) loving aunt, you are a terrific liar yourself: usually no harm is done, but this time is different.

Celia passed the open door, looked in, saw them together and guessed what they were talking about. Celia was very quick in her perceptions. She said, "May as well give up, Sue. I tried it, too. Have you found Monty's gun yet?"

"Monty's—no!"

Celia's face was suddenly rather stony. "Let's have

another look. I think you dropped it here. It's got to be somewhere."

"Probably in the sea, the deep blue sea—" Aunt Addie was about to carol something.

"Come on," Celia said. "Here, Sissy. There's even a fine new sandbox on deck for Sissy. All I can say is hurray for the Coast Guard."

Addie began to croon softly, "I love the Coast Guard— the Coast Guard loves me," to the tune of "I Love Louisa."

Celia gave a quick glance at the bedside table, innocent now of betraying glasses or bottles, and then an exasperated but kind glance at Addie.

"How about a life on the ocean wave?" she said.

Addie checked her little chant. "Oh, I've said that many times. But indeed I hope that our life on the ocean wave will be lovely. Now. Sunny—quiet—"

"I wouldn't count on that," Celia said shortly. "Fact is, I'd like to go home."

Sue couldn't resist. "Back to Palm Beach?"

"Eluethera is nice, too," said Celia neatly and, in Sue's view, quite explicitly; so Celia had been there, too. "Let's ask Wiley if he knows anything about the gun."

"I wish Juan wasn't coming with us."

"Wiley is determined to have him. And Monty is determined on something or other, too." Celia straightened her slender belt. "Come on. We'll brave Wiley. He's really not so bad when you know him. A bit of a crook, but then—" She shrugged and led the way to Wiley's cabin. The doctor was there, however.

"You can't see Wiley. He's very tired, very feeble. Impossible to see him just now."

He closed the door firmly.

"And there's another crook," Celia said glumly but with a gleam of mischief in her eyes.

Twelve

"Dr. Smith? Why, he's a—a fine doctor! A great surgeon! I know."

"He just wants that new wing for your hospital. My guess is he'll stick to Wiley until he gets a promise: in writing."

"You really don't trust either of them! I tell you I know—"

"Doctors have got into peculiar dealings before now," Celia said darkly. "However, I can't see why he'd push Monty overboard. Or scare off Juan with a bump on the head."

"I can't see why anybody would do all that. And stop the yacht in the middle of a fog—"

"In a storm, at sea. Actually, the Coast Guard referred to it as a bit of a blow! To be fair, the boat was stopped dead-still before the 'blow.' A blow!" said Celia indignantly. "But I've got to take Sissy out." Celia spoke to the dog, who was trotting along beside them, "Come on."

So the storm at sea had been only a bit of a blow: a puff of wind perhaps! The fog was definitely a heavy fog, however. And there *had* been two attempts at murder. It was chilling suddenly to remember the old saying that things happened in threes. There was not a sound from Aunt Addie's cabin, or from Wiley's. Everything seemed blessedly content—for the moment, Sue amended uneasily and went to bed after locking the door.

Sun was streaming in the salon the next day when Sue, thankfully without being forced to cling to the rail, found her way to the salon. She was, however, late; Lalie, who was there with Sissy, brought out freshly made coffee.

122

"Everything is in the galley," she told Sue. "I thought you'd never wake up. But I did keep something hot for you."

Everybody else, it developed, was on deck. Even Wiley was stretched out in a long deck chair and covered lightly with a blanket. The air was balmy, the sea was flat as a plate. The wake of their passage sent two diverging paths of white behind them. The cruise had overnight turned into the cruise as it was meant to be, and they were far from land, setting a course for Eleuthera.

Addie was sitting calmly in a deck chair and looking unbelievably pretty in one of her customary pink sport dresses. Celia was in white shorts, which showed tanned and graceful legs; she had a red bandanna tied around her dark hair and she, too, looked fresh and rested.

Altogether it was a beautiful, sunny day, warm in the sun, yet cool enough from a slight ocean breeze.

Dr. Smith sat down beside Sue as she chose a chair. "Now this is the way it was supposed to be," he said. He actually gave her a comradely smile. "I intend to rest and enjoy it. I phoned the hospital last night from the Coast Guard Station. Everything is all right; at least nothing demanded my return. Young Dr. Alry is taking over for me. He'll get in touch if something develops that is beyond him. The radio is working now, so we can get and transmit messages. I need this rest. So that is great, too."

"I've never been this far south, along this coast, I mean." Sue lay back in the deck chair.

"Neither have I. Very interesting, isn't it? By the way, I'd advise Miss—your aunt—to get out of the sun. She's so very fair."

Sue sat up guiltily. "Yes."

Addie, sweetly smiling, moved into the shade and adjusted herself comfortably with a nod of thanks to Dr. Smith. "I was getting a little warm. How nice of you to think of it! How is Mr. Wiley?" She lowered her voice with a glance at Wiley, who seemed to be asleep.

"Doing really very well. Everything considered!" Dr. Smith said. "Your lawyer friend seems to be thriving, too." He glanced at Lawson, who leaned perilously over the rail and looked very nautical in jeans and white sweater, borrowed, Sue suspected, from Stan, for the lawyer was so thin that he'd never have been able to wear anything that fit Monty. He was less grumpy; he was eying the expanse of blue sea with apparent pleasure. "He seems to be taking this unexpected vacation rather philosophically," said Addie admiringly.

"After weathering the beginning of this cruise, I think we are all a little philosophical," Dr. Smith said. "At least we are thankful the worst of it is over."

"And everything running so well and so smoothly. What is that boy's name, Doctor?"

Dr. Smith followed her glance at the rail where the Coast Guard man and Lalie were standing together. Lalie had her head flung back as if she enjoyed the ocean breeze. The doctor said, "I heard somebody—Monty, I believe—call him Jim. Nice lad. That pretty girl—Lalie?"

Sue replied, "Her name is really Eulalie. But Lalie suits her."

"Of course! Charming young girl! Do you know," Dr. Smith said idly, "I had an idea that she was a little interested in the young navy fellow—your old friend, I understand."

Addie chipped in lightly, "Our old friend. We've known him forever. Not that he's old, just an engaging youngster."

"Ah," said Dr. Smith and shut his eyes. Sissy gamboled out of the sun and into the shade. The yacht made her way steadily southward. The sun shone on sparkling blue water. Everyone was content; nothing could have been better.

At least if Juan hadn't been somewhere in the boat, it could have been perfect, Sue thought uneasily.

If there had never been those accidents—accidents? Twice. A third accident?

No, Sue told herself firmly and shut her eyes. No use

thinking of anything but the sun and blue sea and blue sky and the calm motion, the pleasant but desultory talk now and then. Even the appearance of Juan, white-jacketed again, serving the luncheon on small tables, was not precisely unwelcome.

All the same, Sue wished Juan were not again on the yacht.

The young man, Jim, later disappeared, probably to take over the wheel and charts. Monty appeared, rested, shaven, attractive in his blue shorts and white shirt, smiling and handsome. He gave Sue a little affectionate touch on the shoulder and followed Jim to the bridge. In a moment Stan and Lalie strolled along the deck before they settled down in chairs. They were very close and in subdued conversation.

Addie had behaved beautifully at lunch; only one gin rickey, "It's the influence of approaching southern seas," she had said, refusing a second drink. She had not, however, conquered her gift (or weakness, depending upon how one looked at it) for quoting. Sue heard her murmur something about " 'Lest a frightful fiend doth close behind me tread.' " As Sue moved, hoping to quench the flow, Addie shook her head. "No, that's not quite right. But" —she leaned toward Sue and whispered, "I do wish Juan had been left behind."

Juan at that moment was bending over Wiley, apparently urging him to rest, for Wiley shrugged and got awkwardly to his feet. Juan supported him, and as the two departed, Dr. Smith materialized again at Sue's side. "Juan does see to him. Better than I do in some ways. Glad he was permitted to continue on the cruise."

That I'm not, Sue thought but didn't say so.

Addie decided to retire to her cabin. The warm air, she said softly, was making her sleepy. Sue went with her and made a swift tour of the little stateroom. The only bottle she found, however, was labeled and proved to be—for she tasted it—a mouthwash.

So Addie was content. But Addie locked her door again as Sue left; she heard the click.

She hadn't given Monty's missing revolver any thought; she did then but briefly. Clearly, someone had found it, picked it up, placed it in some safe place.

Safe?

Certainly. All was tranquil. Nobody was going to be obliged to shoot anybody. Nobody wished to shoot anybody.

She was not too sure about that. Things go in threes; she wished that ancient and surely nonsensical adage had not come to her mind anew.

She lay on her bed, thinking and watching the lights reflected from the waves dancing along the ceiling.

She was beginning to know Monty as she had not known him before the short, but in its way revealing, cruise.

First, and all to his credit, there had not been the slightest hint of the proprietor in the light touch he had given her shoulder that afternoon. It occurred to her rather coldly that Monty felt that their agreement had been made.

Clearly, too, he was, as Lalie had said, "straight." Perhaps he believed in all the suitable trimmings of romance. So he would wait for what he considered the proper moment for a more loving proposal of marriage.

Certainly Monty was not only a very determined man, but he was also single-minded. He had insisted upon the same people on board who had been there at the time he had taken his dangerous swim in the sea, a swim that he insisted was an attack upon his life. Stan agreed with him about that. But Monty, or Stan, did take the precaution of suggesting that the young Coast Guard man accompany them; an extra measure for safety? Yes, that was likely.

But Monty had also proved himself to be a man of swift and impulsive actions—when he saw Celia he had been instantly very angry; he had got hold of Lawson and changed his will, which probably had previously included Celia.

Perhaps Monty's reactions were the classic reactions of poor-boy-makes-good—or makes a great deal of money; to put it crassly, the strong desire to show off his possessions (the yacht, for instance, in its elegance, overlooking its age and ability). Even Celia, with her beauty and her worldly experience would be a kind of feather in anybody's cap, but especially for Monty.

Certainly now Monty felt assured of himself as to his relationship with Sue. The will was in answer to that. Even his promise to care for Addie was another response.

As if summoned by her thoughts, Monty called from the corridor. "Sue, is this door locked?"

She sprang up and opened it. Monty and Stan both stood there. Monty's face was a little flushed. Stan looked remarkably white. Both came in without invitation.

"Can we talk in here, Sue?" Monty asked. "It's almost impossible to find a place on this yacht for a private conversation."

"Of course, Monty," Sue replied as Stan closed the door behind him and interrupted, "I tell you, Monty—"

"Don't tell me." Monty sat down. "I've made up my mind."

"You're a fool!"

Monty smiled at that and shook his head. "Not me."

"What's all this—" Sue began. Neither man paid her the least attention. Stan shoved his hands in his pockets and leaned against the door. "I tell you it's a perfectly impossible, outrageous kind of thing you are trying to accomplish. I'll have nothing to do with it."

"All right. If you want to get out of it, take a swim. You'll probably be picked up somewhere."

"Oh, Monty, stop and think. You are simply inviting trouble."

Monty shook his head again. Stan insisted. "I say you are and you are doing it deliberately. You should never have continued this cruise. You should never have let that little rat Juan aboard again. I'm sure he has some reason for coming along. And it can't be a good one! You're trying to be police, judge, everything yourself!''

"I'll admit I think he's a liar. But he is fine with Sam Wiley. It's the only thing to do and I'm going to do it.''

"I tell you, you can't. Discover who shoved you in the sea, for God's sake!''

"You do admit you think it was an attempt on my life.'' Monty was not smiling now. His eyes had a steely blue glitter.

"Yes,'' Stan said wearily. "But I don't think you are going to find out who did it and why.''

"But you are going to help me.''

"So I'm supposed to be a detective now, am I? Not me.''

"You'll have to help.''

"Just how? Oh, Monty, this is a preposterous situation.''

"What would you do in my place?''

"I'd go straight home, let everybody off the boat, and put the thing in the hands of the police—''

"Brilliant! A bright boy you have here, Sue! Your dear old friend is content to let attempted murder be simply overlooked and let whoever tried to kill me get safely away—''

"Wait a minute, Monty.'' Stan was beginning to look dangerous. "You're not fair. I said the police—''

"And I said we'll do better ourselves. Be fair yourself, Stan. What would we have to report to police? A fall, they'd say, at the rail. A bloody bump on the head from striking something. A gash on Juan's head. A coincidence. We go home, tell this weak story to the police, and meanwhile everybody on this boat—including whoever tried to kill me—goes along home and the thing is over. Stan,'' Monty leaped forward earnestly. "Don't you see, if we did that, I'd never have a peaceful moment?''

Stan looked at him. "I see your point of view. Sure. But you are basing all this upon your own conviction that somebody on this boat, one of your invited guests, actually tried to kill you.''

''And will try again,'' said Monty, incontrovertably.

Stan hesitated, paced across the small room a couple of times, went back to lean on the door again, and said, ''Don't forget, Monty, that there is at least one uninvited guest on board.''

''You mean Celia. I don't forget that.''

''And that man Lawson. The lawyer. Would he have any interest at all in your death?''

Monty thought that over; his eyes narrowed. ''In a small way, I suppose.''

''What way?''

''I left him some money, and he deserves it. He's been my lawyer since I was a young fellow starting out on a hard road, my friend. A very, very hard road. It is thanks in large measure to Lawson that I never got myself into any legal tangles. He knows the law and he kept me on the right side of it when I just might have strayed on the wrong side.'' He seemed suddenly to recollect Sue's presence, for he shot a quick glance at her and said, ''Nothing dishonest! Nothing out of line! I had better common sense than that, but there are all kinds of snares lying in wait if you don't watch your step. Lawson looked out for me. Sure.'' He returned to Stan. ''I've left him some money but not enough to induce him to shove me overboard, for God's sake! Never!''

''I see.''

And he did see, Sue felt; she thought she understood, too. Monty did have good sense, and in his upward climb he'd have made sure, if only for safety's sake and his own conscience, that he was, as he said, on the right side of the law. She was positive that Monty's conscience was in good working order. As Lalie had said, a little scornfully but affectionately, Monty was straight.

She broke into their heated exchange. ''That Mr. Wiley.

Celia thinks he is a crook." Both men stared at her. "She said Wiley is a crook and so is the doctor."

Monty moistened his lips, but he was angry again; his face flushed. "Celia says! Well, she ought to know. Wiley is one of her pals. Apparently she knows more about the doctor than I do."

Stan said, "Come on, Sue. Why would she say that? Did she give you any reasons?"

Sue began to backtrack. "I'm not sure I can remember. That is, yes . . . She thinks the doctor is too intent on getting that new wing for the hospital. I don't agree with her," she said hastily. "I do know Dr. Smith. He's a great man. As for Wiley, you're not happy about him yourself, Monty. After all, he sold you this boat without letting you know the shape she is in—"

"My own damn fault." Monty's jaw set itself grimly. He thought for a moment and added, "Stan—and not very politely, either—has pointed that out to me. But I have to admit he is right. That fellow at the dock—I must say, Stan, you were very helpful about all that. They took one look at your navy I.D. card and turned themselves inside out—"

"The Coast Guard can't repair boats. But it's true they know how and where to get things done with no time wasted. They'd do that for anybody in trouble. And we certainly were in trouble."

"But we're not going to be this time. Beautiful weather. Beautiful—"

"Monty, you are a fool. If I could swim to shore, I would. If I had known when we set out that you had this wild idea of playing detective in your head—"

"You did know it. You said as long as I didn't endanger Sue . . . Well, I'll not endanger Sue. For heaven's sake, Stan! Sue, of all people! Why, we're going to be married."

Stan's eyes flickered once to Sue. Then he said, "I'm sure I wish you both every happiness!" He swung around and opened the door. He turned back to say, "I'd find that gun of yours, Monty. Too bad the Coast Guard and the navy are so particular about sidearms. Otherwise we ought to have been able to get another gun somewhere. Oh, yes, congratulations.'' Stan shut the door almost gently behind him. It was as if he wished to emphasize his lack of interest in Sue or her engagement.

Monty said reflectively, "I have a feeling Stan came on this trip to Eleuthera simply and solely because you are on board and he's afraid—''

"Monty, I think I'm afraid, too. Let's go back home. It's not too late.''

Monty didn't even consider it. "No.''

"But perhaps Stan is right." I'm sure he's right, she thought.

"Sue, I have thought this over. Very seriously. Very seriously indeed. I'm going to do what I can, and I rather think— Come on, let's forget it. Try to find my gun, will you?''

"I have tried,'' she said desolately. Was a disagreement with Monty not a disagreement at all but simply running up against a stone wall?

"Good girl. Now then, shall we tell the others about our engagement tonight?''

Our engagement? All settled? Sue thought. Of course, in its way, it was settled. "I—I'd rather tell Aunt Addie first.''

"Yes. Certainly. Very correct." Monty rose. "I think I'll just have a talk with Wiley—there may be something in Celia's opinion of him. Of course he is an old pirate, giving me such a sales talk about this boat. But I shouldn't have believed him. Doesn't mean he is a crook exactly. See you,'' said Monty kindly but firmly and departed.

So that was that. Sue stood for a few moments, feeling the steady, very welcome throb of the engines as she watched the sunset glow of pinkish light leave only a faint glimmer on the waves.

Monty did consider their engagement, such as it was, a firm pact.

He was also determined to discover the identity of whoever had attempted to kill him.

What could anybody do about it? Stan was loyal to his friends; instinctively she had always known that. So she was obscurely moved to agree with Monty that he had deliberately remained on the yacht to—well, to protect her? At least he had told Monty he must not endanger her.

It was like Stan, sturdy, as firm in his own way as Monty.

Obscurely again, she rather hoped that Lalie would not be just the right girl for him and caught the thought back before it took off as if it had wings. Then she realized that night had come swiftly and finally and it was time for cocktails and dinner.

This time, regrettably, Addie allowed herself to be affected by the memory of the other nights at sea and tucked away three martinis before Sue could stop her. She also murmured more lines about the frightful fiend that close behind her trod, unfortunately just as Juan announced rather sulkily that dinner was served. Sue was sure he had heard it, for again his eyes took on a kind of somber glaze. But he held a chair for Addie politely and without bashing in her head with the carving knife, which he placed before Monty instead, with the expressed hope that he had not overcooked the roast.

Dinner was handsomely laid out again at a buffet; small tables glittered with spotless napery and silver. Monty, at the buffet, began to whet the carving knife on the bone-handled grindstone. The gleam of the steel and the sound as Monty sharpened it sent a most unpleasant little clutch at Sue's nerves.

She looked around the salon. Everyone was there except the lawyer and the young man Jim. Even Stan had taken a spell away from the wheel. Apparently Mr. Lawson had volunteered to stand watch with Jim, for the doctor commented upon it, helping himself to a rather large helping of beef and potatoes. "Fine meal, Monty," he added. "Think of having all this on a yacht."

Lalie was pouring another martini for herself. She said tartly, "Surely you've traveled by sea before now, Doctor. A yacht—if it's well run—" she interpolated with an unpleasant, if sisterly, glance at Monty—"is not really much different from the usual ocean voyage."

However, at that point they encountered a heavy swell. Lalie grabbed at the nearest stationary object, which happened to be Stan, who held her tightly and said heartily, "Take it easy, Lalie." Lalie disengaged herself, but not too hurriedly.

Celia efficiently filled a plate for Addie.

They went leisurely through all the food, which was indeed well cooked, so Juan did have his uses. There was a little random conversation. Stan and Monty, apparently on good, if rather formal, terms went back to the wheel together.

"I'm in favor of making it an early night," Celia said. "We really are out in the sea now. Sizable swells, obviously, but thank heaven not what we had."

They made it an early night.

It was close to two o'clock when the shot was fired.

Thirteen

It was chance only that brought Sue out into the corridor just before the shot was fired. She had awakened with the sense that some noise had roused her. She lay for a few moments, feeling the reassuring throb of the engines and the rush of the boat through the sea, rocking under slow, long waves. She thought, vaguely, that someone had speeded up the engines.

But surely some very nearby sound had roused her.

Addie?

She crawled out of bed, groped for a dressing gown, and went out into the passage, which was lighted dimly. Nothing moved along it. Unexpectedly, Addie's door was not locked. She opened it cautiously, but she could see, in the faint path of light entering the cabin over her shoulder, that Addie was comfortably nestled in bed, her curls not even disheveled and—Sue sniffed—there was no odor of whiskey, rum, anything unwelcome. She closed the door cautiously again, and retreated to her own cabin. She was in the act of closing that door when the shot came.

It resounded through the stillness of the yacht, above the distant beat of the engines. Without a pause to think, as if someone had told her where to go, she ran toward the salon. It was not lighted, but there was light streaming up from the galley. She plunged through darkness toward the light and stopped at the galley steps. Juan lay in the middle of the otherwise spotless room. There was a growing red pool on the floor and another on the front of his white jacket.

She had been trained for emergency; so, oddly, it seemed to her later, the rules that had been drilled into her operated even then, for she stumbled down to Juan, knelt and put her fingers on a pulse, which should have been there but was not. Try making him breathe?

"But there's a doctor in the house," she heard herself mumble and surged up, out of the galley, across the salon and along the passage to Mr. Wiley's cabin. She knocked, decided that everybody on the yacht had suddenly gone stone-deaf, and pounded on the door.

The door to the cabin shared by Celia and Lalie opened; Celia came out hurriedly, a silk dressing gown floating around her, black hair down, yet neat even then. "What is it? What's happened? I heard something—"

"You heard a shot. Doctor! Dr. Smith!" Sue called.

The cabin door swung open just as Sue lifted a vigorous fist at it again, so she stumbled and almost fell into the doctor's arms. He set her upright, turned back to shout something at Wiley, and said, "What's the trouble? Where?"

"The galley. The shot. I mean Juan in the galley!"

The doctor was accustomed to emergencies.

"All right, Nurse. I may need help. Come with me."

Sue obeyed; an order was an order. Celia followed. By the time the three had reached the galley, Sue was vaguely aware that others had heard the shot and had made the discovery she had made. Stan was there, very white. Monty was there, leaning hard against a table, staring down as if he couldn't believe his eyes. The doctor bent over Juan; his neat white pajama collar showed above his blue dressing gown. Sue had not been mistaken, as for one mad moment she hoped she was. The doctor investigated swiftly but carefully; then he turned Juan gently on his face. Sue had a curious kind of shock when she saw that Juan's mop of coarse black hair had disappeared: there was only a shining bald spot, surrounded by a dark fringe of hair. The doctor leaned over to examine a small spot of red on the back of Juan's white jacket. This grew rapidly as all of them watched.

Finally the doctor squatted back on his heels. "This man is dead. He has been shot. . . . At close range, I would say. Is there a gun on the yacht?"

Monty replied, his voice unsteady, "Mine."

Celia went lightly to stand at his side. "But you didn't shoot him, Monty."

"Me!" Monty turned stricken eyes to her. "Shoot anybody? Certainly not!"

By this time the coastguardsman, Jim, had found his way to the galley and stood staring.

Stan managed to move and spoke to the coastguardsman. "Okay, Jim. I mean it's not okay, but I'll let you know later."

"Yes," Jim said swiftly, tacked on "sir" as a mark of respect, and ducked out back to the bridge.

Monty said numbly, "Is my gun there? Anywhere?"

It was not there. There was no gun anywhere.

"Overboard," Stan said at last.

As if in a nightmare that couldn't be real yet was, Sue thought, this is the third thing. They come in threes. This time it was successful. But why Juan?

In her heart she had suspected Juan of pushing Monty, of saving himself from accusation by somehow getting the gash in his own head and then making for the nearest land.

Stan said flatly, "Looks as if Juan has been the target all along, Monty."

Monty shook his head, still in a dazed way. "Couldn't have been. I'm the one somebody tried to kill—"

Stan said, "But you were using Juan's hammock, remember?"

There was so still a moment that the throb of the engines seemed very loud.

Finally Monty said, "Nothing we can do right now—"

Stan leaped for the salon. "Oh, yes, there is."

"Wait, Stan!" Monty freed himself from his lethargy and also from Celia, as a matter of fact, who was clinging to his arm. "Wait, Stan. *No!*"

Stan's voice came floating back from the salon. "Yes! Only thing to do!"

"No!" Monty pounded after him. "I'll not have it—" Their voices were loud in the salon.

"You have nothing to say about it! It's the law. Hey, Monty, stop that!"

"Get out of my way."

"You can't do that!"

There was a kind of ripping swish and clatter.

Addie's sweet voice drifted distinctly from the salon. "Now boys, don't fight like that."

"Oh, God," said Celia and ran into the salon.

The doctor said, quite calmly, "Apparently Monty has wrecked the recently repaired ship-to-shore phone. Now, Nurse Gates, let's just get this poor man to—to some vacant cabin if we can arrange for one. We ought to leave him here for the police but, under the circumstances, that is not really very practical. Especially if Monty has stopped a chance of getting any police right away. Get a sheet. Preferably two sheets.''

''Yes. I mean, yes, sir.'' Sue was still under a kind of mandate to obey her training and the doctor. Besides, she couldn't continue to stay there in the tight little galley with Juan lying like that at her feet.

Celia had gone, but Sue was not surprised to see Addie in the salon. She was amazed to see Wiley, in wildly striped salmon-and-yellow pajamas, but with his mustache twirled up neatly at the corners, sitting cozily beside Addie with a glass in his hand. She should not have been surprised to note as she passed them that her aunt had a full glass, too. Addie said, ''Don't hurry, Sue. He's already dead, isn't he?''

Sue gulped, ''Yes,'' and ran on.

In the corridor she almost bumped into the lawyer, who backed hastily out of the way but grasped her arm. ''Is it true? I mean Stan and Monty shouting and—is it true?''

''Yes, oh, yes.''

Now for an empty cabin, and, of course, there wasn't one. The yacht had its full complement of guests. Eventually she jerked two sheets off Monty's bed (he was host, even if a host to murder, she reflected wildly), wadded the sheets under her arm, and hurried back to the galley. The lawyer was standing beside the doctor, shaking his head incredulously. She thrust the bundle of sheets in the doctor's direction, refused to look at Juan, and must have gone back into the salon again, because she was suddenly sitting, limp and yet with throbbing pulses, beside Addie. Without knowing it, too, she must have reached out and simply taken the glass from Addie and held it to her own lips, for a stinging drink went down her throat. It was also reviving. Addie murmured gently at her side. Wiley said sadly, ''Poor Juan! Terrible! Been in my service for years. Very faithful. Like another drink, Addie?''

He rose and moved to the bar. He didn't stagger, but it seemed to Sue that the yacht was moving faster, thrusting her way through the seas so the engines were pounding as if at their full strength.

Lalie ran into the salon as Wiley turned and put another glass in Addie's welcoming little hands.

"I heard. Juan—murder. They're fighting up there on deck," Lalie gasped. She had some kind of beach towel wrapped around her, showing bare shoulders and legs and a fine outline of Lalie beneath it.

"Who is fighting, child?" Addie was polite.

"The men! I mean Monty and Stan. Fighting like everything. Give me some of that please, Mr. Wiley."

"Certainly, my dear." Wiley frisked into service at the bar. "Dreadful! All of this! Terrible! Poor old Juan!"

"Never mind about poor old Juan." Lalie sat down and the towel slipped farther, rather to Wiley's interest, for when he gave her a glass of very dark liquid, his gaze lingered. His hand went up then automatically to twist one end of his mustache.

"Never mind about poor old Juan," Lalie repeated, clutching the glass. "I'm thinking about poor old Monty and Stan and—"

"What are they fighting about?" Addie asked again in the most polite voice, quite as if she were inquiring as to the weather.

"The radio," Lalie snapped and drank.

Sue found her voice. "What about the radio? Doesn't it work?"

"Oh, yes." Lalie gulped down more of her drink, sputtered at its strength and said, "They'd got it all fixed up. Didn't work when you sold this pig of a boat, Mr. Wiley."

"Oh, now! Come on! Everything on the yacht was perfect." Wiley settled back into the sofa beside Addie.

"Everything was no such thing." Lalie glared. "You

just told Monty everything was fine and he believed you—''

"Now, now, my dear." Lalie's towel had slipped a little farther, and Wiley twisted the other end of his mustache, eying her with pleased attention.

"Lalie," Sue said shortly, "*why* are they fighting?"

"Because Stan says they've got to report Juan's murder and Monty won't. That's all. Fighting. Monty," Lalie said with an air of judicially weighing the outcome, "Monty is heavier. But Stan is younger and very strong."

Addie murmured, "I hope they'll not hurt one another."

"Juan must have been murdered," Sue said. "So it must be reported as a murder—''

Lalie's eyes flashed. "What else could it be? I heard them yelling about it. Who could possibly shoot himself in the back? Straight through the heart! That's what the doctor said, isn't it? Straight through from the back! Stan said the gun is gone!"

At this point the doctor and Lawson appeared, trudging up from the galley, carrying a long white bundle between them.

Lalie put her hands over her face. Addie watched with mild interest. Sue felt sick. After the grim little procession had disappeared into the corridor, Celia came back into the salon, dropped into a chair, and said, "If somebody doesn't stop Monty and Stan, there's going to be another murder any minute."

"I expect I'd better go," Wiley said.

Celia stopped him, although his gesture of leaving was not very resolute. "Stay right here. I think the coastguardsman is about to clobber both of them. But he said it might be mutiny on the high seas. So he can't quite make up his mind what to do."

"I know," Addie said unexpectedly and rose.

There was a surprised silence as she floated in her pretty pink out of the salon. Sue, Lalie, Celia and Wiley sat frozen, listening to a kind of hubbub above them, thuds,

voices, indeterminate sounds of struggle. All of it suddenly ended.

"My God," Lalie said, "what did she do?"

Addie floated back, ruffles, curls and a smile.

Lalie cried, "What did you do?"

"Oh, nothing. Just slapped them both. Needed it, too.
Such noisy—I'll take a drink, I think, dear Mr. Wiley."

Wiley gave her her own glass and then lifted his in a
rather awed salute. Celia's dark eyes widened; she looked
at Addie as if another person had magically emerged from
the fluffy little pink figure and Celia didn't know just what
to make of this new and rather alarming creature. Lalie
gurgled, said, "Jesus," under her breath, evoking a reprov-
ing glance from Addie, who had ears like a cat's, and
added, almost in a whisper, "you slapped Monty? You
slapped Stan?"

"Certainly." Addie smoothed down her curls. "Only
way. Surprised them, of course! Then the Coast Guard
boy, Jim, began to laugh as if he'd choke. But—too
bad—"

"What is too bad?" Sue cried.

"Well, it seems that somehow Monty had grabbed
something about the radio that stops it working. I believe
he threw it in the sea. What would that be, Mr. Wiley?"

Wiley sighed so furiously that both ends of his mustache shot upward as if at a turbulent breeze. "Might
be anything. Lots of things can ruin a transmitter. As
for the antenna, almost anything could break that—a
hammer, an ax. Can't do anything with the radio without an antenna."

There was another rather stunned silence. Then Celia
said, "So Monty is going to have his way."

Lalie nodded. "Sure. We're going on to Eleuthera. But
that's not all."

"Not all what, dear?" Addie asked, sipping her drink
with pleasure.

"Monty is going to find out who killed Juan and why. Mainly because somebody tried to kill him."

There was something out of kilter there; Sue cried, "No! That first attempt was meant for Juan! Whoever did it thought it was Juan in the hammock! Not Monty. Stan said so. Just now in the galley."

There was another silence. Then Celia said, "Yes. I think I heard him. But I didn't quite take it in. Not just then. Everything was so confused." Her face tensed. "Sue, did you ever find that gun of Monty's?"

"That gun," Addie said, "is at the bottom of the sea by now."

Celia obviously didn't believe it; Lalie didn't either. Sue only hoped it was true. Addie said, "Of course. It must be. Might have had fingerprints, or something." She lifted her glass again to her lips.

The doctor came back, followed by Lawson. Both men looked very solemn. "All right," the doctor said, eying Wiley. "Back to bed with you, Wiley. I'll not be responsible if you continue to carry on like this. Here, let me give you a hand."

Wiley rose with a dignity that was rather marred by the wild stripes of his pajamas. However, he bowed most courteously to Addie, and then in Sue's direction and Celia's and Lalie's. "Ladies," he said politely and stalked out. Dr. Smith eyed him as he left and shook his head.

"That man is going to kill himself," he said dourly. "All this carrying on! Has he been drinking? I see that he has. I advise you ladies to go back to bed. Nothing can be done tonight unless Monty gets a message through by radio."

"He can't do that," Addie assured him. "Broken."

The doctor stared at her, his face redder than usual and yet tired-looking. "Not again."

"Oh, yes. Monty did it."

"But why? Why—"

Lalie replied, "Because he intends to find out who

killed Juan and who tried to kill him." Lalie shrugged; the towel slipped perilously low. Addie uttered a mild remonstration, and Lalie added, "He says he's not going through life afraid that somebody will attack him again. Or Sue."

Fourteen

"Sue!" Celia cried. "Why Sue? She's in no danger!"

"Neither is Monty, if you ask me," Lalie replied. "But he intends to marry Sue, and since she is so close to him he feels that she is in danger, too."

"But that can't be right," Sue said defiantly. There was a curious kind of hollow feeling under her ribs just the same. "If the attack upon Monty was meant to be an attack upon Juan, as Stan said." Sue was very firm so didn't at all like the way her voice shook. However, she was beginning to emerge from a kind of paralysis of shock; the name of Stan, with the image it summoned up of good sense and strength was a help. She took a long breath and appealed to Dr. Smith. "Please, Doctor, I think *you* might help. If you would...well...reason with Monty. You are a doctor."

The doctor gave her a surprised look. "Reason with him? As if he were some kind of psychopath?"

Lalie uttered a short laugh and let her towel slip, but any such unveiling was apparently no treat to the doctor, who merely glanced briefly at her, his eyebrows drawn together. Lalie's slim figure, more than half revealed, was no treat for Lawson either, for he was staring indignantly at Sue. He turned to the doctor. "Why, Dr. Smith! What a thing to suggest! Monty is as level-headed as anybody I have ever known. Known very well, I might say, and worked with for some years. He is a perfectly sound, sensible man."

"Doesn't seem very sensible just now," Lalie snapped.

Dr. Smith was frowning thoughtfully. "On the other hand, there are cases of concussion—" He paused, considering.

"Concussion?" Celia cried.

"I can't diagnose his behavior as the result of a concussion, although he did sustain a severe blow to the head. No, I really cannot say that I have seen any physical signs of it, but his actions certainly are out of character. However—" He shook his head.

"However what?" Addie asked.

"I was only thinking of the odd things a man can undertake when he—when anybody, I should say—has suffered a slight concussion. The person might seem perfectly well, perfectly coordinated, perfectly lucid—and not be at all lucid in fact. It is a difficult field. And an impossible diagnosis sometimes. However—no." He shook his head. "I cannot honestly say that I believe that is Monty's problem. Yet I cannot say it isn't."

There was a short, brooding silence in the salon. Then Addie rose to her feet and the occasion. "He only needs a good talking to. You and I—all of us know that we ought to go straight for—" She turned to Lalie and then to Celia. "By the way, where are we?"

Lalie hitched up her towel and shook her head. "Do you know, Celia?"

"Heavens, no!" Celia's dark eyes flashed.

Addie insisted, "But you must have taken trips with Monty before—I mean on the yacht. Didn't you, Celia?"

"Oh, yes," Celia said quietly. "A few times, actually, before Wiley sold her. Then after Monty bought the boat and had her brought up to the Sound, he took her out a few times. Perhaps I didn't mention it. Sometimes all the way to Greenwich and Larchmont," said Celia and looked demurely down at her hands. "Monty did employ somebody to teach him everything he wanted to know. It was, Monty said, like taking lessons in driving a car."

"Rather different," Sue said, and as Celia looked at her with an amused flash in her dark eyes, Sue added, lamely, "But it *is* different."

"Especially in a heavy fog," Lawson said bitterly.

Celia went on. "Monty was sure he could manage the boat. With Juan's help, of course. Monty said it was easy. He only had to learn about different signals, buoys, charts, lights, all that."

Sue said, "But I thought Monty had had experience with the yacht. Stan thought so—"

"He did have some experience," Celia said. "I told you. He took me—and Sissy—out several times. Of course," she added, "as I told you, those trips were short. And in full daylight. Everything, at least the engines, ran perfectly. Really very pleasant trips," Celia concluded and rubbed Sissy with one foot, for at her name the little dog, up to then a sleepy huddle of brown curls, had sat up intelligently and given a slight, plaintive sound. "Oh, God!" Celia said. "She's got to go out."

"I'll take her." Lalie hitched the towel up again and turned to Sue. "Come with me. Somebody come with me."

"I'll go." Lawson looked almost human for a moment.

Celia said quickly, "Oh, never mind. I'll go. She's my dog."

Actually, Lalie, Celia and Lawson all marched out at the behest of a little brown dog. Sue tried to smile, couldn't, and said, "Doctor, where is he? I mean, which cabin?"

"Not a cabin at all. That is, we found a sort of cubbyhole he used. For heaven's sake, girl, don't look so scared. You've seen street accidents, the effects of violence, all sorts of things brought to the hospital. Why are you so squeamish about one little steward?"

Addie, very quietly, disappeared toward her cabin. She moved so cautiously that Sue suspected a glass in one hand. A bottle, even, was possible. And a very sound idea, it struck Sue for a fleeting instant. But Dr. Smith lighted a cigarette, and she turned back to him. Really, even a doctor—hardened, one supposed, to all sorts of ills—could become too cold-blooded. Sue persisted, "Where did you put him?"

"In a storage place, of course. Below. Next to the engine room. He's not going to trouble your rest, Nurse. Couldn't trouble it, anyway. Where are you going? You don't look well—"

"I don't feel well," Sue quavered and fled.

But by the time she had got down the corridor past Addie's closed door, into her own cabin, banged the door, and thrown herself on the bed in order to have a good attack of hysterics, she no longer could even make herself cry. However, while she didn't grieve for Juan, there is an abysmal distinction between a lively little man, going about in his white jacket, and what she had very nearly stumbled over in the galley.

There is also a shattering awareness of danger when a murder has occurred; she said it, half aloud, half whispering to herself, and decided, hearing herself, that in fact she, not Monty, needed some psychiatric attention.

It was probably an indication of her state of mind that she didn't immediately give much thought to Addie, but when she did, she was impressed by the new Addie's strong sense of self-preservation. And for that matter, good judgment. Imagine slapping Stan. And Monty!

Outside her door, Stan called, "Sue—Sue—"

She was vaguely surprised to find that her legs were a little unsteady. It wasn't owing to the pitching of the yacht this time, although the boat seemed to be moving at the full extent of its powerful engines. Her lethargy was due, simply, to shock.

She steadied herself and opened the door for Stan, who gave her one sharp look. "Sit down!"

"I—I don't mean—"

"Sit down! I don't want a fainting woman on my hands!"

"I'm all right."

"Glad to hear it. You look awful. Oh, Sue." His voice warmed. "I do realize what a terrible thing it was for you. But you are one of the few sensible people on this boat. I can't have you carrying on. Hysterics! What not!"

"Nobody had hysterics!"

"All right. Nobody fainted. Nobody screamed. Everybody was quite in control and—listen, can't you do something about Monty? The man is a fool. He's got to get into the nearest port and report Juan's murder—"

"I know. But I can't control him—"

"Aren't you engaged to him? Aren't you going to marry him? He said so."

"I—why—yes—no, that is—"

"Make up your mind. Are you? Yes or no."

"That is none of your business, Stan! What I'm trying to tell you is, if Monty has made up his mind to continue on to the island, I don't think anybody can induce him to change it. Even the doctor doesn't think he can be persuaded."

Stan leaped to the obvious conclusion. "You asked the doctor to talk Monty out of this? Good for you! Why didn't he try it?"

"Because the lawyer, Lawson, said Monty wasn't at all—that is, that Monty is very sensible."

"I'm sure I hope so." Stan frowned. "Especially since he's got a gun."

She sprang up. "His gun! He found it! It's been missing—"

"Wait till I tell you. He found it a moment ago in his cabin. Just flat out, there on the bed. And now he's got it tucked into his belt and says it's loaded. He began talking wildly about mutiny if Jim and I or anybody insisted upon making for Savannah."

"Oh, no! He wouldn't—"

"No. He's the owner, but of course it wouldn't be mutiny. We'll have to control him, though. Jim has already set our course in that direction but, even at that—Oh, Lord, why did I go on this cruise? For that matter"—he looked at her angrily—"why did you? Just to make sure of Monty? Was that it? Because he wanted you to? Because you've intended all along to marry him? Ever since you got acquainted with him? Isn't that right?"

"Shut up!" Sue must have yelled. She caught her breath, but before she could speak in a quieter voice, Stan began to laugh.

"Sounds more like you! Now if you can lure Monty down here and keep him here—"

"Really, Stan!"

"I don't mean seduce him! Although I rather think I wouldn't put it past you. Never mind! Don't yell!" He sobered. "The fact is, he keeps going around the bridge, and every time he gets near the compass with that damned gun, the compass whirls and Jim and I have to get back on course again and try and keep Monty out of the way."

"Stan, why would anybody leave that gun in his cabin? Monty couldn't have murdered Juan. Not even if he'd had a concussion."

"What do you mean a concussion? From that knock on the head?"

"Yes, but the doctor says he can't be sure."

Stan kicked at a chair leg thoughtfully. "Well, if the doctor can't tell, I don't know who of us can. Concussion, huh? Something to think about. Still . . ." He shook his head. "No. I can't believe that. Monty is too—too—natural, somehow. Misguided, I think, but natural. And I don't think he killed Juan. If we ever get to land and police, they can check on the bullet. The police can't get at the bullet to see if it came from Monty's gun without an autopsy. My guess is that that gun killed him. If so, it stands to reason whoever shot him had to get rid of it."

"Addie said the gun was probably at the bottom of the sea."

"Addie was wrong." He put one hand to his cheek. "My face still red?"

She looked at it and was rather proud in a clannish way to see a slight blotch suggesting the hard application of a hand. "Yes."

"You needn't purr about it. Your aunt packs quite a wallop. Surprised me. Surprised Monty, too. Jim took advantage of it and, not very respectfully, told us both off. But Monty is determined to have his own way, and this gun business only makes him more so. He says that whoever murdered Juan is trying to set Monty up as first suspect."

"Stan, down in the galley, you said that the attack upon Monty was meant to be an attack upon Juan. Somebody who didn't know that Monty was using Juan's hammock."

"Sure. Seems reasonable."

"Then why would that same person try to get rid of Monty, by leaving that gun to be found—"

"With Monty's fingerprints on it."

"My fingerprints are on it, too."

"Yes, I know. Also, you found Juan."

"But I didn't—nobody could think that I—oh, Stan!"

"Anybody can think anything." But Stan's face was all at once very hard and rather white. She had a sudden flashing memory of an incident, years past. She and Stan were sailing in the small Sunfish he had then when an ominous puff of wind came out of nowhere. He had ordered her to duck as the boom swung around; he had ordered her to huddle down and try to balance the boat. It had been, she later knew, a rather perilous few moments until they came into the relatively smooth water near the Sea Cove Club. She could even remember the comforting lines of the Club, stationary in a suddenly frightening world. But then, everything was all right. She was drenched to the skin, and so was Stan; they had gone in Stan's ridiculous old car to Stan's mother's house, where they had dried off and had hot tea with sugar. At least Sue had

had tea. She suspected that Stan, all of fifteen at the time, had quietly gone to the buffet in the dining room, for when he came back there was color in his face.

But that was a long time ago.

"But, Stan, nobody can accuse me of murder!"

"You didn't kill Juan. Don't be an ass. Now then, I'll try to get Monty down here to talk to you." A rather impish spark came into his eyes. "I'll tell him you need him," said Stan and went out. There was something very emphatic about the way he closed the door behind him.

Sue wondered whether or not Monty would come to talk to her; she rather doubted it.

She was right to doubt; Monty—nobody came near. She listened at intervals and heard only the slap and wash of waves and the steady throb of the engines. There was no way to know what they had decided; she could not bring herself to venture on deck and confront Monty. The catch was, she suddenly realized, it wasn't Monty she was afraid of confronting. It was the very quiet, very hushed boat, making its steady way along to—well, where? Eleuthera?

The fact was, she was afraid to walk along that dark corridor and creep along the dark, not quite steady deck.

She locked her cabin door.

There was a steady motion, a repeated but rather gentle slapping of waves against the boat; she didn't think she had slept at all when somebody knocked at the door.

With a rush the picture of Juan—little, dark, brooding Juan—in the galley came almost before her eyes. His unexpectedly bald head added a rather macabre note to the memory.

Lalie called, "Wake up, Sue!"

She stumbled out of bed and opened the door. Lalie, already in shorts and a shirt with the ends tied around her bare midriff, came swooping in. "You look as if you'd slept! How could you!" she cried accusingly.

She rubbed her eyes and surveyed Lalie's slim, rather ribby midsection. "I'll bet you did, too!"

"Not a wink," said Lalie cheerfully and then backtracked. "Well, some. But all night I kept seeing things."

"So did I. What's happening?"

"Nothing, really. Celia made some coffee. There's food if you feel you can eat."

"Is anybody eating?" Sue was all at once, however, conscious of wanting coffee, food, anything to fill a kind of chill hollow.

"Oh, sure. Everybody," Lalie said airily and then denied it. "Not much, of course. What do you expect? Everybody sneaking looks at everybody else and thinking, Did *you* kill Juan? Did *you*?" She pushed back her long hair. "However, Lawson had a hearty breakfast. Fixed it himself, as a matter of fact. I think Monty came and went. Haven't seen Stan. But that handsome young man, Jim, ate like everything. Of course, he's only a kind of observer. None of all this—that is—oh, you know what I mean— none of it has anything to do with Jim. He wasn't even with us during the fog trip. If you want anything to eat, better make it snappy. Lawson is holding a kind of—not a trial, but an investigation. Times where we were here or there. What we saw here or there. Now then," Lalie added, "put on something pretty. Do you good."

I must look like nothing on earth, Sue thought. A glance in the mirror confirmed her notion. She went to work, splashing, brushing, dressing in clean clothes that Lalie tossed at her. Lalie said, "You look nearer the human race. Don't get upset now. It isn't a trial but—" Lalie added sourly, "damn close to it. Come on."

It was indeed rather like a trial, for everyone sat around in the salon or perched on chairs or tables. Addie had contrived to get a comfortable chair near the bar, which, Sue saw quickly, was locked, at least it was closed, so probably Monty had locked it. Monty or Celia.

Even Wiley was there, looking much better, very natty all at once in white trousers, blue jacket with brass buttons, gleaming white turtleneck sweater; with what was left of his hair showing the marks of a wet comb and both ends of his mustache twisted upward smartly. He wasn't, he couldn't be paying court to Addie. Or could he?

Monty was not there, Stan was not there. Jim sat on the edge of the seat and, catching Lalie's eye, rose courteously and offered his chair. Lalie accepted with a very sweet and feminine smile, patting his arm as she sat down, upon which Jim smiled and put his hand over hers. Dr. Smith, sitting astride a straight chair, turned around so his arms were folded across the back of it, observed the interplay, for he slightly lifted an eyebrow, as if quite aware of feminine wiles but neither approving nor disapproving.

Celia was pushing a cup of fragrant coffee into Sue's hand. "Go on. Drink it." Celia's shining black hair was neat, not a strand out of place, but her make-up was a little heavier than usual. It did not, however, quite hide the dark circles under her eyes.

Sue gave her a grateful nod and sipped her coffee.

Lawson was speaking in a rather rasping voice, "And that is all you know of Juan, Mr. Wiley?"

There was an air of an inimical prosecutor about the lawyer. He must have cast some doubt upon Juan's character, for Wiley twisted one end of his mustache; then he adjusted some gold-rimmed spectacles, which, oddly, made him look even more dandyish, although possibly like a nineteenth-century model.

"Everything I know," he replied lightly. "He came to me originally through an employment agency. No faults that I know of. Good man. Good cook. Good caretaker. Slept here on the yacht." He sighed. "I'll miss him."

Lawson's mouth tightened; he had the thin, firm lips of a born investigator and a man who can keep secrets. "That's all you can say about him? No possible motive for anybody to shoot him?"

"None that I could even guess about." Wiley hitched up his gleaming white trousers.

The self-appointed prosecutor persisted. "What did he do on his days off? I suppose you did give him days off."

"Why, certainly." Wiley's eyes flashed behind the gold-rimmed spectacles. "What do you think I am? A slave driver? Not," he added reflectively, "that Juan would have let himself be slave-driven."

"Yes, yes. But what did he do on his days off? Go to the movies? Go to the beach? Go to a bar? I gather he wasn't married."

"Well, really, my dear fellow, how could I possibly know? None of my business." Wiley paused, seemed to search his memory, and said tentatively, "I believe he had a sort of hobby."

Lawson leaped at it like a fish at a juicy bait. "What?"

"Rather dull," said Wiley disappointingly. "He liked to jog on the beach. Swim. He had a camera. Took pictures along the beach, anywhere. All sorts of things." He seemed to search his memory again and added, "I believe he developed them himself. The photographs, I mean."

"Pictures. H'm." The lawyer brooded, then shot a piercing glance at Wiley. "Ever see any of them?"

"Yes. I suppose so. Only waves and things. Nothing I thought very exciting."

"He might have been interested in the bathing girls," Lawson suggested.

The doctor stirred. "Come now, Lawson. No point in suggesting—" He stopped, for Wiley sat up, jerked off his eyeglasses, revealed eyes that had turned as chill and faintly blue as an iceberg, and shouted in a high-pitched voice, "Don't you dare insinuate anything nasty about Juan now that he is dead and can't defend himself! He was a good servant, smart, honest."

Lawson did look faintly ashamed. "No, no. Wouldn't suggest anything out of the way or— Now then, that's all you can tell me about Juan? You don't even know any former employer?"

Wiley settled back in his chair with an air of triumph.

"I've told you. I suppose I did know once. Before I employed him. Can't possibly recall." He turned to Celia. "Do you remember, Celia?"

Celia was leaning, but gracefully, calmly, it seemed, against the corner of the vast bar. She lifted her black-fringed eyes. "Why, no. Now that I think of it—no. I vaguely remember when he came to work for you. No, I'm mistaken. He was working for you already when you left your big house and bought the co-op near me. That's when I met you—some party or other, I think. No, I really can't say anything of Juan's life prior to the time I saw him serving drinks in your apartment."

"But he must have had a family somewhere. Or friends," Lawson persisted.

Wiley shook his head. "Don't recollect that he ever mentioned a family. Or friends, for that matter."

Lawson looked slightly baffled. "But we've got to notify somebody, somewhere about his—his—"

"Death," said Addie flatly.

Lawson was growing irritated. "What else?"

Addie lifted her prettily curved brown eyebrows and became specific. "Death by murder."

Fifteen

Wiley's mustache jerked upward a little, revealing his white teeth. Addie added pleasantly, "Has anybody searched Juan's possessions?"

This created an odd sort of consternation. Everyone looked at Addie. The so-to-speak prosecuting attorney swallowed hard, cleared his throat, and said, stuttering a little, "I don't know."

Addie immediately followed up on her victory. "Then wouldn't it be a good idea to do so?"

"Oh, yes, certainly. That is—" Lawson tried to resume his air of being master of all he surveyed. "I believe that is Monty's responsibility. At the time he was murdered, Juan was in Monty's employ, so I feel he should do any such investigation."

The doctor said, "My dear fellow, Monty did that last night. Told me he found nothing of any interest."

Lawson's face developed two pink spots in his cheeks, and he reversed himself without discernible compunction. "Monty is taking *too* much authority. Monty has no right to keep us out here. Way out at sea. Far from police—or— far from everything that is proper in a murder case. Even busted the radio," said the lawyer angrily. Then he appeared to regret, slightly, the undignified word he had used and substituted, "Put the radio out of commission. Monty's actions alone are most reprehensible. Could not possibly be defended in court. He'll pay dearly for this high-handed procedure, I'm afraid. And I don't intend to defend him when that time comes! Now then." He shot a swift glance all around, fastened upon Sue, and said, "Now then, Miss—er—Sue. You were the last person to see Juan?"

Sue straightened up, sparked into defiance by his tone. "No!"

"What? But you said—"

"Surely, Mr. Lawson, the last person to see him alive was his murderer."

"M'm. Well, but how did you happen to be there so quickly?"

"Because I heard the shot."

"Heard the shot," the lawyer said meditatively. "Heard it or—now let's see. The gun—at least a gun—was found on Monty's bed. Were your fingerprints on it, do you think?"

"Probably."

"Probably. Do you mean you—"

"I didn't shoot him," Sue said. "Don't question me

like that! Why in the world would I shoot Juan? Or anybody else?''

"One never knows," the lawyer said unpleasantly and turned to Wiley. "Did Juan ever have any money to speak of?''

Wiley started. "Money! Only his salary. He may have done a little betting—but as to real money, no.''

The doctor's face was flushed; he shouted, "Are you suggesting blackmail, sir?''

"Not at all, not at all," said Lawson smoothly. "I'm only interested in knowing why Miss—Miss Sue here— found it necessary to be so near the galley. She says it was the sound of the gunshot that brought her. She says Juan was already dead. How did you know that, Miss?''

"I'm a nurse," Sue said shortly. "I don't have to be told.''

"She's a good nurse, too." Dr. Smith was losing what patience he had. "See here, Lawson, you have no right to carry on like this.''

Lawson returned his angry gaze imperturbably. "I have every right. I am a lawyer. I am a citizen. Indeed, I have every right to make a citizen's arrest.''

Addie said mildly, "What on earth is that?''

"What I said. Arrest!" the lawyer replied sharply. "And also to order Monty to report this murder. Even if we must lock up one of—''

"One of us?" Wiley said.

Addie wasn't to be downed. "Lock up how? In handcuffs?''

"Lock up in a cabin. Tied up, if necessary. The only thing needed is reasonable proof. Such as—'' He turned to Sue. "The fingerprints on that gun.''

My fingerprints are certainly on it, Sue thought dismally.

Celia walked quietly over to stand beside Sue, almost defensively. Celia knew that Sue had had the gun.

Celia lifted her lovely dark head and told a really whopping lie. "I don't believe there is any way we could identify the fingerprints here. Anyway, my fingerprints are on it. I'm not sure just where. I think on a table somewhere."

Sue couldn't let that go. "No, Celia. You are—are mistaken. He gave it to me. So my fingerprints are probably on it."

"Now, Sue." Celia whirled toward her, and Sue said, low, "Thank you. But let's stick to facts. You do remember—"

Celia whispered, "Let me handle this."

"No, you can't do it this way."

Lawson strode toward them. "So we have a little collusion here," he said almost triumphantly. "Just whose fingerprints? Just who took the gun—"

A loud commotion from the deck directly above stopped him. Stan was shouting, "And give me that or I'll paste you one—"

Monty shouted, too, "Stay away from me, you young fool. I've got the gun—"

"You won't have it long!"

Monty burst into the salon, Stan with him, either shoving or grasping at Monty.

Monty stopped so short that Stan stumbled over him and brought up against Sue, who caught his arm. Once on his feet, Stan yelled, "Take that gun away from him or shut him up somewhere! I don't care which!"

There was, not remarkably, a certain amount of confusion, voices, questions, general hubbub until Monty roared above it all, "It's my yacht. I'm the owner. I'll do what I please. You don't get this gun away from me!" Whereupon he brandished it threateningly. Lalie gave a scream. Wiley started up, his hand over his heart, and Addie said, "Stop it this minute! You ought to be ashamed of yourself, Monty. You, too, Stan. What's all this about?"

Monty glowered at Addie. Stan replied, "He has that damn gun and he won't stay away from the compass. He keeps coming over and looking at it. Jim and I try to set the course again but the instant Monty gets near—" Stan shrugged. "You know what happens."

"What happens?" Addie asked with interest.

Stan gave a wildly exasperated gesture that nearly knocked Sue back against her chair. "It whirls around. Then Jim and I have to get the yacht back on course. Sometimes Monty sneaks up, and we don't know it until we're off course again. Take that damn gun, somebody. Drop it overboard. Lock it up. Or lock Monty up. We'll never get anywhere unless you do."

Lawson rose. He and the doctor began what struck Sue as a rather reluctant approach to Monty. She didn't blame them for a certain lack of zeal, for Monty was waving the gun around and shouting that it was loaded.

Stan jumped at it from behind; Monty leaped for the doorway and escaped. Stan followed him. The echoes of some rather violent shouts and remarkable language lingered behind them.

Lawson sat down. Wiley mopped his head and replaced his eyeglasses; the doctor stood, baffled, as if for once in his life deprived of command; and Lawson said, muttering, "Fingerprints! A hell of a lot of fingerprints on it now."

Addie rose. "Dear me! Boys will be boys." Shaking her curly head, she went out after Monty and Stan.

There was not this time, however, a prompt and smug return of Addie. Instead, feet pounded along the corridor. Addie squealed. Wiley shot up from his chair and ran out, evading the doctor's clutching hand. There was another confused but brief hubbub. Sue said quickly to Celia, "Don't claim anything about you and the gun. You didn't have it. I do thank you, but—"

"Don't thank me." Celia's dark eyes were fixed upon the doorway. "I wonder what your aunt is up to now."

Apparently Addie wasn't successful, for in a moment she returned, her curls drooping rather like Sissy's when the dog was seasick. She shook her head at Lawson and the doctor. "Couldn't get at him. Locked himself in his cabin. But—'' She brightened a little. ''He has the gun with him.''

There was a heavy silence, except for a certain pounding on a door somewhere.

Addie sank into her chair. ''That's Stan. Kicking at Monty's door. Cursing, too. The language these boys do learn! Thank you.'' Lalie had contrived to move sufficiently to bring Addie a drink. It looked like water. Sue was not at all sure it wasn't vodka.

Addie took it gratefully. It had to be water, for even Addie could not swallow that much vodka without so much as stopping for breath.

The pounding stopped. Footsteps came running along the corridor, but Stan did not enter the salon.

Addie sighed. ''I expect young Jim has got us back on course again. I do wish Monty were not so stubborn. It really can't be right. Not reporting all this.''

Lawson said sternly, ''He's breaking the law, that's what he's doing.''

''But you did say something about arresting him, didn't you?'' Addie said. Sue looked at her sharply; her voice was just a little too sweet.

Lawson glared at her. ''Anybody who wants to arrest that raving maniac can do so. Not me.''

''He's not a maniac!'' Sue said hotly.

Celia came at once to her support. ''He's anything but a maniac. You said so yourself, Mr. Lawson.''

''I may have made a mistake,'' Lawson grunted sourly. ''These emotional explosions can occur without much warning. A concussion, perhaps. Right, Doctor?''

The doctor nodded, but absently, for there was another burst of voices, and then silence from the deck.

Lalie who had started for the deck, stopped abruptly. ''The new man, Jim, seems to have left his post to hear the row. Stan is telling him off. I'll never go on another cruise in my life,'' she said with sincerity.

There was a tacit agreement in the silence with which

this resolution was received. Sissy chose this moment of acquiescence to start another ruckus, for she bounced up from the galley, fastened her eyes upon Lawson and stopped, obviously remembering the kick he'd given her. She started, belly low and menacing, toward the enticing view of the lawyer's bare ankles and growled.

Sue, nearest, collared her. The lawyer tucked up his feet and swore vividly while Sissy made little rumbling sounds of fury, like a small thunderstorm.

The doctor said, "Come on, Wiley. Back to bed with you."

"Oh, no." Wiley settled back in his chair and smiled.

"Oh, yes," the doctor growled, a growl that was considerably louder but not quite as menacing as Sissy achieved. "If you don't want my hospital to have that wing sooner than you intended."

"Doctor! You mean it is in his will?" Addie cried. "How very tactless to mention it that way!"

"How very rude," Lalie said.

Sue thought, And how very blunt. Dr. Smith was always blunt. But he stuck to the truth, so patients not only accepted it, they demanded it.

She said to Wiley, "The doctor is right, Mr. Wiley. That's what you pay him for, you know. Why not follow his advice?"

"Oh, the hell with the doctor," Wiley said daringly, expanded his rather narrow chest, and gave his waxed mustache a jaunty twist. "The sea air is good for me, Dr. Smith, as long as it's not foggy. Always has been. I'm fine."

Lawson cautiously lowered his legs, which he had prudently got under him as Sissy advanced upon him.

"What we've got to do is find somebody who can control Monty. Or at least influence him," he said positively.

Wiley glanced at Celia. "Celia, Mrs. Hadley, is a—a long-time friend of Monty's."

Lalie jumped at it. "Yes, Celia! You talk to Monty. If anybody can stop him, you can."

The boat gave a slight, almost imperceptible swerve. Wiley cocked his head on one side. "Maybe nobody will need to talk to him. Unless I am mistaken those two young men in the wheelhouse are taking advantage of Monty's having locked himself in his cabin and steering for the nearest port."

Monty, however, had realized that, too. His door flung open and he marched along the corridor. His footsteps trod heavily up the deck.

Addie said dreamily, "I do hope he left the gun in his cabin."

Lawson sprang up. Sissy drew back her lips and snarled, showing all her teeth. The lawyer didn't quite snarl back but gave that impression as he and the doctor both plunged out into the corridor.

Lalie sat back, a quiet little smile on her mouth.

Sue cried, "They'll get the gun! Then we can make for—"

Celia shook her head. "Now, really, Sue. Monty wouldn't leave that gun to be found. He's got it with him and—" She lifted her shoulders lightly. "He'll see to it that we go the way he wants to go. Monty has made up his mind."

The doctor came back heavily. Lalie said airily, "No soap? I mean no gun?"

The doctor grunted. Lawson returned, too. "I tell you he's breaking the law! And so are we if we let him go on this way. Besides there's the heat. That body—" He looked at the doctor.

Dr. Smith nodded briefly. "I know. The weather is getting warmer every minute."

Lalie put her hand over her mouth. Addie said, "How about a burial at sea? I've always thought how lovely and tranquil that must be."

This contribution to peace was not well received. Lawson snarled again; at least he lifted his lip. Lalie said after a moment, "I should think that Stan and Jim between them could just overpower Monty and—"

"Monty," said the doctor, "has the gun."

"Even so . . ."

"Oh, Lalie, nobody wants to run full tilt into a gun!"

Wiley said thoughtfully, "You know, Celia, when we were interrupted I was about to ask you to use your influence upon Monty. This is really a very uncomfortable situation."

Lawson commented angrily, "Uncomfortable! It's downright illegal. We may all find ourselves in jail!"

Celia lifted her slender black eyebrows. "You don't really believe that, Mr. Lawson. This is Monty's doing and Monty's alone. But as to influence, no. I'll not even try to influence Monty once he's made up his mind. Come on, Sissy."

Sue went out with Celia, thankful to get away from the ugly atmosphere in the salon. That was due partially to Lawson but perhaps also to the natural feelings of suspicion and fear on the part of the others. She had scooped up Sissy under her arm and Sissy cast back threatening glances toward Lawson. But once they were on deck, everything seemed better. The sea was blue and quiet; the sun was bright; the sky was flecked with tiny white clouds. Sue took some long breaths and felt better, but it was of course an entirely false feeling of safety. Within that luxury yacht lay the body of a murdered man. And within that luxury yacht there existed somebody capable of murder.

Celia leaned on the rail. Sue put Sissy down and thwarted a notion on the poodle's part to return to her prey in the salon. "A single-minded dog," she said to Celia. "Now then, why did you say your fingerprints would be on the gun and not mine? That is, I thank you for trying to save me embarrassment or—"

"Or suspicion?" Celia said dryly. The light breeze lifted her black hair. She looked out to sea steadily. Sissy gave up and trotted off to the sandbox.

"I don't really know," Celia said enigmatically. "Perhaps because Lawson's high-handedness really made me mad." After a moment she added, "Perhaps because I like you, Sue."

"Well, I like you, too."

"All the same, I don't intend to give up Monty to you. You understand that."

Sixteen

The small waves rushed past them. The breeze seemed softer and certainly warmer.

This, Sue thought as she had thought before, was an odd matter-or-fact, woman-to-woman kind of conversation.

Celia waited for her to reply, and as Sue said nothing, Celia put a strong hand over Sue's. "I know you must hate me—"

"No, I don't. Not possibly."

"But, I must be fair and—the point is, I intend to marry Monty. I want you to know that."

"All right," Sue said helplessly. "But Monty will have something to say about it."

"Do you mean he has actually asked you to marry him?"

"Yes, that is, in a way."

Celia didn't ask in what way, as Sue expected. She said only, "Don't count on it. All right, Sissy. We'll go back to the courtroom but please don't even look at that lawyer. He'll have you up for resisting arrest or something worse. And by the way, Sue, there is such a thing as a citizen's arrest. But I think the catch is that the arrestee, so to speak, is not likely to cooperate. Certainly not Monty. And I am perfectly sure he didn't kill Juan. He's only single-minded about going on, like this, instead of heading for the nearest police. Look here, Sue, when he talked of marriage—you say he did talk of marriage.''

Sue nodded.

''And you said yes.''

''I—that is—in a way.''

Celia didn't even bother to look at her; she watched the blue sea and blue sky. But she said, ''You keep saying 'in a way.' Surely a man says either will you or won't you. And a woman says yes or no.''

Again Sue collared Sissy, who was sneakily advancing toward the salon and Mr. Lawson. Celia waited a moment. ''Perhaps it wasn't very romantic?''

''I don't think Monty is the romantic type.'' That was safe to say.

''Or,'' Celia said smoothly, ''perhaps there is another man. So you didn't quite jump for joy when Monty approached the subject.''

''No other man,'' Sue said stoutly. ''Monty wants marriage, and I'm going to marry him.'' Sue hesitated. ''I'd like to be friends, Celia. But I suppose we can't be.''

To her surprise, Celia turned, smiling, her dark eyes warm. ''I'm sorry. I like you. But I intend to get Monty myself one way or another. However, it's nice to have to fight somebody you like. That is, no, I'm not sure it is nice, but anyway—I think—'' She paused and finally said soberly, ''I really think we could be friends. Sounds mad, doesn't it?''

''But that's not the only thing that's out of kilter on this boat.''

''I know. Murder. And by simple reckoning, also a murderer. Where are you going?''

''To Juan's cabin.''

''Monty searched it.''

''He might have missed something.''

Celia eyed her. ''I wouldn't go near that cabin if I were you. It's just a cubbyhole, really. I've seen it. Juan has made the yacht his special domain for years, the whole time he worked for Wiley. Don't do it, Sue.''

"Come with me.''

Celia shrugged. "I don't want to. But I will. Come on.''

Sissy, naturally, went with them, pausing only to give a growl toward the salon and Lawson. They all seemed to be talking; Addie's fluty voice could be heard rising above some of Lawson's magisterial pronouncements.

Juan's cabin was called a cabin merely for the sake of a name; it was literally a cubby hole.

After they had sorted out the few things that obviously belonged to Monty, there was nothing among Juan's stored-up boxes and suitcase that could possibly indicate a reason for his murder. White jackets, dark and threadbare trousers, neat little shoes. A wig below some underclothes.

Sue found that, and her fingers shrank from its coarse black texture. Celia smiled. "He always wore a wig. He was almost entirely bald. Didn't you notice that when the doctor turned him over there in the galley?''

"Yes.'' Sue felt a little faint; the muggy air in the cabin, the slight motion of the boat? No, it was the feel of the coarse hair. She dropped the wig on one of the boxes.

Celia said, "You'd better get out of here. You look a little odd.''

"I feel odd.'' Sue gave a rather shuddering glance at the wig and followed Celia into the airy width of the corridor.

Celia said, "I'll go and find out what our self-appointed prosecuting attorney is having to say. Look here, Sue—'' She lowered her voice. "Your aunt is quite a woman. If I had to pick the most likely person on this boat to do murder it would be your aunt.''

"Aunt Addie! Why, she wouldn't kill a—''

"I'll bet she's swatted hundreds of them! I'll go further. A tarantula wouldn't have a hope if it tangled with her.'' She looked out across the water absently and suddenly gave a little laugh. " 'She'd fight a rattlesnake and give it two bites.' See? I've caught your aunt's habit.''

"Who said that?"

"I don't remember. Yes, I do. Harry Leon Wilson. Sue, has your aunt ever acted? I mean professionally. Or—well, or in amateur shows?"

"Why, no. I don't think so."

"A pity. Talent wasted."

"She isn't acting. That is—"

"Not all the time? I suppose you have a kind of sense of when she's putting on a show and when she's not."

Sue thought it over. "She does go all dramatic sometimes."

"Dramatic! Carries on, you mean. With an eye to the gallery. Come on, Sue. Tell me the truth. Has she always been like that?"

Sue thought that over, too. "She likes to get the full excitement out of anything."

"I'll bet she never made a good story worse."

Sue laughed, remembering some of Addie's tales, which even as she told them Sue had known were somewhat, occasionally more than somewhat, exaggerated. "No harm in that."

"Except when she's maundering on about who killed Juan, who helped him out of the salon the other time even if he did say he was alone. I'll bet she didn't actually see who if anybody was with him that night. I hope not," Celia said seriously.

Sue hoped so, too. "I'll talk to her again."

"You'll not get anywhere." But then Celia laughed. "And I'll tell you something else. She doesn't really drink as devotedly as you imagine. Believe me, that woman could stop drinking any time she decided to." Celia patted Sue's shoulder. "Never mind. I don't think she killed Juan."

Sue had rallied. "Stan said, right away, there in the galley, that whoever it was who tipped Monty into the sea thought it was Juan in the hammock."

"I know. And Monty still clearly believes that he is the target."

"Oh, yes," Sue said dismally.

"So we go on. Until somebody does something to bring Monty to his senses."

"You can't?"

"I don't propose to try. I told you. I intend to marry Monty. I don't intend to cross him about anything. He doesn't like it. Come on, Sissy."

She strolled toward the salon. Sissy debated but prudently chose Celia to follow.

Sue was all at once overcome with uneasiness and a feeling of utter distaste for the court of inquiry Lawson appeared still to be holding in the salon. She didn't want to go up on deck and, just perhaps, witness another conflict between Monty and Stan. Having no other place to go, she went to her own cabin and was rummaging in the narrow drawers of the tiny built-in chest near the bed, hunting for a scarf she seemed to remember packing, when her fingers encountered something sharp and stiff, some kind of paper. She dug it out with the help of an emery board and found it was merely a yellow envelope, enclosing several small photograph negatives.

Juan had a hobby, photography.

Her thoughts leaped to an obvious possibility. Since Juan apparently had lived on the yacht, what was more likely than that he had quietly made use of one of the large cabins rather than his own cubbyhole? Especially in the warm weather of the coast off Palm Beach. Perhaps he had not mentioned this little departure from the rules to Wiley. Possibly, too, Wiley wouldn't have minded so long as Juan kept the place clean.

But this small envelope of negatives had been forgotten.

It seemed a plausible explanation, although there was nothing certain about it. Sue was sufficiently curious to hold the negatives, one at a time, up to the light. They were very small, set into cardboard holders, so she could only see blurs of sea and ships or parts of a boat. Possibly there were figures, some in the water, a h what might be waves. But though she scrutinized each one, there was simply nothing she could identify. So then Juan—if it had been he—had merely indulged his hobby, tucked away these negatives, and forgotten them.

In view of the eager surge of hope for some clue to Juan's murder, this was not unlikely but disappointing.

She had closed the door to her cabin. She was sure that she had closed it, but she was conscious of a slight motion somewhere behind her as she stood holding the negatives up against the light from the porthole. She thought she felt a slight current of air and whirled around, but the door was closed.

Had she heard it close? She wasn't sure. She wasn't sure of anything.

She thrust the negatives into a pocket of her jeans; she would turn them over, she supposed, to Wiley, Juan's former employer. Or Monty.

She lay on the bed for a long time, thinking and trying not to.

Also wondering what, if anything, had developed in the salon.

Celia was right about Addie's affection for drama. Addie didn't precisely lie, but she was not what one could safely call an accurate reporter. Somehow her account of an incident was often highlighted in a dramatic way. Probably, she thought, Addie had merely glimpsed Juan's white jacket in the dusk of the corridor and assumed that he was being assisted by someone.

But to anyone who didn't know Addie, this statement could have been taken as fact; only Celia's observant eyes had noted Addie's flair for rather fanciful embroidery. And certainly Addie did have a pragmatic and very strong will concealed below that charming façade of helpless and appealing femininity. Hadn't Addie seen hard times for herself and for Sue approaching? Hadn't Addie very sensibly grasped the nettle, sold the big house, bought a cottage at just the right time before real estate values for small places rose so dramatically? Hadn't Addie supported Sue's plan for taking nurses' training?

Hadn't Addie very quietly, very gently and very powerfully encouraged Sue's marriage to Monty?

The answer was yes. But that did not mean she would kill anybody, especially somebody she didn't even know, like Juan.

She had backed down over her former statement about seeing him and the dinghy dropped into the sea. Naturally, Addie had simply decided that she had allowed her story to lead her into dangerous waters, so she had resorted to stout denial. It was, Sue suddenly remembered, a favorite ruse of Addie's. Anything she didn't choose to admit, after her lively fancy had gone too far, she simply denied, and such was her charm and appeal that people accepted it, knowing perfectly well that Addie was lying but completely unable to thrust her lie, so to speak, down her throat.

Now Addie's course was clear. Deny anything that might make trouble.

It was prudent. If not wise. Yet there might be more than a grain of truth in her words.

Celia's remarkably friendly kind of defiance was surprising. Celia meant everything she had said: she was determined to marry or at least keep Monty.

Sue would have to see about that. She couldn't help liking Celia, and that made her own prospects of marrying Monty a little more hazardous but did not shake her determination. She reminded herself that she had arrived at that decision in cold blood, with sensible thinking. Regardless of how much Sue liked her, no former mistress of Monty's was going to change it.

Stan interrupted her brooding.

"It's Stan," he shouted from outside the door. "Can I come in?"

"Yes. It isn't locked."

Stan came in and glowered at the door and then at her. "Should be."

"Oh, Stan, nobody is going to hurt me. Why would anybody—''

"Why would anybody try to murder Monty and fail, but succeed in killing Juan?"

"Stan, you said that the attempt upon Monty was intended as an attempt upon Juan.''

"That's what I think. That's what everybody would think except Monty. He's still got that damn fool notion in his thick head that somebody is after him. If he doesn't take himself and that gun away from the wheel, either Jim or I will see to it that he gets another dip in the drink.''

"Oh, don't, Stan. He'll—certainly, he'll—''

"Simmer down? Not Monty.'' Stan sank into a chair and rubbed his eyes.

"What are they doing in the salon?''

"Nothing, I think. The doctor is pacing around the bridge. Lawson is sitting in a deck chair making notes on some legal-sized pad of paper that apparently he brought with him. In which,'' Stan said acidly, "to make the notes for Monty's new will. Now this great legal mind is fancying himself a detective. God knows, he might succeed. But forget about that. I came to ask you to do something.''

"All right.''

"You should be cagey and find out what it is first. But I'll tell you again. I'll send Monty down here with his gun and you keep him here.''

"But I—how—''

"You ought to know how to please him. Just keep him away from the compass. You're engaged to marry the man, aren't you?''

"Why, I—yes—that is not—that is—''

Stan flung himself out of the chair and out the door. He stuck his head back in. "By God, if I ever get engaged to marry a girl, she'll know it,'' he said and disappeared.

Monty, however, did not come to her cabin this time either. If Monty did not have a concussion, it was certainly overconfidence in his own common sense that had given him a mandate to find the enemy and deliver him to justice. She thought back to her knowledge of the symptoms of a concussion and failed to find anything that suggested it in Monty's behavior. But she was no authority. Clearly Monty did not intend to leave the deck that night. He would stay there, with the gun, keeping himself wide-enough awake (and keeping Stan and Jim wide awake, too.)

Months, or perhaps only hours, had passed when Lalie turned up, again with food, rather higgledy-piggledy tea sandwiches that she shared with Sue. "No lunch, and it's late afternoon. Nobody likes to admit they are hungry," Lalie said, munching. "But everybody is sort of sneaking into the galley—avoiding the place where they—no, you—found Juan." She chewed and added, "Celia mopped it up. I must say she's got guts. But don't let her lick you, Sue. It's you Monty wants to marry. Here, have another."

"What else are they doing?"

"I told you. Sneaking into the galley. Sneaking some drinks, too."

Sue stopped a sandwich on the way to her mouth. "Aunt Addie?"

Lalie considered it. "No. She's busy charming that man Wiley. They are already like twin souls. Want a new uncle, Sue? Not for very long, if your doctor friend is right. But still, Wiley is loaded, I'd say. Monty told me he has a house he's trying to sell for five million. Five—" Lalie shook her head. "I can't count that far. Five million seems a terrific lot of money. But Monty says Wiley is so good at selling things that he'll get the money he asks. Like he got money from Monty for this lovely broken-down yacht." She polished off the remains of the sandwiches. "Do you happen to know what time it is?"

Sue wore a stout wrist watch, not the jeweled (and, she was sure, very costly) one Monty had given her. And probably had given one like it to Celia, she thought briefly.

"It can't be six o'clock! I must have forgotten to wind it. What an idiot! In the hospital I always kept it wound."

"Looks like a hospital." Lalie eyed the utilitarian time-piece and rose. "I suppose Stan and Jim, with Monty to watch them for fear they'll start for the nearest port when his back is turned, will stay on deck all night." Lalie yawned. "It's been a long day. Almost sunset. I wonder where in hell a port is."

Sue locked the door again after Lalie had sauntered away. Lalie was very like Monty sometimes; anybody would have known that they were related for they had the same confidence, the same pleasant warmth of manner—and possibly the same determination, but channeled in different directions. She suspected that Lalie would have yielded to common sense and headed for the nearest port herself.

Later Sue went to the galley, where Celia and Lalie were rather absent-mindedly making gestures of preparing some kind of dinner. Sue made automatic gestures, too, and didn't bother Addie, who was quiet and thoughtful. Nobody was precisely merry. Stan turned up, and Lalie became very busy, bringing his food, leaning on his chair, her arm around the back of it, while he ate. Lalie could make her eyes sparkle and her lips smile invitingly without half trying, Sue thought tartly as she fixed a tray for Lawson, who grunted his thanks.

Nobody seemed to want to talk. Everybody seemed to keep a watchful eye upon everybody else.

Natural, Sue thought, but also rather unpleasant, very unpleasant indeed.

Good-nights were perfunctory and appeared to suggest that a really restful night on that yacht was not to be expected. She saw Addie to her cabin and at last crawled into her own bed, trying to let herself be lulled to sleep by the motion of the boat.

She couldn't have locked the door! That was her first vague notion when she felt something stir in the cabin.

It was not a sound, exactly; it was barely a sense of motion somewhere near her that roused her from sleep.

Her heart began to thump so hard that, oddly, she was afraid someone might hear it.

Well, then say something, she told herself. Speak to him—her—whoever it is. Better than that, shout. Yell! Scream!

No: she didn't dare show that she was even aware of any presence in the cabin. She wasn't even sure of a presence—but yes, she *was* sure. There was the faintest, smallest kind of rustle or click somewhere.

There was the sound of the engines, pounding away. There was the steady wash of waves. There were the tiny creaks and sighs of the yacht, which could be heard most clearly at night. It's like a house, she thought vaguely; like Aunt Addie's cottage, it comes alive at night. But this was not the safe little cottage. This was a boat on the high seas, carrying murder.

The small yet definite little noise came again, and she recognized it as the faint click in the tiny chest of drawers. It was near her bed. So whoever had opened and then closed that drawer had to be very near her.

She tried to steady her breathing in the hope that that would steady her wildly thudding heart. She had an impulse to thrust her head under the blanket and was so frozen with terror that she couldn't move. If she made the slightest move, then whoever was there, so near her, would instantly know that she was awake and aware of him and would instantly—no, no, her mind cried; not murder me! No, no!

But there was or seemed to be a rather sudden cessation of sound.

In the dense darkness she couldn't possibly be seen. Neither could that stealthy visitor be seen.

After a moment, which seemed like a year, there were faint sounds, growing softer and farther away. She listened with all her nerves, all her body, everything about her as still as a frightened bird when a hawk hovers overhead.

But then—oh, then there was a perfectly clear and unmistakable sound of the door being opened; there was a slight current of air across her face. The door softly closed, the current of air was gone, and she heard a key turn in the lock.

It was a key. It had to be a key.

Eventually a kind of strength seemed to return to her paralyzed body. She sat up. Instinctively she knew that she was alone; also, however, she felt that she must be very quiet. It was probably only a minute, but it seemed much longer before she summoned up the courage to reach out into the inky darkness and turn on the tiny bedside lamp.

Naturally, there was no one prowling around the cabin. The intruder had gone. She had heard that departure. Hadn't she?

There was no doubt in her mind about that. Someone had been quietly searching the cabin. For what?

At that, she got cautiously out of bed.

There was no visible sign of any search and nothing else unusual except there was the key to the door lying on the carpet.

So whoever had visited her cabin had used some other key to enter. He could have pushed out the key on her side of the door, quietly used his own, and quietly but very quickly, as if alarmed at something she had not known, departed after first pausing to relock the door with his own key.

Monty had keys.

As evidenced by his intrusion into Aunt Addie's cabin, Wiley had kept his set of keys when he turned the yacht over to the new owner. Juan must have had a set also, and who knows what might have happened to those keys!

Then search the place for herself, especially the tiny built-in drawers near the bed.

There were three small drawers; the upper two were

very shallow. The lower drawer was deep. Every one of the three showed signs of a hasty yet fumbled search, but a definite search. Scarfs were shoved to one side, lingerie was piled up any old way. There had been no attempt, or no time really, even to try to give a semblance of order. So whoever had been searching her cabin had not cared whether or not the search was discovered. He had been careful only to get away when he heard something, she couldn't even surmise what, that alarmed him.

That, or he hadn't found what he had expected to find.

It was an uncomfortable reflection, made worse when she put her hand below the tiny bedside table and found Juan's wig.

Seventeen

It was as coarse, as ugly, as horridly sticky as it had been when she found it in Juan's cubbyhole.

She dropped it with a kind of sickening aversion.

She turned swiftly to the bathroom and scrubbed her hands furiously. Drying them, she thought, at least she hadn't screamed. That was good.

The fact was, however, she couldn't have screamed. Her throat had simply locked. She couldn't have spoken, let alone scream for help.

Besides what help could have been given her by anybody?

Some common sense would have been useful, yes. A sound assurance that although sulky little Juan was certainly still on the yacht, he was not, so to speak, in a position to walk around, leaving his horrible little wig wherever he chose.

With that, something hideously like a giggle came up in

her throat. Hysterics! Somebody had said he didn't like hysterics. And fainting women.

She didn't care for either herself.

All the same, she shoved the repulsive wig almost out of sight, using a slipper to propel it under the chair. Then she more or less collapsed on the bed and huddled there.

After a while she remembered Juan's telling Addie just to ring if she wanted anything. There was a small mother-of-pearl button near the door. Why not ring?

But Juan wouldn't answer.

She was getting very cold, not from the night, which was balmy and warm, but from another kind of chill. She wouldn't ring, for certainly she did not want Juan to come in answer!

And now, she knew, she was getting almost over the border into absurdity.

So she must do something. There was a perfectly logical course for her; she could use the key that gleamed from the carpet, open the door, go out into the corridor and up to the deck and find Stan, Monty, Jim. Anybody. And tell them what had happened.

But what *had* happened? Someone had come into her cabin, using another key. Someone had searched the few places there were to search. Someone had left Juan's horrid coarse black wig. And then gone.

What could anybody do about that?

Searching the entire yacht would only emphasize what everybody knew; there was a murderer on board.

After a while she realized that she did not even have the courage it would require to open the door and walk out along the corridor and up to the bridge. Once there, yes, she'd feel like herself. But getting there was something else.

After a while, too, she wondered about the time. It felt very late—or, rather, very early. Almost dawn?

After a while, too, from sheer nervous reaction and

weariness, she found that she had dropped over against the pillow.

When she heard Lalie at the door, she opened her eyes. Her bedside lamp still burned, but it was clearly a sunny day. She was cramped and cold and thought that she had had a most hideous nightmare. Certainly it had to be a nightmare.

It was no nightmare. An ugly little patch of coarse black hair lay, like a lurking beast, half hidden under the chair.

Lalie was shouting, "Hey! Breakfast is over."

Aunt Addie's high soprano joined Lalie's voice. "She's only overslept. Tired to death, poor dear. Oh, why did I say that? Sue, *will you open this door?*"

Sue got slowly, stiffly, out of bed and fumbled her way to the door, remembered the key on the rug, stooped to get it, gave a kick to Juan's wig, hiding it more surely under the chair, and as Addie sang, " 'The snail's on the thorn, the bird's on the wing. . . .' " Sue unlocked and opened the door.

"I thought you didn't like Browning," Sue said crossly.

"I hate him." Addie was always good-natured. "Come on, Sue. We're going to have a burial at sea."

"We are not!" Lalie gave Sue a sharp look. "What's the matter with you? You do look terrible."

Sue tried to grasp at aroused common sense. "Aunt Addie! What do you mean, a burial at sea? You can't mean Juan—"

"Oh, yes." Lalie took over, pushed Addie and herself into the cabin and hunted through Sue's small supply of clothing. She snatched out navy-blue shorts and a white shirt. "Here. Put these on. Too warm for jeans. And hurry up. A trial is going on and friend Lawson is acting like a hanging judge."

"Judge Jeffrey," said Addie and seated herself. "Sue, it's lucky your legs are tanned. And pretty."

"Hurry it up," Lalie advised. "You never heard such a racket. Everybody is fighting everybody else."

Not everybody, Sue discovered when she got to the salon, cooler in a way, owing to the shorts and shirt, but hot with apprehension. Addie trotted on ahead, singing, "'When the saints come marching in,'" which even at that moment struck Sue as extraordinarily inapt.

Stan was not there; Jim was not there. Monty was not there.

Otherwise there was what Addie would probably call a full complement, plus coffee offered her promptly by Celia and accepted as promptly by Sue.

Only Celia gave Sue so much as a glance with the welcome coffee.

Lawson was expounding. ". . . we can't just shove him into the sea. There's got to be proof of the corpus delicti for the police!"

Addie had instantly picked up the thread. She settled herself near Wiley, who gave her a positively voluptuous grin. She said, "Why?"

Lawson scowled. Dr. Smith sat in his favorite position astride a small chair, reversed so he could lean his elbows, belligerently it seemed to Sue, on the back of it. "I think you are all wrong, Lawson."

"Corpus delicti," said Lawson ponderously, speaking to Addie, "is the heart of the case . . . I should say . . . in layman's terms, the murdered man. Corpus—"

Addie didn't giggle but looked as if she might. "Oh, I studied Latin, Mr. Lowery—"

"Lawson" came in a rumble from the lawyer. Addie went on, "But in this connection, really—no, I don't think I ever heard that particular phrase. May have read it. But now, '. . . *nil nisi bonum*.'"

"Yes, yes," Lawson said impatiently.

Celia, leaning on the mahogany bar, said softly, "Wouldn't it be a good idea to find out what Monty thinks? It is his yacht."

Lalie, sitting with long legs crossed, hugged her knees

with her thin arms, shrugged the T-shirt tightly across her shoulders, and said, "Monty won't have it."

Lawson thundered, "I tell you, Monty is breaking the law every single instant he goes on with this fantastic—"

Lalie interrupted. "All right. Monty is breaking the law. But I know Monty better than any of you—that is—" Her blue-gray eyes flickered once toward Celia. "Better than most of you," she corrected herself, but not too blatantly. "And I know what he'd say to this idea of simply dumping poor Juan in the sea. First, of course, he's got to have that whatever you called it, corpus something. That's to show the law when he gets around to it. Or I should say when he has discovered who murdered him."

It seemed to Sue that there was an instant chill in the salon. From its windows on the port side, sunlight streamed in and there were glimpses of the blue sea. Lalie crossed her legs the other way and continued, "Besides, Monty wouldn't think it was at all proper. No, now don't stop me!" Somebody, Lawson or the doctor, had made a motion, and Lalie checked him with an emphatic shake of her blond head. "I tell you, I know Monty. He's a straight-A square. From the backbone out. He'll never consent to such un-an—"

Addie helped her out. "Unorthodox behavior. I expect you are right, Lalie."

"Oh, yes," Celia said rather absently, looking out beyond the salon to the blue sea. "Monty is conservative. Born that way."

"You should know," Addie said, so pleasantly that Celia merely gave her the fraction of a glance. Addie did have the grace to blush slightly. "I mean, Celia has known him for a long time—"

"Not as long as I've known him," Lalie broke in. "Why, I've known him since I was born. He'd never consent to letting you just slide old Juan into the sea."

"Then," said Dr. Smith, "we do it without consulting

Monty. After all, we have to think of the health of the rest of us.''

Lalie considered it and shook her head. Celia considered it, her dark eyes steady. Addie sat with her pretty hands folded, looking at nothing. Sue eyed her warily; Addie was thinking of a suitable quotation.

The doctor stirred. ''Wiley, you have a bad color,'' he commented abruptly. ''It's very warm in here. Can't somebody turn on the air conditioner?''

Wiley gave a kind of cackle. ''Air conditioner! My God, friend, this yacht was built long before anybody ever thought of air conditioning. However, there used to be fans somewhere.'' He glanced vaguely around. And Addie found her theme, although it was not quite appropriate. She sang softly. '' 'Now the day is—is o-o-ve-rr, Night is falling near—' Or is it 'fast'?'' she interrupted herself to ask. ''Odd how one can so seldom remember hymns. Now if anybody said, 'Happy days are here again'—or—''

''Aunt Addie,'' Sue said threateningly.

''There now, certainly I don't mean it is a happy day when we consign a loved one to the deep. That is, he was not exactly a loved one—unless, of course—'' Addie turned a sweetly apologetic gaze upon Wiley, who smiled dotingly and twisted one end of his mustache. ''Unless you felt he was a good and faithful servant— Oh, that's it!'' Addie cried. '' 'Here lies a good and faithful servant—' ''

''He'll not lie long,'' Dr. Smith said shortly. He turned to Celia. ''Aren't there sharks in these waters?''

There was an instant's horrified and perceptive silence.

Dr. Smith looked at them one at a time, cleared his throat and said, ''He's gone. He'll never know—''

''Don't!'' Lalie cried.

Celia said slowly, ''Yes. There are sharks in these waters. Not often, however. Not many.''

Wiley had wilted. Now he perked up. ''Very seldom, my dear Celia. Very seldom. Miss Addie, really, I can't remember more than two or three times when a shark has been sighted anywhere near where—'' He faltered. ''That is, near wherever we are now.''

Addie, who had apparently been brooding, said suddenly and plaintively, ''My niece doesn't like my singing. Or my habit of quoting. I am so sorry.''

Wiley put his hand over Addie's, which was on the arm of her chair, placed conveniently near Wiley. He eyed Sue defiantly. ''This dear lady can do as she wishes. For my part, I think it a very charming practice. There, there, dear lady.'' He patted Addie's hand.

Sue was sure she saw the very slightest smile touching the corners of Addie's pretty lips, although her eyes were cast down modestly. Good heavens, Sue thought; can this be an ancient—well, call it mature—romance blossoming? But Wiley was so very ill that a doctor had accompanied him. At the same time, Addie was innately kind and maternal and would probably be at her best in caring for Wiley. And who knows? The sea air, Wiley had said, was good for him. He had indeed seemed to take on a more vigorous attitude toward life recently.

The doctor, distracted by no such sentimental fancies about Aunt Addie and his patient, rose with an air of decision. ''So we'll see to this without telling Monty. Come with me, Mr. Lawson. I'll need help.''

Sue rose. ''No! You can't do that without telling Monty.''

Celia sighed. ''All right, Sue. I'll tell Monty.''

Lalie rose. ''I'll go, too. There'll be fireworks.''

''No, fireworks, '' the doctor said. ''I will assume responsibility. Simply a reasonable reaction to Monty's high-and-mighty determination to take that poor—oh, never mind,'' he said sharply to Addie, who started to speak.

But she got out a few words. ''If we only had a wreath to throw after him into the sea. That's the way they do it in the movies.''

The doctor's voice rose over Addie's wail. ''All right, Lawson. Now then, *you women stay here.*''

Celia and Lalie both sat down, exchanging only looks of disapproval.

Addie snuggled her hand more closely into Wiley's hand, which was certainly not unreceptive. The doctor fastened a commanding eye upon Sue. "You take charge, Nurse. *Nobody is to move. Nobody* is to talk to Monty or those two young men. Understand me?"

"Yes, Doctor." Sue's voice didn't quaver; to her own surprise, it was perfectly calm and obedient. What was she—a woman or a mouse?

She was a qualified nurse; but she was also a woman and a frightened one. Somebody had certainly entered her cabin during the night; she couldn't dismiss that unwelcome visit as a nightmare because there was Juan's terrible little wig.

She had not even mentioned her nightmare—or rather, the perfectly sure visit on the previous night and the revolting proof of its reality. There was no real reason for her reticence, but there was a suggested reason that she had refused even to admit to herself. She did so, then. The wig actually seemed to imply that Juan was not dead at all, that he had contrived to slide around the yacht, to enter her room, somehow to lose that ugly wig and then disappear.

This could not be a fact. All her rational processes of thought rejected it wholeheartedly. Wholeheartedly?

She decided that she really must pull herself together, conquer such bizarre and extremely unnerving reflections, and accept the truth.

The plain truth was that someone had taken Juan's wig and left it in her cabin.

She might tell Monty, but not in his present angry state of mind. Stan? No. Celia, Lalie? Perhaps her prudence in keeping that unwelcome visitation to herself was based upon a sound and sensible instinct. She couldn't just then identify the instinct. She only knew the extremely unpleasant fact that Juan's wig had been left in her cabin. Who would remove that wig from Juan's things? Who would leave it in her own cabin? Was it a kind of subtle threat? No, it had to be merely accidental. But all the same, somebody (but not Juan, oh, not Juan!) had entered her room, very, very stealthily; searched very quietly and then fled, still very quietly, but perhaps dropping the wig.

There was no way to guess why anyone would be carrying Juan's wig around with him. Certainly she could not so much as surmise any reason for searching her cabin.

As certainly, however, sometime and soon, she would risk Monty's unpredictable state of mind and tell him of the nightmare that was indeed not a nightmare.

There was only the steady sound of engines. Finally Addie rose, gave Wiley's hand a reassuring pat, and tiptoed to the salon entrance.

Celia saw her go and sighed. Lalie started to rise, stopped, and adjusted her scanty blue shorts. Celia, as well, was in shorts. The whole cabin was too warm. Wiley felt the heat also and opened his shirt.

Lalie and Celia both jumped up as a kind of hubbub arose suddenly in what seemed to be a recent custom on the yacht. Men's voices; men's footsteps, running, pounding along the deck and into the salon! The doctor came first, marching along steadily. Lawson came next, panting and wiping his face with one hand. His eyes had a curious glitter. Then Monty burst in, shouting, "Who did it? You've got to tell me. Who did it?"

Stan came after him. Jim followed Stan. The doctor caught Sue's arm and said, "It's all right." He turned to Monty. "Take it easy."

Lawson cried nervously, "Behave yourself, Monty. Nobody—"

Stan came across to Sue. He said in a low voice, "Batten down the hatches. Prepare for rough weather." She stared up at him, and he added, quite coolly but with an edge in his voice, "Juan is gone."

"Juan—" Sue began, but Monty shouted, "Who did it?

I tell you I'll find out. I had to have his body! Somebody got rid of it. Where is it? Who's responsible?''

The doctor wiped his cheeks. ''Now, Monty, don't have a seizure. The fact is—''

''All right, all right! What is the fact? I tell you—''

''I'm trying to tell you. Juan's body has disappeared.''

''I know that!''

The doctor went imperturbably on, ''And a very good thing. In this weather.''

''But I had to have the body—''

''No,'' the doctor said firmly. ''You've got to consider the health of your guests. This weather—my God, Monty! Thank whoever tossed that—I mean to say—'' Addie had given a faint scream, but the doctor, who had the ears of a cat, had heard it and he softened his words. ''I should say committed that body to the deep—''

''I never thought of it like that,'' Addie murmured.

The doctor continued. ''. . . was very sensible. A very sound act!''

Monty looked almost villainous, unshaven; his usually kind and reasonable eyes were swollen for lack of sleep, and worse, one hand was upon the bulge at his belt, below his shirt, which only a gun could make. ''No. Altogether wrong!'' he shouted and then lowered his voice. ''I tell you it was wrong! How can I ever convince the police that there was a body! That there was a murder! And—'' Monty's voice lowered; he said in a measured way, ''and that there is still a murderer on this boat.''

Sue moved nearer Stan and wished she had his presence of mind.

Not that, for the moment, he seemed to have much presence of mind, for he, too, suddenly shouted, ''Jim! Get back to the wheel.''

Jim was hanging over the bar, staring. Now he gave the doctor a frenziedly imploring look, gulped hard, and said, ''I did it.''

Monty whirled upon him. ''You did it!''

The doctor took command. "Perhaps I misled you. Perhaps I ought to have told all of you at once. Jim did not do it single-handedly. He helped me." He paused deliberately and lighted a cigarette.

Monty turned almost scarlet, stared at Jim and the doctor, and swore. Addie recovered sufficiently to cry, "No, no, Monty! Such language! I'm sure they did it for the best of motives."

Lawson had apparently got his breath, but he was very angry. He all but jumped at the doctor, who puffed on his cigarette and squinted up his eyes to avoid the smoke. Lawson, too, resorted to shouting. "You did that! You let me go with you and discover that the body was gone and you never said a word. You let all of us think—"

"All right, Lawson. Yes, I did all that. Saw no reason for explaining just what I did and—it was this way. Calm down, Monty. And sit down before you have a stroke. You are young to have a stroke, but if I ever saw anybody on the verge! *Sit down!*" he thundered.

Monty sat down, staring at the doctor and at Jim, who said, miserably, "I thought you understood. Of course I helped him."

"So you helped conceal a crime. Just when did all this go on?"

"I didn't mean—" Jim faltered, and the doctor took over with a rather theatrical, if unintentional, flourish of his cigarette.

"Naturally, I asked him to help me. Now just wait, Monty," he said peremptorily as Monty gave every appearance of a volcano about to explode. "I'll tell you. You'll admit the weather is getting warmer and warmer."

Monty gave an angry nod. The doctor went on. "I had to consider the health of your passengers. Believe me, Monty. That's my job. Save health as long as possible. So I knew what must be done. I went up to the bridge. Stan was at the wheel. I don't know where you were. Anyway this young fellow, Jim"—he waved the cigarette at Jim, whose face was a bright pink—"Jim had dozed off on the little bench just back of the wheel. Stan didn't see or hear me. I nudged Jim and beckoned. Once on deck I explained the situation. He understood."

"I was half asleep," Jim muttered. "But all the same." He straightened, mopped his forehead, and said smartly to Monty, "It was a good idea. Hygienic. The doctor explained—"

".So," the doctor continued, "Jim came with me. We buried Juan at sea. Very quietly, of course. But I must tell you, Miss Addie, also very respectfully. And very sensibly, too. Not that I expect any of you to agree with me. Until you think it over."

There was a pause while quite obviously everyone was thinking it over and quite as obviously even Monty calmed down a little. "But you ought to have told me," he said.

"You wouldn't have permitted it." The doctor looked sorry and undoubtedly was. "I had to go along with the idea of a burial at sea. Proposed—or at least approved—by Miss Addie."

Sue said boldly, "But, Doctor, wouldn't it have been better to have told us right away, this morning, just what had been done?"

"Oh, yes. Yes, I'm sure you are right. As it turned out, it would have been very much better. But—" He turned to Monty. "You see, we were having a discussion this morning—"

"About a burial at sea," Addie piped up.

Sue said, "And nobody wanted you to hear of it, Monty. You or Stan. So finally the doctor and Mr. Lawson went down to get the body and—"

Monty turned a dangerous red again. "We can go back and try to find it! How far back—"

Stan spoke up. "No way of finding him or anything. We don't know where—"

"Monty, we can't go back to look for him." Sue said. "And I think"—she braced herself—"I think whatever Dr.

Smith did, and however he did it, was right. Another day of this sweltering heat—you'd have endangered all our lives. Your own, too.''

Jim, having prudently withdrawn to a corner, muttered something about air conditioning and refrigeration. Stan cut him off. "Not on this ancient lady. Go back to the wheel. The ship can't run itself indefinitely.''

Jim straightened. "All right. Sir,'' he added as an afterthought and marched out with a relieved and rapid tread.

Stan leaned against the bar, his rather tired-looking T-shirt limp from heat and his jeans wrinkled. "Now let me get this straight. First you, Doctor, and Jim put Juan overboard. You preferred not to let Monty or anybody else know of it—''

"Certainly,'' said the doctor. "Monty would have raised hell.''

"Damn right I would,'' Monty muttered savagely.

Stan took up the saga. "Then this morning there was, I take it, some discussion about what to do with—with the body. Heat and all that. So you insisted upon burial—''

"At sea,'' Addie piped up.

Stan went on. "But you let everyone believe that Juan's body was still on the boat, even after they all agreed with your plan? Right?''

"Certainly,'' said the doctor again.

"I can't see why you didn't just tell them the truth. Then and there.'' Stan, too, was getting angry.

"I tried to explain,'' the doctor said. "I thought it just was not the time and place. Everybody seemed a little . . . upset. Except Miss Addie. But I really thought it would be better to—say, break the news in a different way, to lead up to it gradually. I rather wanted Lawson's backing, I suppose.'' The doctor seemed to debate, smoking and pursing up his eyes to avoid the little white wreaths. "Probably it was my own instinct for self-preservation. I wanted a lawyer on my side before I tried to explain the situation to—well, Monty, to you. I knew you wouldn't like it. However, I do apologize to you, Lawson. I see I made a mistake. But I'm not versed in law and—"

Monty shoved his hands in his pockets and strode over to the doctor. "You have more than that to explain. Even with the heat, it seems to me you were awfully eager to get rid of the body. Do you know something about the murder?"

"Now, Monty. Don't carry on like that. I warned you—"

"Did you kill Juan yourself?" Monty shouted. "Did you try to kill me?"

"I didn't," the doctor said quietly. By chance, probably, a little puff of smoke drifted into Monty's face. The doctor saw it. "Oh, I'm sorry! Now, really, Monty, I didn't try to kill you. For heaven's sake, I have no reason on earth for killing you. Pull yourself together."

Celia said, "He did save your life, you know, Monty. Remember—"

It didn't satisfy Monty. He shot a furious glance at Celia. "After he'd hit me over the head and then dumped me in the sea! I tell you he tried to kill me and then when he found it wasn't going to work—"

Stan sighed. "All right, Monty. If you can prove that, then we'll start for the nearest port this minute." He turned toward the deck.

Monty shouted after him. "No we don't! You stay right here. Can't you see that now there is no body that I can show to the authorities and prove that there was murder? This fine doctor of yours"—he shot a steely glance at Sue—"has disposed of the—the evidence."

Stan turned back. "There were plenty of witnesses to the murder." He looked at Lawson. "Couldn't there be a sort of affidavit, all these witnesses affirming the fact of murder—"

"Clouds of witnesses," Addie said musically. "Clouds..."

Sue counted and said firmly, "Eight. Nine, with Jim. But that ought to be enough. We all saw Juan—"

Monty was still smoldering. "Nobody can say what he died of."

"I can," the doctor said. "Come on, Monty, I assure you I don't intend to kill you! Why on earth—"

"I don't know why!" Monty was like a handsome but goaded bull. "But I think you did."

"All right." The doctor was agreeable. "Think as you like."

Stan said, "I've had enough. We're going in to port."

Again he started for the deck. Again Monty stopped him, this time with a grasping hand on the arm, which took Stan by surprise and whirled him around. In an instant, however, Stan had freed himself with a scarcely visible dexterity.

Just then Sissy trotted in.

Addie gave one look at her and screamed faintly. Wiley stared and put out an arm for Addie, who drooped against it.

Sue nearly screamed, too; only her hands at her mouth stopped her.

Sissy gave a pleased look around and dropped the thing she had clenched in her teeth on the carpet; she then lay down with the black matted object between her paws and wagged her tail. It was quite as if she had brought a treasure to them. Instead, she had brought Juan's black wig.

Eighteen

Sissy, Sue reflected later, must have a strong sense of drama. She even thought of reincarnation, for it occurred to her that Sissy might have been an actress in another life.

There couldn't have been a better (or worse, depending

on one's viewpoint) time for dragging in that ghastly souvenir of Juan.

Even as that unwelcome idea occurred to Sue, Sissy further proved her instinct for the dramatic. She fastened her sparkling brown eyes upon Lawson, picked up the wad of hair, galloped over to Lawson's feet, and dropped it before him. She then looked up but didn't wag her tail; instead, she growled, quite as if she intended to blame him for the wig, for Juan's murder, for everything she didn't like on the yacht. Lawson again tucked up his feet and yelled, then checked himself and glowered at Celia. "Can't you control that creature?"

Celia was looking rather frightened herself as she recognized the wig. "But that—" she began and moistened her lips and said, "but that—"

"Is poor little Juan's wig," said Wiley, still holding an arm around Addie, who had revived and was regarding the wig and Sissy with much interest.

Now was the time to tell everybody of the visitor in her cabin the previous night, Sue told herself firmly. But an inner voice said equally firmly, "Keep your mouth shut. Not now—tell Monty and Stan later. But not now."

Because that visitor must be within a few feet of her, looking merely normal, quiet, interested (but not unusually interested) in the little tumult Sissy had produced.

Wiley's mustache was turning down a little. "Was Juan wearing his wig when he was shot?"

For a moment nobody answered. Obviously it was a dangerous topic; if somebody said yes or no, either reply might serve to proclaim that person's highly questionable knowledge of Juan's appearance at the time of the shot.

Wiley bristled and removed his arm from Addie—who didn't need it at all and sank back comfortably into her chair—and continued, "I tell you that was Juan's wig. Don't you believe me?"

"Yes." Sue made up her mind. "He wasn't wearing it when he was shot. I remember noticing when the doctor turned him over, there in the galley. He was almost completely bald.'' She took a breath and added, nailing it, ''No wig.'' She didn't add, But I saw the wig later in his cubbyhole and last night somebody got into my cabin and searched and left the wig there. Not yet, she told herself again. There were simply too many crosscurrents, too many eyes fastened upon the wig, too many ears listening, including the ears of that nightmarish visitor.

But Sue couldn't entirely refrain. She said, ''You have a most gifted canine there, Celia. She can open doors, explore rooms—''

Monty broke in, ''I searched Juan's cabin.''

''Below his underwear?'' Sue asked as if she'd got the bit in her teeth and couldn't quite stop herself. ''The wig was there. Celia and I found it.'' She almost galloped ahead; she did manage to stop.

Stan said, eying her, ''You look very white, Sue. Better come up on deck. Get some fresh air.''

''Thank you. I'm all right.'' What a lie that was!

Stan shrugged. ''You don't look it. But if you say so.'' He paused to scoop up the wig. ''I'll just throw this overboard,'' he said and left quietly.

Monty cried, ''How did the dog get that damn wig? Something peculiar is going on here!'' It was a remarkable understatement.

Dr. Smith put out his cigarette in the only ashtray that had turned up; rather, not an ashtray but a large saucer. Clearly Monty, Wiley, Juan had disapproved of smoking. Probably Juan, observing the doctor's stubborn habit, had produced at least a receptacle for ashes. She could almost see Juan in his white jacket carefully emptying the saucer, washing it and replacing it on a convenient table.

The doctor went over to Monty. ''Look here, Monty. I'll have Lawson make out a paper stating the exact circumstances. I'll add my professional opinion; that's simple. Only one possible medical opinion. We'll all sign the thing. Then when the time comes we'll hand it over to the authorities. Lawson will make it legal. Right, Lawson?''

Lawson, with one eye on Sissy, nodded. ''Oh, yes. Certainly. I'll make it legal,'' he said as if uttering a threat.

''But we are not going to change course,'' Monty said. ''I'll get at the reason for all this first!''

Music drifted into the salon, became louder. It defined itself as a popular dance tune. Celia looked wearily toward the porthole. ''A cruise ship,'' she said.

Everybody looked for an instant toward the portholes as the music grew louder. Sue could see the cruise ship sailing past them, returning, she supposed, to New York. The decks were crowded with people. The ship was near enough for her to note their holiday attire, sport clothes, shorts, bathing suits. There was much waving and shouting mingled with the band music. Lalie said in her ear, ''I say, that girl's got a good bathing suit. Like one I didn't bring!''

The object of her admiration was for a moment near enough to display the suit, what there was of it. Addie, peering over Sue's shoulders, said, ''Why, Lalie dear, you could have packed it. Wouldn't have taken up any space at all. There's nothing to it. Just little triangles. Quite charming.'' Addie was unpredictable.

''Sure. The skin,'' said Lalie with a teasing sparkle in her eyes, ''needs air.''

''That much?'' said Addie blandly. ''But I'm sure you are right.''

The ship went on, taking its happy holiday makers and its cheerful if blaring music along with it. Sue turned away from the porthole, rather as if she were shutting out the normal world and turning back into another nightmare. Nothing had changed.

Sissy was growling softly. Dr. Smith had disappeared. Lawson, a man of one mind, had gone to a table and had been supplied with paper and a pen—by Celia, apparently, for she stood by him, watching as he wrote. Addie said softly, " 'Ships that pass in the night.' "

"It's not the night," Sue snapped.

Addie paid no attention. Monty had gone—probably to the deck—because just at that instant the yacht gave a rather violent swerve. Celia gasped, "Oh, dear! Something happened about the compass. That—yes, of course."

"I know," Sue said grimly. "Stan and Jim laid out a course to the nearest port while Monty was down here—at least Jim did, and Stan helped him as soon as he got on the bridge. And then Monty—"

"Got on the bridge, too," said Lalie, still looking wistfully after the disappearing cruise ship and quite obviously wishing herself upon it.

Celia sighed. "Oh, yes. So we're now back on course to Eleuthera."

Lawson looked up, frowning. "But, my God, that will take days. And nights. I tell you Monty is bending the law."

"You said that thing you are writing will fix that," Sue reminded him rudely.

"Oh, that! But we've still got to report—"

Addie said gently, "Oh, thank you, Mr. Wiley. How very kind! Just what—how very kind—"

Sue, on her way to the deck and the talk she must have with Monty, whirled around. Wiley had taken a chain, loaded with keys, from somewhere about his thin person. He was inserting one key into the door of the bar. He turned it, smiled, and reached for a decanter. Addie stretched out her small white hand and secured a rather large glass.

"Oh, no!" Sue wailed softly. Nobody listened. Lalie, instead, said warmly, "A good idea, Mr. Wiley."

Sue gave up. Let them all eat whiskey, she thought bitterly, or rum, or vodka, or whatever. The idea of eating anything drew her attention like a magnet to a large plate of sandwiches, which she hadn't noticed before, on the table near the bar. Evidently it was late, noon or past noon, and either Celia or Lalie had sensibly arranged the food. She took a sandwich and went on deck, up to the bridge, munching, where she found Monty swearing at Stan, Jim and the doctor.

"You've changed course again! If I turn my back for a few seconds, you change course. I will not have it!" He reached for the wheel. Stan shouted at him. Jim shouted. The doctor said, "There goes the compass again."

"Get his gun," Stan cried. "You hold him, Doctor. I'll get the gun."

Sue tried to get out of the way. Monty backed off and waved the gun at the doctor, Stan and Jim. "Don't come near me! Don't you dare. All right," he said. "I'll stay away from the wheel if you promise to stay on the course."

"To Eleuthera?" the doctor said.

"Certainly. And before we get there I'll know who did this—"

Sue tugged at Monty's arm. "Please . . ."

He had the gun in one hand now but he was far enough away from the compass, apparently, to suit Jim and Stan, who were now bent over the chart desk and wheel. "Please, Monty," Sue repeated.

"What? Oh! Sure."

He looked down at her and, though rather slowly, his good-looking face recovered its usual pleasant and intelligent look. "Easy, dear. What is it?"

Stan yelled, "Get him away from here! Doctor, shove him out! This place is too small."

Jim said loudly and dismally, "Damn compass is still whirling."

The doctor went to Monty and put a hand on his arm. "Listen, Monty, a while ago you suggested that I tried to murder you. Wouldn't it have been easier for me just to let you drown than pull you out?"

"Sure," said Monty. "But I still think—oh, come on, Sue."

The doctor, however, walked along the side deck after them. Monty, with one hand on the gun at his belt and the other on Sue's arm, firmly drew her away to her cabin. "Only place we can talk," he said and swung the door open for her. "Next time I buy a yacht I'll have some kind of little study for the owner. Books and chairs and—" His pleasant mood changed. "But I'm never going to buy another yacht! You know what, Sue?" He closed the door after them and sat down, but kept one hand on the gun just the same. "You know what? I'll bet when Wiley bought this boat, he intended to refurbish her completely, spend all kinds of money. But then he decided it would cost a lot more than he planned. So the old fox sold her to me." All at once he grinned, the handsome, rather boyish grin Sue liked. "Wiley is a good name for him, come to think of it. Now then, what's on your mind, Sue?"

Sue automatically picked up her wrinkled jeans and turned to the shallow cupboard. Over her shoulder she said, "I'm to be your wife. Is that right?" She adjusted the jeans on a hanger.

She heard a note of surprise in Monty's voice. "Sure. Just as soon as we can arrange things."

"Well, then—"

But Monty went on, rather diffidently, "I suppose your aunt will want a real fine wedding. Church. Reception. Lots of guests. All that." He added more positively, "So do I, of course. The works. But I expect it'll take a little time to arrange. Perhaps several months. Next—well, not next year, but—"

She turned back to face him. "Monty, I've got to tell you something."

There was a flash of an emotion she could not identify in his eyes. "Mean to say you've changed your mind?"

"Oh, no, no. Something else. Last night somebody got into my cabin. I told you that wig of Juan's was with his clothes when Celia and I searched his cabin. But then—then whoever was here, right here, last night, dropped the wig. Sissy found it here.''

Monty's reply was unexpected. "Goddamned nosy mutt!"

"No, no! She only—she's a nice little dog. You're not listening.''

"I'm listening." He did listen as she went through the entire brief yet unnerving incident. Even then, in full daylight, with Monty, big and strong, sitting there facing her, even then the recital of it sent little quakes up and down her back.

Monty said at last, sensibly, "Any idea who it was?''

"I told you. I don't know. I only knew—''

Monty interrupted, "Had to be that doctor.''

"Monty—''

"No, don't try to protect him, Sue. Had to be the doctor. Who else was prowling around last night? Throwing poor Juan into the sea! Tell me, who else?''

"Monty," Sue said firmly, "it was not the doctor. Just believe me.''

"Then who was it?''

"I tell you, I don't know—''

"Then," said Monty irrefutably, "if you don't know who it was, how do you know it *wasn't* the doctor?''

Sue was getting a letdown and a surge of impatience at the same time. "Why are you so insistent about Dr. Smith? Why would he search the place? Why would he have Juan's wig and leave it here? But then, why would anybody just leave it here?''

Monty gave her a peculiarly penetrating glance. His eyes, usually so friendly and kind, had taken on a steely glint.

His silence was so curiously indicative of sudden and extraordinary thought that Sue waited a moment before she spoke. "What on earth is wrong, Monty?''

"You're in love with that doctor!''

"Monty!''

"I can tell."

Sue got her breath. "But I'm not. How could I be? I hardly know him except through my work at the hospital."

"All nurses fall in love with the doctors," said Monty pontifically.

"But they don't! At least I don't! Dr. Smith! Monty, you really are—"

"I am what?" he asked dangerously.

"Off the beam," Sue said far too frankly, for Monty's eyes were really sparking with fury.

"You think I'm out of my head because I am going to find out who it was that tried to kill me and did kill Juan. And then—" said Monty with an air of drawing a logical and only conclusion, "then dumped his body overboard. There's your fine doctor for you. You can't tell me! You defend him every time anybody so much as asks him a question! You flew at me, just now like a—like—" He paused and said, defeated, "Like something or other. Not the way my fiancée ought to act. I want an explanation."

"See here, Monty! You couldn't be further from the truth. Me! In love with Dr. Smith! It's just not possible. Why—why, you remember. Surely you remember. He couldn't even think of my name when he first saw me on the yacht. That first night. Remember?"

Monty was silent for a moment, then found a reason. "Smoke screen! Sure! Didn't want me to know about your—" He bogged down. "I mean his—well, anyway, didn't want me to know."

"God give me patience! If our married life is going to be like this—"

"Don't talk to me. I can tell. It's the doctor. He is the reason you've been so—well, sort of touch-me-not. Know what I mean? Funny, I never thought of it before."

"Don't think of it now!"

"You don't like to talk about our wedding! Oh, I've noticed. You don't have any—any enthusiasm," he said lamely and looked like a surprised, saddened little boy.

Oh, come on, Sue said to herself: he's not a little boy. And as a matter of fact, he had not shown any glorious enthusiasm himself, she thought unexpectedly. But then, he was older than she, more accustomed to self-control over himself and events. Nevertheless, something about his indignation over the relationship he assumed between her and Dr. Smith seemed just a trifle—she hesitated, hunting for a word and thought—overdone. Almost as if he really wanted to quarrel. Wasn't it?

But she said placatively, "Just believe me. I can't see why on earth you would think the doctor—"

"Then what was he doing in your room last night?"

"But he wasn't—anyway it wouldn't have meant—" Her wits were thoroughly scattered.

"He was out and around last night. No, Sue. You've done your best, but you can't fool me—"

"I'm not trying to fool you. I'm only telling you the truth. For heaven's sake, if you don't believe me, talk to the doctor. He'll tell you the facts. After he's nearly died laughing," she added waspishly.

Monty gave her a long, stately look while he appeared to debate within himself. Then it came out. "If not the doctor, then who?"

"Monty," she began feebly.

"Who? You just don't act as I expected you to act. So I know there's some other man."

Sue rallied. "If you are referring to the fact that I didn't leap like a fish swallowing bait when you talked of marriage—no, I didn't. I certainly didn't! You said—whatever it was you said—"

"I told you I'd just made a new will in anticipation of our marriage. Leaving money to you. And to your aunt. What else was that but a proposal of marriage? Answer me! Didn't you see that?"

"I—yes. Yes, of course I did. But I—everything was hurried and somehow— Oh, I don't know!"

"I know," said Monty firmly. "You've got some other man."

"No. I haven't! Let's not quarrel, Monty."

He gave that some silent reflection. Finally he sighed. "All right, then. Things are all right between us. But that doctor—"

"Don't give him another thought."

Suddenly his mood changed. "I've got to give thought to everybody on this blasted boat," he said gloomily.

"Wouldn't it be better to head for the nearest port?"

Sue had heard of, but had never actually seen, a red rag stirring up a bull. She had an uneasy feeling that she had just done that very thing, for Monty shot up from the chair. "I've told you! I've told everybody. I'm going to get at the reason for all this. Damn it, come here."

Without waiting he caught her in his arms. It was a hearty, warm embrace and kiss, she was perfectly sure of that. Everything was fine. "So," he said, releasing her and smiling, like himself, good-natured, affectionate and friendly.

"That's better." He laughed. "I've not got much sense. You and the doctor! What an idea! Let's forget it." He laughed confidently. "Forget it, I mean him. And my notions. Fact is, I'm overtired and very . . . all these things . . . everything . . . upsetting and . . . never mind."

He nodded, smiling, and went out. The door swung slowly to after him.

"But what about the wig?" Sue cried, and sank down into a chair.

Monty had paid little if any attention to the wig. His only worry had been that Dr. Smith had ventured into her cabin for romantic reasons. Later, certainly, he would think of the wig and investigate.

She had always known Monty was a most attractive man, cheerful and good-natured, rather childish in some ways, perhaps, but not in his money-making talents. But it was true that all of them were depressed and deeply concerned about a cruise that had become so tragically different from the trip they had expected.

So what do I do now? she thought.

She might tell Stan about the wig: he would listen and he would not accuse the doctor of being her clandestine lover.

But Monty wouldn't like it if she went to Stan with the problem of the visitor stealthily searching her cabin. And Monty, with that alert sense he had displayed, would somehow know that she had discussed it with Stan. Not that she was afraid of Monty, she reminded herself; it was only more conducive to an agreeable situation if she didn't arouse Monty's quick, almost eager, suspicions.

But at any rate she didn't have a former lover on the yacht as Monty had; and Celia, in spite of everything, was still there, still beautiful, still acting almost like a wife to him.

It did seem ironic that he should take such a strong position on the subject of another man in Sue's life with Celia as one of his guests, uninvited but a guest nevertheless.

It was clear, however, that Monty would be an affectionate, friendly husband.

She did rather vaguely examine that word "friendly." It was a good word. But she wasn't sure it was the right description for a lover.

His determined pursuit of his own decision, defying all legalities, might be incomprehensible, yet there must be some reason for it.

However, there was no real suggestion of ambivalence (or concussion?) in Monty's actions. He was simply a man who could make up his mind and assert himself. She became aware of the fact that the door was gently swinging inward. There was no reason for her heart to jump up into her throat. Monty had merely not quite closed the door. But as she watched, it continued a silent slow motion inward, toward her. There was no sound, no motion other than that of the quietly moving door. It stopped.

Someone was watching her, slyly, through the slitted opening.

Nineteen

That could not be. There was nobody who would creep up to the door, stealthily open it, and then simply watch her, not speaking, not moving, only watching.

Yet she was terrified.

She couldn't control her heart, her breath, her body. She couldn't even scream. She couldn't cry, "Who is it? What do you want?" She sat frozen, all but hypnotized, and then the door was shoved widely toward her and Sissy frolicked in.

Sue stirred; then she plunged up and toward the door, but the passage outside was empty of any human being. The observer, whoever it was, had swiftly vanished. Sissy jumped and pawed at her, gave her a long look, and said almost in so many words that she wouldn't be responsible for anything if Sue didn't take her on deck at once.

There was only the sound of the engines, reliable now, pounding steadily, and the wash of the waves.

Sissy gave a bark.

"Oh, all right, Sissy. You're a fine, intelligent dog, and I am perfectly sure you wouldn't fall overboard, but we'll stick to the drill and get your leash."

It was always rather comforting to talk even to a little dog. Sissy wagged her tail agreeably, and Sue went to the door of the cabin Lalie and Celia shared. It was closed. There was no answer to her knock, so after a second she opened the door. Sissy's leash was hanging over a chair, along with Lalie's jeans. Nobody was around anywhere; nobody who could have silently opened her door and watched her, because, Sue told herself, there was no reason for so peculiar an exercise in espionage. Sissy gave an approving little yelp and bounded toward the deck. Sue followed.

She had a quick glimpse of the salon. Lawson was still writing, slowly and carefully, tipping his head on one side to scrutinize what he had written, nodding with satisfaction, going on. He looked as if he hadn't so much as taken a breath since he began to write, certainly not as if he had very quietly walked to her cabin and opened the door—and probably whoever had done that had paused to listen to her conversation with Monty. But then, where had that quiet watcher gone when Monty opened the door fully and walked out?

Probably into a nearby cabin. The nearest of the cabins, C, was used by Wiley. The other, opposite her own, was used by Addie. Sissy gave a tug that jerked the leash from Sue's hand and bounced up on deck. Sue ran after her. But canny little Sissy prudently made her way to the sandbox, which now was placed modestly on the port-side deck instead of on the wide afterdeck.

It seemed mandatory to Sue to discover, if she could, just who had opened that door and waited so slyly, peering in at her.

She and Sissy ambled on to the wide deck, where a rather curious scene presented itself, for Addie, Wiley, Lalie, Celia, Dr. Smith, Jim—in fact, everybody but Stan and Monty and Mr. Lawson—simply sat in a row of deck chairs, but somehow without conveying any suggestion of ease. Nobody talked. Nobody seemed to be doing anything at all; it was a grisly kind of torpor. On the horizon was another boat, a thick, stodgy, but big boat steaming along. Sue was sure that everybody before her was conscious of that boat, whatever it was. Everybody eyed it; nobody moved or spoke. It was as if they had been hypnotized or frozen in listening, guarded positions, prepared at any instant to hear or see something hidden or near. It was the frozen listening of, say, some helpless prey trying to hear the stealthy pad of a ravenous and lethal beast.

It was so strong an impression that, in another moment, Sue felt she would adopt the same attitude, straining all her senses to hear or feel a savage but silent advance. She was actually relieved to see Lalie toss back her hair and Addie take a long breath and move her lips as if repeating some quotation.

At least they were all alive, not entirely overcome by quiet terror. Instead of joining them, she went to the bridge, to find Stan, glasses at his eyes, apparently watching a boat that was smoothly crossing ahead of them in the distance. He was aware of her presence. "Looks as if we are nearing a more popular lane of shipping. Want to look?"

He gave her the glasses; as she held them to her eyes, the distant boat seemed to leap much nearer. She could see its bridge and someone in blue uniform at the wheel.

"I wish I could talk to them," Stan said. "That fool, Monty! He knows just enough about electricity and a ship to do as much damage as he can. You've been talking to him, haven't you?"

"Yes. I got nowhere."

"It's so idiotic. Where is he now?"

"I don't know." Suddenly she remembered that he had not been one of the watchful figures on the deck.

"Did you try to talk sense into him?"

"I tried. Honestly, Stan, he's very upset—"

"Upset!" said Stan nastily. "What a word!"

"But I mean—it's not at all nice."

"If you can't say any more than that! Give me the glasses."

He held the big binoculars up to his eyes. "Maybe Jim knocked him out. But I don't think so. Monty will turn up with that blasted gun. If he'd even give us a chance to jump him."

"If you do that—Stan, Monty really is upset! Don't laugh. He's likely to—to—"

"Shoot somebody? I don't think so."

"Will you listen to me for a minute?"

He glanced at her briefly. "Sure. Sit down."

There was a narrow bench. She sat, letting the breeze touch her face and lift her hair, and looked at the vast expanse of blue sea and blue sky and one—no, three—ships traveling placidly along, all far away but oddly reassuring by their very existence.

"Why did you get so worked up when Juan's wig turned up? I thought you were going to faint."

She swallowed hard. "I thought so, too. Listen—"

Stan looked at her very seriously as she told him about the ugly incident of the night before. Once he said something under his breath; it sounded fierce. She went on.

He didn't actually speak until she finished. "So when Sissy brought that wig in—" She stopped because her throat seemed to close up. Stan said, "My God! Why didn't you say anything? Why didn't you yell last night, scream, do something—anything—"

"I was scared."

"You told Monty all this?"

"Yes, of course."

"What did he say?"

"He said I was in love with Dr. Smith and trying to defend him."

"He said *what*?" Stan jerked around to stare at her. She nodded.

Stan laughed. It was a short, not very amused kind of laugh. "I hope you put Monty straight about that."

"I did. That is, I think I did. Stan, that boat—over there. Isn't it near enough to see if you—"

"If I what?" Stan said shortly. "Lean over the rail and shout yoo-hoo?"

"But you have a string of signals and—"

"Had. Monty got away with every single one. Even the yellow-fever one." Stan half grinned, but then became altogether too sober again. "Sue, what did the guy want in your cabin?"

"I don't know."

"But you said whoever it was searched the place."

"He did."

"Or she did," Stan murmured. "Did you miss anything?"

"There wasn't anything to miss. I mean—heavens! No jewelry! Only a few clothes—that kind of thing. Anyway, I haven't missed a thing. Honestly, there is nothing gone and there was nothing for anybody to take."

After a moment he took up the glasses again, apparently focused them upon a sturdy-looking ship plowing its way along, and put them down with a sigh. "Monty is such a fool about this."

"But can't you just ask—"

"What do you suppose I've done! Over and over, and he just waves that damned gun around, and the plain fact is, if Jim and I—or any of us, all of us, for that matter, got together and tried to jump him, that gun would go off. Sure as you live. The catch is, it might hurt somebody."

"Oh!"

"Monty wouldn't mean to hurt anybody. At least I can't believe that he would. But in that kind of free-for-all things do happen." He leaned over, looked at a chart, made an infinitesimal correction of the wheel, and added, morosely, "But I can't say I like being sensible. Not in this particular fracas. You don't seem to realize, Sue, that that little guy was murdered."

"*I* don't realize it!"

"And the murderer is right here on this boat."

"*Stan, I know that. Everybody on the boat knows that!*"

"You needn't yell."

"If you would just take a look back there, on the deck. All of them sitting around, not moving, as if they're scared to breathe. Listening for—oh, I don't know what. Somebody creeping up with a—an ax. Or something. They are all thinking the same thing. Which of us—which one—when—what is to happen? I can't bear it.''

He turned to her. ''Well, there. Don't take on!''

''There's something else. Monty was in my cabin talking to me. And when he left, the door opened just a little bit, and somebody was out there, in the corridor, watching me through the crack.''

He grasped her shoulder. ''Who?''

''I don't know. I ran to the door—when I could move. There wasn't a soul in the corridor. Nobody anywhere. All the doors were closed. I don't know who it was, and if we don't get into a port soon, any port, I tell you we'll all be gibbering idiots.''

''I'm doing my best, Sue.''

''Doesn't Monty ever sleep? Couldn't you get the gun away from him then?''

Stan's face was set again. ''It's been tried.''

''Who—''

''I tried it. Monty had the gun under him, he was right on that bench, I thought he was asleep. He was asleep. But the instant I gave the smallest touch to the gun, he jumped up and waved it at me. He really is not in a very reasonable state of mind.''

''How could he be? All this going on! The yacht he bought! The guests he invited—''

''Not all of them.''

''But Celia wouldn't kill anybody!''

Stan took a long breath. ''That's what we all say to ourselves. Celia wouldn't. Lalie wouldn't. Your aunt wouldn't. Wiley wouldn't. The doctor wouldn't—at least he's probably killed a patient or two, but not with a gun and certainly not intentionally—''

''How about Lawson? He has a motive for getting rid of Monty.''

''But Juan was the one who was killed. It's reasonable to believe that Juan was the object of attack all along.''

"But what's the motive? Juan had no family, Wiley said. He also seemed to think that Juan hadn't much money. I can see why somebody might not really like Juan much, but you have to have a stronger motive than that for murder."

Stan half smiled. "I know quite a few people I don't like—in fact, I can't stand. But I don't go around shooting them. Too much affection for my own skin, for that matter. Sue, did whoever it was who searched your cabin last night have a light? I mean a flashlight, any kind of light? Even matches?"

"No. I'd have seen that. I only heard him—her—whoever. And then this morning there was that ghastly wig. Oh, somebody was there, Stan! All the things in the drawers were shoved around, out of place. Nothing gone—just pushed around."

"Then our mysterious prowler must have been looking for something he could recognize by touch."

She considered it. "Yes, I suppose so."

"Did Celia use that cabin on her various trips with Monty on the boat, do you know?"

"Why yes. Yes, she must have used it—"

"Occasionally, anyway," Stan said with a wry twist to his mouth.

"All right. You don't have to keep talking about her and Monty. That's in the past. Honestly, I didn't see a thing in the cabin that might have belonged to Celia. Ever."

"Did you look for anything of the kind?"

"No. Why should I?" She was on the defensive again, as so often happened when Stan spoke of Celia and Monty.

"Curiosity, I should think. After all—"

"Stop that."

"Stop what?" Stan asked, far too innocently.

"You know what. Don't act like this. I'm so—so—"

"Worried?"

"No! No! That is—" Her unsteady voice betrayed her. "Scared. I can't help it."

One hand left the wheel and came out again, this time to pat her shoulder rather gently. "I know, Sue, I know. Way we all feel. Where is Wiley?"

"On the deck with the others. They look just perfectly terrible. A deadly sort of apathy, yet you know that they are all nerves—listening and thinking and accusing one another and—"

"Is Monty with them?"

"No! No, he isn't!"

"What is he doing do you suppose?"

"Listening to you two," Monty said pleasantly from behind Sue. Sissy, who had jumped up to sit beside Sue on the bench and let the breeze ruffle back her long ears, gave a sharp bark and leaped down, wagging her tail. This time Monty was friendly and leaned over to pat her. The gun made a bulge under his shirt, and Sue actually put a hand out to seize it, but Monty straightened up, knew precisely what Sue had been about to try, and said, "Now, now, none of that, darling."

She tried another appeal. "You'd feel terrible if by any chance somebody was hurt. I mean if that gun went off and—"

"I'll see to that. How we doing, Stan? I'll take the wheel."

It was an order; Stan so accepted it, but reluctantly. He, too, cast a longing look at the bulge below Monty's shirt and tried another approach. "You're not the kind of man just to shoot anybody, Monty. You keep threatening us, but if I made a grab for that gun you wouldn't hurt me."

Monty replied in as friendly a manner as Stan had used. "I wouldn't mean to hurt anybody. But the fact is, I'm on the ragged edge of—I don't know what, but something. So is everybody else. I might pull this trigger just because— oh, because," Monty said almost pathetically. "Don't make me, Stan. I don't want to hurt anybody—except whoever murdered Juan and tried to murder me."

There was nothing to be gained by Stan's insisting that

Juan had been the intended victim all along. Monty had apparently closed his steel-trap mind, and there was simply no way to get it open.

Of course, Sue reflected, that quality in Monty was one of those characteristics that had made him such an extraordinary success. Stan sighed. "All right. We are back on the course to Eleuthera, so watch out for the compass. Off Charleston—quite a way off Charleston, by the markers I've been able to spot. But on the course you want. Monty, will you let me put into Charleston or—"

"No!" Monty flared with anger.

Stan shrugged. "Okay. Mind if I talk to Wiley?"

"Not at all," Monty replied, still politely, but with a sudden gleam of interest in his eyes. Stan, however, merely ducked out of sight.

Sissy jumped up on the bench beside Sue. Monty took up the glasses and said, "You and Stan are very friendly."

Oh, dear! Sue thought, another Dr. Smith phobia. "Of course we are friendly. Why not? Monty, I think someone was outside my cabin while you were there talking to me."

He put down the glasses with a thump. "What do you mean?"

"When you left, you closed the door. Then—after a while—somebody opened it. Only a little. I could just see the crack. But someone was there. Did you see anyone in the corridor?"

"No. Who do you think it was?"

"I don't know. I couldn't see."

"Then how do you know somebody was there?"

"I just felt it. Watching me."

He thought that over. "Why didn't you do something about it? Look to see who it was at least and—"

"Monty! I know someone was watching me and I—well, I couldn't move. Then the dog came in. She shoved the door wide open, and by the time I got to the door and looked along the corridor, nobody was there."

He considered it, frowning. "Your imagination."

"No! I tell you I knew. Please believe me."

He considered that, too, and finally said, "Is there anything you know—or have—anything at all, Sue, that just might give the murderer the impression that you know who he is?"

"No! If I'd had the slightest idea of that, I'd have told someone."

"Me?"

"You, of course!" He mustn't get started on the doctor again.

"So there isn't anything. You sure?"

"Yes, I'm sure. Good heavens! We are living in a nightmare. If you'd stop talking about that gun and pretending you might shoot somebody—"

He peered through the glasses again. A small plume of smoke vanished on the western horizon. Finally he said slowly, "You don't really know me very well, Sue. That is, you know me as I am now. But not other things. I mean—oh, when I was a boy. The point is, I survey the situation and make up my mind as to what I must do; then," he said simply, "I have to try to do it. So far I have succeeded. In life, that is. Not on this boat. Yet."

The words struck a spark of recognition in Sue. "Didn't some famous general—"

"Sure. I read it when I was a youngster. Size up the situation, then take action. And stick to it. I don't remember what general said that first, but it's a good thing to remember. I wasn't well educated, you know." He was not really on a tangent. "I very much wanted to go to one of the big universities. There wasn't enough money. That is, my father didn't have it. I couldn't take the money from Lalie's mother. Don't know why. Just a stubborn kind of kid. Anyway, I wouldn't."

And you're still stubborn; luckily, perhaps, she didn't say it.

Monty's face took on its most gentle and friendly

expression. "Lalie's mother was a sweetheart. She'd have given me anything. I don't know why I couldn't take any more than I had to—that is, of course, I guessed that it was her money that supplied considerable luxury for all of us. But money flat out for my education? No. I've tried to make up for all of her kindness to me. I've tried to do what I thought best for Lalie. I may have made mistakes. I really don't believe Lalie had anything to do with Juan's death."

"Lalie! Whatever would make you think that? She couldn't have."

"I hope not. Jesus, I hope not. But she's kind of a rambunctious kid. Gets herself into problems every so often. Nothing very serious yet. As far as I know."

"Lalie wouldn't—"

Monty continued, "So far, and as far as I'm sure of, only such things as speeding. Drinking when—she shouldn't have driven. Getting some strange friends out to the house, and—the fact is," he said miserably, "I suspect there's been some drug-taking—pot, pills, maybe even cocaine. Nothing I could nail down, though. I have talked to Lalie, reasoned with her. Sometimes I thought she accepted what I told her. But sometimes she keeps talking about the generation gap—"

"I know," Sue said shortly and with indignation. Monty paid no attention.

"And, of course, in a way one does exist. I'm older than Lalie. Years older. And I've been so damn busy. She talks about the great world. Thinks I don't know anything. But—" He sighed. "That's her age. I never knew so much in my life as I thought I knew at eighteen. Lalie's age. At twenty or so I began to see that I wasn't so damn smart. Lalie's getting over it. She's a really nice kid at heart. But she can get herself into some of the damnedest messes. I've always gotten her out. So far."

Sue swallowed hard, liking Monty wholeheartedly. "She's all right."

"I keep thinking, just suppose. She travels around. With a batch of pals who are like her in some ways. Not deep down. Lalie's got sense. But she doesn't always act as if she had."

"But Juan—"

"That's what's on my mind. I can't sleep—can't—" He shook his head miserably. "She spends time anywhere she feels like going. East Coast, West Coat. Miami, Palm Beach, San Francisco, Acapulco, Las Vegas. Anywhere. She has enough allowance to go where she pleases and—and do as she pleases. Last winter—" He fiddled with the glasses, rubbed one lens on his shirt, and said, "Last winter she was in Palm Beach. All along the East Coast, actually. With a lot of friends. Some of them—maybe not vicious but not very desirable either. Juan was in Palm Beach and up and down the coast sometimes. What I'm afraid of—" He took a long breath. "Sue, just suppose she got herself into a mess that Juan somehow found out about and tried to blackmail her and she decided there was just one way out and took the gun—she knew I had it—and shot him. Didn't give herself time to think. Didn't realize what it would mean to her. And to me and the rest of you if it came to that. She's still a child in many ways."

Sue waited a moment, seething with questions, with refutations, with defense of Lalie and with a dreadful recognition of the possibility of truth in Monty's apprehensions.

"But Monty! What about the attack on you? She wouldn't have shoved you into the sea."

He turned a sad, even anguished face to her. "No. She couldn't have meant to do that. Stan may be right about Juan as the intended victim. She could have been so frightened she wasn't thinking."

"She would never have left the gun! That gun! There in your cabin."

"Oh, that. She'd have been so scared and frantic that the only thing she could think of to do at that moment was to put the gun back where she'd found it. She knew I'd protect her. She didn't mean to cast any suspicion upon me. Can't you see? She was just a frantic child.''

Sue had to persist. ''But Monty, then why did you accuse the doctor?''

''I only hope I'm right! That is—no, I don't hope I'm right about that. I just don't intend to let Lalie get into trouble.''

''But if what you think possible does prove to be truth—''

''I'll see to Lalie,'' he said vaguely. He turned back to the wheel and said, unexpectedly, ''Why do you think I've insisted on this course of going ahead on my own? Everybody thinks I'm out of my mind. I'm not that. Not exactly. Can't you see—I've got to prove that it wasn't Lalie before I turn things over to the police. As,'' Monty said grimly, ''anybody in his senses would have done at once. I know that. But I've got to think of Lalie. That's why I don't want you to mention this to anyone.''

So: not ambivalence, not concussion, not even plain pigheadedness. Only ''I've got to think of Lalie.''

Monty said gravely, ''I have to do what I think safest.''

Stan reappeared on the bridge deck. Sissy sprang down and gave a happy bark. Stan looked very strange, something hard about his jaws and very bright in his eyes. But he said quietly, ''Want me to take over again, Monty? I think Jim is about to come along. When he can leave Lalie.''

Monty's face tightened at mention of Lalie. ''All right. Thanks.'' He left abruptly, the gun now showing at his belt.

Stan didn't speak for a moment. He went to the chart desk and the compass, swore and said, ''Monty is such a fool! Stood right here with that damn gun. Why did you let him? Now I've got to get us back—'' He muttered to himself.

Sue didn't even prepare a defense. She was thinking too hard of Lalie.

Stan at last turned to her. "I know who killed Juan," he said in a quiet voice and then whirled completely around and clapped his hand over her mouth. *"Don't say anything!"*

She gurgled behind his hand. He leaned over close to her ear. "Shut up now. Don't let on to anybody. I've got to prove it. But I know."

Twenty

She made wild flutters with her hands. Stan took them to be promises and released her. She silently moved her lips *"Who?"*

"I told you. I've got to prove it first."

At that moment Jim marched briskly onto the bridge, glanced at Stan and Sue and said, "Go ahead. I guess anything can happen on this ship! But honestly, I don't think you ought to choke such a pretty girl. Sir," he added with a grin, which he tried to conceal as he turned to the wheel.

Stan didn't show the slightest discomfort as far as Sue could see. And if Jim thought Stan was strangling her, let him, was Jim's conclusion. Stan was his superior.

Jim was indeed a well-trained young man, Sue reflected briefly. Dr. Smith came up. He had some papers in one hand and was scowling ferociously. "See this!" He thrust the papers at Stan.

"What are they?"

"Lawson's. I thought he was preparing a simple statement, but he's written the whole thing. *Read it!*"

Stan was rapidly scanning the words. "Seems fairly accurate."

"Oh, it's accurate. No question of that." The doctor got

out a cigarette. "But I'm not in favor of signing it. Never!"

Stan said, rather dryly, "You look at it, Sue," He handed her the closely written sheets.

Sue took the paper, which rustled. She read rapidly, turning the pages. Lawson's handwriting was firm and legible, and certainly he included everything he knew; even Addie's affection for certain alcoholic beverages and Monty's threatening them all with the gun.

She longed to tell them why Monty had taken so remarkable, indeed so illegal, as Lawson had unmistakably indicated, a course.

The fact was, now she understood his reasons, she liked Monty better than she ever had, even when she decided to marry him if he asked her.

But her thoughts were whirling. Stan had said he knew the identity of the murderer, and Jim had come before she could somehow wheedle Stan's conclusion out of him. Of course, Stan being Stan, she might not have been able to induce him to tell her what she really had to know.

With another layer of her thoughts she tried to concentrate on Lawson's carefully concocted statement.

It was indeed carefully concocted. Without accusing anyone outright, Lawson had certainly in the wiliest way in the world made implications.

The first one, she had noted, concerned Monty, and that was fact rather than implication. Monty and Monty alone had dictated their avoidance of proper legal procedures.

In Lawson's meticulous handwriting the truth looked rather black for Monty.

She seemed to be thinking hard on two levels, which was more or less difficult.

Monty—well, suppose he was right about Lalie. On the other hand, he had definitely accused the doctor. Celia had, in a lefthanded way, all but accused Addie, even if her reasons weren't very clear. She herself had suspected Wiley.

Celia had said Wiley was a crook. She had certainly had

more knowledge than anyone else to draw upon in her stated opinion of Wiley; yet when that came down to analysis, it didn't appear to have much basis in fact.

Sue wondered, reading and rereading the lawyer's accurate and extraordinarily damaging words, if anyone had yet thought of accusing Stan.

Jim was the only one of them completely in the clear.

That, at least, was comforting.

Stan was beginning to fidget. "Now, Sue, it doesn't take you that long to read—"

"It seems correct," she said slowly.

"A little detailed," Stan said stiffly, looking over Sue's shoulder. "No need to write about—about Wiley that way." He read it aloud, "'Mr. Samuel Wiley, former owner of the yacht, claims that he has a bad heart but he is extremely active, nevertheless.' How about that, Doctor?"

The doctor scowled. "One of the many things I don't like about it. Wiley is my patient. I know his physical limitations."

"And there's Miss—your aunt's—weakness, Sue," Stan said crossly. "No need to mention that! Surely that fool lawyer doesn't think she got drunk and shot Juan. What reason does he suggest?"

"Obvious," the doctor said disapprovingly. "Read between the lines. He suggests that Juan stopped her opening the bar."

Sue had reached that item and began to boil. "That's not fair. Aunt Addie wouldn't hurt a—" She stopped, remembering Celia's skeptical observation to the effect that Addie could cope with a rattlesnake, let alone a tarantula, and of all the people on board, Celia herself could choose Addie as a likely contender for the very dubious spot of murderer.

"I don't like it at all," the doctor said and lighted his cigarette.

"You really ought not to smoke, Doctor," Sue surprised

herself by saying. ''You never let your patients smoke. You always say—''

''Do as I say''—he gave her a rather tight-lipped smile—''not as I do.''

Jim suddenly yelled, ''Goddamn this compass! Leave the bridge everybody! I mean everybody! Get that lighter out of the way.''

Stan didn't even look around. He took Sue's arm and practically shoved her out of the way; he gave the doctor a push, too.

''Well!'' The doctor began explosively.

Sue said, ''Oh, never mind. What can we do about this—this affidavit?''

''Lawson says it might be the only thing that could keep us all in the clear—if Monty ever decides to give up this childish gun play and permit us to get to a port. Any port.''

The fresh breeze blew a whiff of cigarette smoke away from Sue. It was, in fact, a rather pleasant scent. ''That is,'' the doctor added, ''all but one of us.'' He tucked his handsome lighter in a pocket.

Sue said, ''But, Doctor, Monty—'' No, she owed it to Monty not to explain against his wishes. Yet he was so alone, in a way; everybody doubted him, everybody thought he was acting the fool.

''The heart hath its reasons which reason cannot know''; the quotation, which Sue felt, ruefully, was certainly apropos, floated through her mind. That would have pleased Aunt Addie, who clearly felt that there was some appropriate comment applicable to almost every situation in life.

Even murder?

''It wasn't right of Lawson to describe Aunt Addie as a—well, as a drunk.''

''Not quite,'' Dr. Smith said acidly. ''Amounts to the same thing. Lawson is a conceited, pompous bastard. *Isn't he?*''

''Well, I—yes.''

The doctor gave her a fleeting glance of approval. "Now you're showing good sense. Anything you can do to induce Monty to get us to shore?"

Her sudden flare of defiance failed her. "No, not yet—"

Dr. Smith nailed that at once; he jerked his head toward her, his eyes steely. "What do you mean?"

Sue backtracked. "Nothing. Nothing at all—"

"You said 'not yet.' What did you mean by that? Come on, Nurse, no secrets in this affair. Too serious. Why did you say not yet?"

"Because that's what I think," Sue said shortly and walked away, Sissy dancing along beside her.

The afterdeck was no longer tenanted by silent bodies in a dreadful, frightened state of inactivity. Indeed, it was tenanted by no body at all, which, in one way, she couldn't help reflecting, was good. So she sat down and began to read, more carefully this time, the paper Lawson had written. The more closely she read it, the more malicious it became. His favorite word was "claim."

Monty "claimed" that somebody had struck him and then lifted or pushed him into the sea. Monty "claimed" he did not know and could not guess who had done that. The very word "claim" seemed to suggest that there was no proof.

She read on. Lawson all but pointed a finger of accusation toward his long-time (but when Monty saw this report it would certainly be Lawson's erstwhile) client.

Monty had "claimed" that he found a gun on his bed in the cabin he was using. Monty threatened them all with the gun in order to force them to continue at sea, rather than put in for the nearest port and police. Monty had disabled the ship-to-shore phone; Monty had broken the antenna of the radio. Monty had thus prevented their signaling for help. That was fact, no getting around that.

At last she finished and clutched the papers in one hand, ruffled Sissy's topknot with the other, and stared out to sea.

Lawson had omitted nobody. He even said that Jim (here was a blank; he probably didn't know Jim's surname) had been a part of the agreement to keep on going.

He couldn't, however, hint that Jim had anything to do with the first ugly episode, Monty's dip in the sea.

Celia Hadley had been a long-time and very close friend of Monty's. There was an implication that she had known that Monty had made plans for a new will (here Lawson wrote modestly that he, being a lawyer, had drawn up the document) providing for Miss Sewall Gates. However, the lawyer could not state with any degree of accuracy the depth of Mrs. Hadley's feelings or any of her actions.

So thus it was Celia's turn for a very sly, very neat innuendo.

And after Sue, Lalie. Sue read Lawson's comments about Lalie. The young half sister, for whom Monty was trustee, was a very young lady, and there was no reason to accuse her of murder. However, it was possible that she had had some acquaintance with Juan during a visit in Palm Beach and the Miami neighborhood the previous winter. He realized, Lawson had written (slyly, Sue thought) that there was considerable traffic in drugs, fought against valiantly by the authorities but spreading its tentacles stubbornly in that part of the world. However, Lawson had added, he certainly had no evidence that the young lady had had any connection with drugs.

Sue noted bleakly that his report of herself was probably more damaging than any other item. She could almost see the written words again, black and neat, on the shining blues of the sea. Miss Seweall Gates would have been the recipient of a very large sum of money if Monty had drowned. This was according to the new will, which had been insisted upon by Monty so vehemently that he had summoned the writer, Lawson, to the yacht; telephoning to him in the night (that is, about ten o'clock) to demand his presence the next day for the cruise that had proved to be not only difficult but, with Juan's murder, tragic. Miss Gates had much to gain by Monty's death at sea.

Miss Gates had found the murdered man and claimed (that ugly word again) that she had been in the corridor, intending to see her aunt, when she heard the gunshot. She had then, she claimed, gone quickly to the galley and claimed that she found Juan there. The lawyer, politely and, in Sue's opinion, sneakily, suggested that in order to reach the galley, Miss Gates had been obliged to pass through the salon and obviously must have seen anybody emerging from the galley or crossing the salon. He left an implication there: was Sue protecting the murderer or had she shot Juan herself?

Altogether, Dr. Smith had had every reason for his fury with the report. Lawson had written it all out, sparing himself; the doctor had desired him (Lawson) to accompany him (Smith) to help with Juan's body; when the doctor had him alone, he explained that he had already disposed of Juan's body, his explanation being that the weather was warm and growing warmer. Thus, the doctor, who had been trained to save lives and prevent sickness, considered it a threat to both ends to keep the body any longer, since there was no proper refrigeration. He, the doctor, had not explained this urgent priority at the time he had succeeded in enlisting his (Lawson's) presumable aid. His reason, the doctor claimed, was that he hoped to enlist the lawyer's backing before he told others on the yacht that he had procured the assistance of Jim (blank) during the previous night and disposed of the body, thereby in effect doing away with the corpus delicti.

Sue imagined that the lawyer had felt rather satisfied with this Latin phrase.

Was there anybody he had left out? No. Even Stan: a childhood friend of Miss Gates, so they claimed; no one had suggested that there was anything at all in the way of affection between Lieutenant Brooke and Miss Gates. However, it could not escape close reasoning (the lawyer implied that his own was particularly acute and logical) that if a warm affection did exist between the lieutenant and Miss Gates, and if she came into a large sum of money through the death of Mr. Montgomery, the young lieutenant and Miss Gates could possibly expect to profit by it. He added, quite superfluously, in Sue's enraged opinion, that he must admit he had seen nothing that indicated collusion between the lieutenant and Miss Gates, but while he had been trained to observe people's actions, he might yet have failed to note numerous mutual agreements or disagreements among the passengers on the yacht.

His report would not be as fully complete as he would wish it, he wrote (unctuously, in Sue's opinion), if he failed to include what he knew of the murdered man, Juan Ibarra. This was very short. An employee of Mr. Samuel Wiley; according to Mr. Wiley, a faithful servant, caretaker and steward of the yacht, no known relatives, no known motive for his murder, unless such a motive existed in the preceding notes. He added no known connection with any underworld figures and no known supply of money other than the salary paid by Mr. Wiley.

He wound up by suggesting gratuitously that all members of the yachting party be detained for interrogation and he would be pleased to answer every question it lay within his ability truthfully to answer. He was theirs most faithfully.

In short, Lawson had written neatly anything that might suggest guilt on the part of everybody, even Jim, on the yacht. Except, of course, himself. He alone was guiltless.

Sue crumpled up the papers and, without thinking it over, went to the rail and tossed them overboard.

No one, she was sure, saw her do it. If anybody asked her about it she'd say—well, what would she say? Only the doctor knew he had shown her the papers, which amounted to legal arguments, she thought parenthetically, enraged. The doctor might be rather pleased if she simply told him the truth.

And yet—and yet, somewhere within the papers, which by now were scattered pieces of white floating, separated, upon the sea, gradually disappearing, there had to be a grain of truth.

Stan had read it all, but he had read it swiftly. It hadn't infuriated him. He might, indeed, not have absorbed it all, for clearly his whole attention was fastened upon his discovery.

There was simply no way she could think of to induce him to tell her more.

Perhaps he wasn't sure that he could prove his statement. It was possible, she thought coldly, that he'd never be able to prove it.

She wished she hadn't let her angry impulse lead her to destroy the papers. It would have been wiser to show them again to Stan—and to Monty. Let them deal with the lawyer and his affidavit.

It had been a mistaken impulse on her part; she realized, with a certain chill, that, looked at another way, it might have gone far to clear all of them of guilt. On the other hand, it might have merely induced a long bout of inquiry and even a trial. A trial! If the lawyer had his way, every single one of them, with the possible exception of Jim, might have been part of a disagreeable trial. If not as a murderer, then certainly as suspiciously involved material witnesses.

In any event, his accusatory account was gone, and she didn't think he would write another one. She also began to wonder where Addie was, where Celia was, what everybody was doing; and she noted that the sun was going down rather rapidly.

She looked out toward the west, where the sky was rosy and so lovely that it seemed to deny the darkening shadows at the east. Dr. Smith came out from a side deck. "Oh, there you are!" he said. "Well, Nurse. You did read your friend the lawyer's neat little accusation of every single one of us."

Sue nodded.

"Give it back to me. I want to show it to the others. They've got to see just what the lawyer thinks. Legal mind!" he said with scorn. "If he thinks that of every single one of us, he's not fit to act as a lawyer!"

"I don't have it," Sue said flatly.

"Oh, who took it?"

Sue waved one hand out to sea. The doctor stared, understood, and instead of showing anger or even irritation, suddenly chuckled. "Good for you! Best thing to do. Ignore it. And the lawyer."

"But, Doctor, Juan was shot to death. We can't get around that."

There was a sudden whirr and splash on the port side of the deck, and both turned to look. Sue had only a swift glimpse of delicate, winged creatures, flourishing merrily above the sea, then dropping back in it.

"What's that?" she cried.

Dr. Smith was lighting a cigarette. "Flying fish. Seldom seen so near the coast."

"Are we near the coast?"

"Usually it's porpoises," the doctor went on, puffing fragrant smoke. "Lots of porpoises around here. They are likely to play in the mornings. Very pretty."

"I thought you said you had never been along this coast before," Sue said idly.

"Oh! Did I say that? It's true in a way. I meant, not to stay, merely a flight by plane. Stayed a few days. Then by plane back to the hospital, not much to see or remember." He tossed his cigarette over the rail and said gravely, "I take it you *have* tried to influence Monty."

"Yes. But"—she braced herself—"I really think that Monty is a very sensible, fine man. Whatever he decides to do is . . . well thought out." It was the most she could say without breaking the confidence Monty had made her.

The doctor squinted up his eyes and surveyed her. "I see. Monty has given you some reason for his preposterous behavior. Odd to see a man who seems so very calm and self-controlled in such a nervous state. I wonder what is actually in his mind."

She shook her head. The flying fish had swooped back to their natural habitat. The sky was darker, although there was still a rosy light on the water.

Dr. Smith said bluntly, "Now see here, Nurse, you've been trained to be observant. You're no fool. You couldn't have graduated and gone into work at the hospital unless you were fully qualified. So now, what is your frank and honest opinion about who shot that steward?"

For a moment she was deeply thankful to Stan for having kept his conjecture to himself so she could answer truthfully, "I don't know." But she added savagely, "I know who I'd like to accuse!"

"Lawson. I agree. But I rather fancy he's too cautious a bird to permit himself to be deeply involved in anything at all. Probably leads a completely harmless and legal kind of life." The doctor sighed. "Too bad," he added frankly.

"I think I ought not to have thrown away his papers," she said slowly.

"Can't get them back now." The doctor was quite cheerful. "Matter of fact, once Monty saw that thing, Lawson would have lost a client. It's getting toward dinnertime. I'll see to my patient." He glowered again. "And that fool lawyer says Sam Wiley would be able to haul a man as big as Monty over the rail, after first knocking him out. Lawyers!" said the doctor with vitriolic disapproval and strode off around the side deck.

It had been an awful day. Sue remembered having seized one of the sandwiches when she left the salon, but it seemed a very long time since then. She would find Addie first and keep her away from the bar as much as possible. Her cheeks burned as she thought of the lawyer's appraisal of Addie—and of each of them, for that matter.

She must think hard about Stan and his statement: "I know who killed Juan." Hadn't he said it in a positive way, as if he were entirely certain? Stan did not make statements of which he was at all uncertain.

What kind of proof did he need? She should talk to him now. At once.

She didn't.

Addie was already seated in the salon, near, too near, the bar. However, Lalie was standing at the porthole. The bar was closed and apparently still locked.

Sue waved at Addie, who smiled and asked where Celia had gone.

"I don't know. I'm going to wash my face."

"You see," Addie asked pleasantly, "dear Celia has the key."

She didn't need to say what key. Lalie turned and grinned. "Watching the cruise ship, Sue? It's coming up fairly near us. About to pass, I think. You can hear the orchestra. Must be having dinner and dancing and more fun than we are," she finished on a doleful note.

The distant music, clearly for dancing and merriment, was louder. Addie sighed. "How very nice! I do wish—" She stopped.

Lalie finished wryly, "You wish we could be there, don't you? So do I." She turned back to the porthole to watch, wistful in the very droop of her shoulders. The music was so clear that the boat must be very close.

Lalie could not possibly have got herself involved in anything so deadly serious that— No, no! Sue thought. Lalie wouldn't shoot anybody ever! Monty's fears were logical in their way, but wrong. And even in a mood of terror and frenzy, Lalie wouldn't drop the gun in Monty's cabin.

Or would she?

Sue turned abruptly along the passage. Wiley's door was open and he was sitting in a chair, staring into space. He looked up as he heard her.

"Come here, Nurse."

"But I—"

"Come here, Nurse."

"Oh, all right. What is it?"

"Shut that door. I don't want to shout so everybody on the boat can hear me."

Sue closed the door. If he hadn't said "Nurse," she'd have paid no attention to him—or at least little. But the very word was like a demand upon her. "Yes, Mr. Wiley. What is it?"

"That young man of yours—"

"My—"

"Oh, I don't mean Monty. I mean that young navy man. What does he mean asking me so many questions? Seemed real satisfied, too. As if I'd told him something he wanted to know."

"You mean Stan—"

"Sure. Now then, I want to know. Why did he ask me if Juan used the entire yacht when he lived on it? I mean, when I was in my house. Or my apartment. Come on, I want to know."

Twenty-one

Sue sank down on the edge of the bed, something a nurse was trained sternly never to do. Wiley twiddled his mustache indignantly. "And why was he prowling around your cabin so long? Now don't say he wasn't. I peeked through the door, opened it a little—the door to your cabin, I mean—and there he was, hunting around that little built-in chest of drawers."

"Stan did that?"

"I'm not out of my head! I know what I saw. Now why?"

"I have not the faintest idea." Sue got her breath and rose. "I'll ask him."

He nodded. "All right. You do that. Not that he'll tell you unless he wants to. I know that type of man," said Wiley enigmatically.

In her own cabin, nothing, simply nothing seemed disturbed in any way. Yet Stan had told her in so many words that he knew who had shot Juan and that she mustn't tell anyone. But why and how could he have found evidence in her cabin? He couldn't have; there was nothing to find.

But chillingly, one or two phrases of Lawson's accusatory innuendo recurred to her. He had written, "Miss Gates claimed that she had been in the corridor . . . obliged to pass through the salon . . . must have seen anybody . . . crossing the salon."

And indeed something, someone just might have been hiding in the heavy shadows of the salon when she ran across it to the lighted galley.

That much of Lawson's speculative account just might be true.

It was an unnerving thought. She tried to recall every instance of her haste toward the light; it had been an instinctive reaction; she wouldn't have gone near the lighted galley if she had paused to think. But since she had, could there be any truth in Lawson's suggestion? Yes, there had been time for the murderer to slide swiftly out of the darkness and make an escape while she stood transfixed, staring down at Juan and then carefully seeking a pulse that no longer beat.

She had to talk to Stan about that, too. In short, she must talk to Stan and persuade him to tell her his own suspicions about the murderer. Yet she rather felt that Wiley was right when he said Stan wouldn't tell her anything unless he wanted to, and clearly he didn't yet want anyone at all to know whatever it was that had convinced him. "I've got to prove it," he had said.

Lawson's indictments had been speculative, yet not entirely without some basis. The only persons who had escaped, or at least partially escaped, a suggestion of blame were Jim and himself.

She went on again; it was a short list. Lawson's case against Addie was weak; nobody in their senses would take a shot at a steward simply to get at the locked liquor cabinet.

Monty had certainly not escaped; there was his stubborn decision to continue the cruise and the gun found in his cabin. The lawyer made the most of it. She was thankful that Monty had confided to her his real and, to him, very urgent reason for behaving exactly as he still continued to behave. She wished she had discovered his plan for unmasking the murderer. But Monty had grown secretive; it must be a part of his business success; he could smile and smile but never be a villain. She was sure of that.

Then, Celia: the lawyer's idea of a motive was very clear about that. Lalie: same thing held good. Stan's suggested motive was exceedingly improbable.

Who else? Wiley! Certainly he was able to move around, with considerable alacrity; he really couldn't be quite the invalid the doctor said he was.

People have been known to summon up a most remarkable reserve power physically; Sue knew that. And he just might have had some long-buried quarrel with Juan.

She rather wished again that she had not been so infuriated by the sly, cautious innuendos Lawson had intruded into an epistle that he must have enjoyed writing. She remembered his smug expression of absorption as he sat in the salon writing, to judge them all.

Probably she ought to be thankful he had not elected to build an entire case against one of them. He had certainly been more satisfied to employ words as he might have employed shrapnel, seeking everybody he could touch.

She rather dreaded seeing him again in the salon with the others, knowing what he thought of every single one of them.

As it happened, she needn't have been concerned about that.

She roused, realizing that the sun had gone down completely and a sudden darkness had fallen upon the sea swiftly, as it does when the sun drops out of sight.

She decided to change, and her only dress that might have been called suitable for dinner was still hanging in the infinitesimal wardrobe, stained with sea water from the first night when they had, all of them—yes, she reminded herself, everybody but Lawson had joined in pulling Monty out of the sea, and, of course, Wiley, who had stayed in bed. The blue cotton dress she had worn for dinner at the Club (so long ago, it seemed) was still reasonably fresh. Her jeans had fallen from the hanger, and she replaced them. She did what she could to freshen herself up and went to the salon.

Stan, Lalie and Celia were in the galley; she could hear them and catch glimpses of them. She ought to have helped prepare dinner.

Addie was already seated in the salon, dimpling at Wiley, who again was dressed very foppishly. Jim was not there, obviously; somebody ought to tend the store. Monty came in soberly, in a fresh and unwrinkled beige jacket and slacks, looking handsomely brushed, shaven and tidy, except for the bulge at his waist, under the jacket.

Lawson—she looked around and felt a kind of shock of astonishment, for Lawson was not there. It occurred to her that it was just as well; she didn't trust her powers of dissimulation to so much as speak to him or, indeed, remain in the salon with him without showing her anger.

Yet a curious little voice whispered within her: Lawson had certainly pointed out the various weaknesses in her own, in everyone's, statements. These statements might be questioned at dangerous length sometime in court.

It was not a pleasant thought. But when there is a murder there must be some kind of inquiry, and unless Monty succeeded in his stated aim of finding the murderer, or unless Stan proved whatever his own conclusion was, it would be a thorough, careful and inclusive inquiry.

Lawson, however, as a rule was very prompt about mealtimes. The doctor sauntered in. Stan came in from the galley, gallantly taking a tray from Lalie and putting it on the table. Wiley whispered something to Addie and took her glass to the bar.

Stan went back to the galley to take a stack of plates from Celia, and Monty asked, "Where's Lawson?"

For a fractional instant it was so silent in the salon that the throb of the engines could be heard clearly. It was almost as if a rope had been suddenly jerked around everybody in the salon, cutting off breath and speech. Then Stan dropped the stack of plates on the table with a hard clatter. Wiley, caught in the act of pouring from a decanter into Addie's glass, kept on pouring, although a steady stream of amber liquid splashed down on the table. Addie gave a muffled, ladylike little squeak, and Lalie shot out of the galley. "What did you say, Monty?" Her voice cut sharply into the silence.

Monty glowered; all his good nature had vanished. "I said, where is Lawson? Why is everybody looking so—so guilty?" Monty finished.

Stan was the first to return to a kind of normal condition. He went to Monty, put his hand on Monty's arm, and said quietly, "Don't get upset, Monty. He just hasn't come to dinner yet."

"Find him!" Monty suddenly shouted.

"All right, all right, hold everything." Stan went briskly (too briskly, Sue thought) down the passage toward Lawson's cabin.

Monty, Dr. Smith, even Wiley started after him. Lalie gave a kind of scream, and Celia appeared from the galley. Addie put both hands over her mouth. Sue tried to restore some sense of order and cried urgently, "He's all right. Just not ready for dinner!" She stopped as her voice quavered upward. Lalie gave her one glance and ran into the passageway.

All at once, there were sounds again everywhere. Sue found herself out in the corridor, watching the men, watching everybody. The door to Lawson's cabin was open, but Lawson was not there.

They searched; they searched the same places over again.

Lawson was not anywhere on the yacht.

Jim, miserably hauled into the salon by Stan, explained that he hadn't thought the splash he had heard meant anything.

Splash, Sue thought numbly.

Monty took Jim by the shoulder. "When did you hear this splash?"

"I don't know exactly. Some time ago—"

"How long?"

"I tell you—wait a minute, you've got me confused."

"What was this splash? Where?"

"I tell you it was just a splash. A kind of heavy splash."

"Didn't you go to look?

"No," Jim cried. "I never thought of a man overboard."

"Oh," Addie wailed softly, "man overboard. Just like Monty—"

Stan said, "All right, Jim, all right. Now just tell it slowly."

Jim swallowed but jerked his shoulder away from Monty and said, parenthetically, "You've got a grip like a horse. Sir," he added and, massaging his shoulder, replied to Stan, "It was just a splash, a heavy splash."

"Where?" Stan asked.

"Somewhere aft."

"The deck?"

"Maybe. I'm not sure. At the time I only thought vaguely that there must be some big fish in these parts. You know, like a shark or something. I never—" Jim gulped and looked sick. "I swear I never thought of a man. That cruise ship was passing. The orchestra got louder."

"We were here!" Lalie cried. "Aunt Addie and Stan and Celia! We were watching the cruise ship. We didn't hear anything like a splash."

Dr. Smith stared at Jim. "What do you think now?"

Jim murmured sickly, "I guess I think it was a man." He glanced around defiantly. "That's what you all think. Isn't it? He's not anywhere on the boat. You've looked everywhere. Haven't you?" he asked Stan, his voice unsteady.

"Yes," Stan said. "Oh, yes. I'm afraid we have."

Celia gave something like a sob and went to Monty, who (absently, quite as if from habit, Sue thought in some little segment of her consciousness) put his arm around her. She leaned against him, her dark eyes wide. Lalie stood like a very pretty statue, chiffon blouse and blue jeans—and again, as a matter of fact, with nothing under the chiffon blouse, which unimportant item did not occur to Sue until much later. Addie, single-minded, the only one quite composed, approached the bar.

Monty took a long breath, pulled out a handkerchief, wiped his forehead, and turned to Stan. "My God! I don't know what happened to him."

"But you do know," Stan said. "He's not on the yacht. He didn't jump into the sea, did he?"

"No! Never."

"You knew him," Stan persisted. "Did he ever show any signs of—"

"Never," Monty said hoarsely. "Never. But this shows . . . this proves . . . here, Stan, take my gun. And you and Jim set the course for the nearest port. If you can find one."

Stan didn't move. Jim stuttered, "You mean to say, you've given up? Sir?"

"Didn't I say so? Get up there now, you two, and find

out where we are and—here—take the gun, Stan. Throw it into the sea. Anything. I don't want it—'' He tugged at his waist, he shoved at his jacket, he turned a bright red and shouted, ''Who took that gun?''

''Monty!'' Celia cried. ''You must have it. Let me—'' She pounced upon him. Lalie flung herself into the search, too. There was a swift background hubbub as they tousled Monty around, hunting pockets, jerking off his jacket and searching it, pulling out his shirt, rumpled and shoved him around as if they were his aunt and his mother—or, rather more specifically, his wife and his sister. Monty emerged from the turmoil looking ruffled, smoothing his hair as if somebody had grasped even at that with searching fingers. He paused, gave a shocked look around, and shouted, ''Where is everybody?''

Addie replied gently, ''Gone.''

''Somebody else has the gun now!'' He whirled and ran, tugging his jacket on as he ran. Celia and Lalie exchanged glances and ran after him.

Sue sat down.

''A good idea,'' Addie said to her comfortably. ''Nothing else to do. I do hope Monty doesn't get so worked up he makes himself ill. And I can't believe Mr. Wiley would take that gun. Of course, he was the first one out of the salon. He *might* have the gun.'' Addie thought that over. ''But then, Monty was so upset, he wouldn't have noticed. Almost anybody could have taken that gun. Fact is, I thought of it myself. That lawyer—well, he wasn't a very pleasant man, but still, I never thought he would do—'' Addie paused. ''Do whatever he did to invite whatever was done to him. Would you have thought so?''

''I don't know what I think,'' Sue said truthfully. ''Aunt Addie, when did the cruise ship come along?''

Addie widened her soft brown eyes. ''Why, you were here just before it passed.''

''I know. But who else was here in the salon?''

"Oh, what you mean is who wasn't here. Who could have pushed Lawson overboard?"

"No—I—that is—"

"Yes," said Addie. "Now let me see. You left to freshen up. Mr. Wiley was here. Celia and Stan and Lalie were in the galley—no, no, I'm wrong!" She sighed. "You see that cruise ship took a while passing. I could hear the music for really quite a long time. I should say—" She thought seriously. "Yes, I should say at least fifteen minutes between the time when I first heard it and when it had passed us and was so far in the distance I couldn't hear anything and—" She sighed again. "That doesn't really prove anything, does it, Sue? Too bad. Could have been anybody. I mean, I didn't push him overboard. I know that. But—" She shook her head. "Fact is, Lalie was in the salon when I came in. I remember the two of you talked about another cruise ship coming. After you left, Stan and Celia turned up. I wonder—yes, I wonder what happened to Lawson's copy of Monty's new will."

"What? Why—" Sue paused, surprised. "Aunt Addie, I'm sure Monty has a copy. The will doesn't matter."

"Not if Monty has his own copy of it. Do you know why Monty suddenly made up his mind to head for the nearest police?"

She was struck by something rather complacent in Addie's voice. "Do you?"

"No," Addie said. "That is, not really. But I did wonder if he thought that Lalie had got into some kind of trouble while she was in Florida and that Juan learned of it and—but clearly, Lalie didn't have anything to do with the lawyer's—that is, his disappearance."

"Man overboard," Sue whispered.

Addie heard and nodded. "Yes, I'm afraid so. Nothing else to think. I'm sure the lawyer wouldn't have jumped overboard. No, no. Quite out of character. But Lalie was right here, has been ever since I came to the salon. Monty must have realized that, too. So now he knows that Lalie had nothing to do with Juan's murder. So right away he gave up his harebrained scheme. It was really to protect Lalie, wasn't it?''

"Monty told you."

"Didn't need to tell me. I can see through things. That is—" Addie paused and said with obvious regret, "some things." As Sue gave her a searching look, Addie flushed a little. "Not everything. I do not know who shoved the lawyer overboard, as someone must have done. Not that I care very much. But murder? Dear me, I don't think either the lawyer or Juan deserved murder. Unless, of course—" She broke off.

Sue, curious, tried to pin her down. "Unless what?"

"Oh, Juan struck me as a kind of—kind of what I believe is called a hit man."

"You can't mean that! Juan taking pay for killing anyone!''

Addie did look just slightly disturbed. "No, I didn't mean kill anyone. I only meant . . . that is, if I had a secret I didn't want known and Juan knew it, I wouldn't put it past him to try to make me pay for his silence. Yes, I know how that sounds, and don't tell me I read too many books. Juan just struck me as a type that—" She stopped.

Sue said, "But it was Juan who was shot."

"Yes, of course. That's why. I mean, I think that could be why."

Just for a second some scrap of conversation seemed to nudge Sue. Some comment, nothing she could pull out of her fleeting memory and examine.

So it couldn't be important. Addie said, "I wonder how Wiley is getting along. He looked rather odd, you know. I saw him hurry—well, almost stagger—out into the corridor."

There was a sudden clatter of feet and clamor of voices along the passage. Sue had a quick glimpse of Stan, Jim and Monty, tumbling over one another, then vanishing to the deck. All her trained instinct told her to inquire about

Wiley. She half rose, and Dr. Smith called to her urgently, "Nurse, Nurse!"

"I told you so!" said Addie.

Sue hurried out to the doctor, who waved at her, beckoning. "I need some help, Nurse. My patient has taken a bad turn—"

Actually, though, Wiley looked quite comfortable, flat out on the bed and pretending to keep his eyes shut, for Sue could see a betraying glitter below his eyelids. The doctor had his black bag open and took a syringe, closed the bag neatly, removed the plastic cover, and plunged the needle into a small vial of medicine. "I'll just give you a spot of a sedative, Wiley. It can't hurt you."

"Might kill me," Wiley said, flaring his eyes open and jerking himself up to a sitting position.

"Listen," the doctor snapped with small patience, "if I wanted to kill you now, before you've made your will giving us that new wing, we'd never get it. At least from you. Now, lie back and keep still."

Wiley gave his mustache a rather baffled twist but, catching the doctor's eye, obeyed.

"Swab it off, Nurse," the doctor said, removing the syringe.

She did, quickly.

"There, now," the doctor said. "You'll feel better in a minute."

"Unless I don't feel anything," Wiley muttered contumaciously.

Dr. Smith half smiled, took his bag, nodded at Sue, and went out of the cabin and into her cabin, next door. The nod obviously meant "Follow me."

Wiley seemed to be resting. Sue let herself out of the cabin and into her own. Dr. Smith closed the door. "He's all right?"

"Seemed so. Sleepy-looking."

"He's a good man, really. I'd like to save him." The doctor glanced out the porthole. "Seems to be quite a lot of shipping around us all at once. Wiley wasn't sure where we are. He thought possibly Charleston. But then he said the boys had been really pushing the engines. We might even have got as far as Jacksonville.''

Sue joined him at the porthole. There was indeed increased shipping, small boats for the most part; there were also bigger boats, cargo boats.

''The boys didn't waste much time after Monty told them to go ahead and make for the nearest port,'' Dr. Smith said thoughtfully. ''Wonder why Monty changed his mind so suddenly. I really thought''—he gave a dry chuckle—''that just perhaps he hadn't much mind left to change.''

''Monty,'' she said hotly, ''is perfectly rational.''

''Maybe. Certainly hope so.'' He had turned away from her, and she heard a soft click. ''Now, Nurse, kindly hand me that snapshot of Juan's.''

''Hand—what?'' She whirled aound and stared and then stared harder, for the doctor's black bag was gaping open; he held a revolver in his hand. *The* revolver! Monty's revolver!

She literally could not speak. The round hole of the gun was pointed straight at her.

''You do know what I mean. Juan let slip that he had hidden it here. Then I couldn't find it. So you must have it. Give it to me.''

''*Give you what?*''

''You know. It's not a lot really—''

The fragment of a conversation suddenly recurred to her. She repeated it. ''Not a lot! That's what Juan told you. I heard him. You said—you told him something about seeing to something. Yes! Juan said, 'Not a lot for you,' and you said, 'No need to get excited. We'll see to—' and just then you both heard me and turned around and looked—looked—''

''You heard too much.'' His voice was steady, his eyes were steady, the gun did not waver by the fraction of an inch. "You heard too much. Juan was a blackmailer. He had something that would have broken me completely. Think, Nurse. Isn't my life and my work more important than the life of a mean little blackmailer? My job is to save lives, and I do. And I'll save more. Good men, good people who give something to the world. That's what I've done. I intend to keep on doing that. So hand over that snapshot."

He meant—he must mean—one of the negatives she had found.

A gun, even if one doubts the firmness of the intent to pull the trigger, is still a potent argument. But Sue tried. "You couldn't shoot me—"

"Look at it sensibly. In honesty I can say that I'm just more important, more valuable than you are. There are other fine nurses. Only one me."

It was said so reasonably that it carried conviction. She tried to fight back. "There are other fine heart doctors—"

"Give it to me. Hurry up."

"You couldn't shoot me—" she repeated.

"I'm sorry. But I'd rather shoot you than end my life and the lives of many more patients. They call good doctors ruthless." He spoke in a fantastically conversational way. "The fact is, sometimes we have to be ruthless for the general welfare."

"If you shoot me, you can't explain it, you can't—"

"I can. You are wasting time. I don't want to. If you hand over that picture I'll let you go."

"But I'll tell everybody—"

"Go ahead. What a story! Your word against mine. You claiming that I actually threatened you with a gun! Who would believe you? Certainly I'll not shoot—if you give me that snapshot—"

"They are not snapshots." Too late she regretted her admission, but it was impossible to retract it. "Only negatives."

"You looked at them! I saw you. I opened the door and you were examining each one."

"Not really. There are only a few tiny negatives, framed in a kind of cardboard. I didn't see—"

"You saw this particular negative. Under a strong light— magnified. No." His voice took on a coaxing tone—his bedside manner, which, unfortunately, she recognized. "I'll not shoot you, once I get that one snapshot."

Memory was again supplying her with a small fact, scarcely noted at the time she had witnessed it. She couldn't stop blurting it out. "He didn't know your name. He recognized you when he saw you. Yes, he was looking at the baggage tags and saying something to himself— something like 'It can't be, but I'm right.' Why, it was only then that he found out your name!"

Dr. Smith's mouth jerked downward. "And decided at once to blackmail me. Made a very quick plan—knew the value of those negatives to me and hid them here."

"Why here?"

The doctor shrugged. "Thought it safe, probably. Didn't think I'd look for them here. Hand them over. I tell you, I'd never hurt you. You know that."

She knew that she could perhaps gain time. "Wait a minute. My jeans. I put them in the pocket—"

"Get them!"

"All right."

Her knees were perfectly steady as she crossed to the jeans. Her hands didn't shrink from the damp chill of the denim. But then, suddenly, panic caught her, for the pockets were empty. She hunted; she turned the pockets out. She was trembling now, for the tiny cardboard-mounted negatives simply were not to be found in the jeans. Were not to be found anywhere. She started to pull out drawers, she hunted through her one small handbag, she felt tears on her face.

The doctor said, in a low voice, "Where are they?"

"I don't know," she faltered, and the doctor suddenly

fell forward on the carpet and the gun went off, blasting the whole place, her ears, the cabin, the whole world.

Twenty-two

Somebody snapped on the light.

All the time she and the doctor had been holding the strange conversation in a dusky light from nowhere. Sue was on the floor, on her knees, leaning forward, staring, as men tumbled and rolled on the carpet and, she realized, fought.

One thud, then another. Voices. Swearing. Shouting. Voices from people at the door, shrieks from somebody— Lalie, Addie, Celia—high soprano yelps from Sissy, who somehow wedged herself into the fray.

Abruptly the scene dissolved into a vividly marked charade. Stan and Jim were fighting. Sissy was nipping whatever ankle or leg came her way. Celia was pulling at Monty, who had suddenly got into the battle, and Dr. Smith had vanished.

The gun lay on the carpet. The air had a peculiar acrid smell. Wiley stood in the doorway staring.

Jim yelled, "Let go, you—"

Stan yelled, "Jim, where are you? Help—"

"I'm here," Jim shouted. "You've got my leg. Let me go—"

The whole place changed. Jim, Stan were on their feet and running. Monty had already gone. Celia and Lalie didn't pause to question but disappeared after them. Sissy marked her own pursuit by yelping at the top of her voice.

Wiley tried to follow but staggered into his room, and Addie, in a rather stunned way, moved after him and into his cabin. Sue heard her. "Now then, Mr. Wiley. Back into bed. You know what the doctor—"

Sue decided simply to wait. Nothing else to do.

But she listened and listened and heard only a confused uproar from the deck. Her thoughts, however, raced wildly.

Unexpectedly, the noises seemed to settle into quiet. The steady throb of the engines was again audible. Celia came to her. "You aren't hurt, are you?"

"Hurt? Why, I—no, I don't think so!"

"Stan wants to know. Well, Monty wants to know, too. Your doctor friend is getting away fast! He seems to be a pretty good swimmer."

Sue swallowed hard. "We may be near the shore."

"The men are on deck."

"I'm coming." But there was nothing she could do except tell them, all of them, what had happened and hope to find the little negatives that had meant Juan's life.

She followed Celia along the passage, glancing in at Wiley's door, which was open. Addie was sitting beside Wiley's bed. She nodded but didn't move. Probably had already got herself a drink, Sue thought unkindly but, as a matter of fact, mistakenly. Addie was simply thinking very hard.

When they reached the salon, Lalie shoved a glass into Sue's hand. "Drink it. Monty wants to know how you are."

"Awful," said Sue truthfully. "But, no—Dr. Smith didn't hurt me. Nearly scared me to death, that's all."

"That's enough." Stan came in from the passage. "Give me one of those, Lalie. Monty's coming down. Jim is at the wheel. We ought to be in port by morning—sooner perhaps. We've been going at top speed."

The yacht, indeed, was straining and quivering; the glassware in the bar clattered musically. Sue grasped for a chair.

Monty came in. He was flushed and disheveled and sat down with a groan. "We didn't even try to get him out. He's gone by now."

Celia said, "Better this way, Monty. Really better. He's a very able and gifted man."

"Also a murderer," Stan said shortly.

"But you said Juan was a blackmailer—" Monty began.

"Sure," Stan replied. "Juan and his little hobby of photography. Developed negatives here. Kept them on the yacht, where he lived. Soon as he recognized Smith he knew what he had, so—this is a guess—he thought a safe place to hide his precious bit of blackmailing was in Sue's cabin. Only my guess. Seems logical." Stan sat down, stretching out his legs wearily.

"Stan, you got to my cabin in time," Sue whispered.

Stan heard her. "Sure. I was watching."

"You knew who the murderer was?"

"Oh, yes. I did. Then. I'll spell it out. First, that cigarette lighter of his. Worked on a battery. I didn't catch on for a while; too long, as a matter of fact. Every time the doctor got close to the compass it whirled around. It was purposeful. He tried to delay us in order to give himself time to do something about Juan. Same thing happened with the gun Monty was carrying—" He sat up. "Where is that gun?"

Addie had come quietly into the salon. "Oh, I have it," she said gently and drew it from some clinging chiffon fold of her pink dress. "Here it is. You see, somebody kicked it on the carpet, and I thought I'd better keep track of it. And now I'll take—"

"Yes!" said Lalie approvingly and leaped to the bar.

But unexpectedly, Addie changed her mind. "No," she said decisively. "Mr. Wiley shouldn't drink, and I think it is a good idea for me, too. Perhaps," she added rather wistfully.

"But that can't be the only reason for saying you knew—" Sue had turned to Stan, who said, "No. The point is that of course he had access to Wiley's keys, so he could go anywhere on the yacht. That was another thing.

Juan had taken a photograph of him. Recognized the doctor. Apparently saw his way to money—''

"I know about that," Sue said quickly. "I heard them talking on deck, and the doctor admitted—'' There was a strained silence as she repeated all that she knew.

Then Stan said accusingly, "Too bad you didn't think of telling anybody about what you heard them say."

"Too bad you didn't tell me to look out for Dr. Smith," Sue said meanly.

Stan yielded. "Yes, it was. Nearly cost you your life."

"But that horrible wig! Why did he leave it in my cabin—''

"Don't think about it, Sue," Stan said. "No way to be sure of his motive, but he had one, even if it was only to confuse you—if, say, you heard or saw him and he had to get out fast. Certainly you'd have stopped to look at that—but I don't know. He'll never tell now."

Monty stirred uneasily. Celia went to him. "Let them talk. I mean, let Stan tell it."

Monty quieted down at once. Stan shoved his hands in his pockets and went on, rather doggedly, for his tale seemed mainly one of errors committed. "I couldn't believe it was the doctor. Not until Sue told me her cabin had been ransacked and I searched it myself and found negatives all neatly framed in pasteboard and—here is the very dangerous one he had to have." He dug into a pocket and held up the small square. "You can't see much until you get a strong light behind it. But it's the doctor. In the sea, beating a woman over the head. And keeping her under the water—''

Celia gave a half-scream. "Monty! Remember! Three years or so ago, wasn't it? That yacht that caught fire and went down off the coast. All the boats in the area gathered around to help, so most of the people on it were saved. A few were lost. Too few life preservers, they said."

Stan said soberly, "The doctor certainly had one. A woman was apparently trying to hang on to it. Smith simply clobbered her off. Juan got the picture. There are some others, but this one is fatal to the doctor. Here it is.''

Monty groaned again. ''Keep all the negatives. We'll need them when we try to explain this to the police.''

Sue said in a small voice, ''So he *had* been along this coast by sea. He said he hadn't been, but he knew about flying fish and porpoises and—'' Her voice quavered off to nothing as there was a sudden, shattering jar. It was like a bomb, the yacht, the world shaking.

Sue was flung to the carpet. She had a blurred glimpse of Stan leaping out the door. Monty had his arms tightly around Celia. Addie was on her knees. Lalie was scrambling up from a melee of broken glass.

Sue was still trying to get on her feet when Stan stuck his head back in. ''Jim hit a buoy. No lights, he said. Nothing. But the boat is all right. Just hold everything.''

Monty didn't even look at Sue, who finally dragged herself up by a chair and settled into it, thinking confusedly what a handsome couple Monty and Celia made.

I mustn't think that. But I do think it. Oh, never mind, not now. Sue looked for Addie, who also was staring at Monty and Celia. She turned to Sue and smiled. ''I think it's fine, really. Don't feel sorry, Sue. As good fish in the sea, you know.''

''I don't know!'' Sue said hotly, but paused, allowed some stubbornly buried idea to rise in her mind and accepted it. ''Yes, Aunt Addie. I mean, no. I'm not sorry.''

''Really like his wife,'' Addie said warmly. ''As I said from the first.''

Neither Monty nor Celia seemed to think that an explanation was necessary, or even excuses on Monty's part. Sue was aware of an unexpected inward giggle.

Inspired by the giggle, she rose, walked across to Monty and said, as seriously and gravely as she could, ''I forgive you.''

Monty stared at her for an instant, then began to turn red. "Well, you see—"

"Oh, I see."

Celia twisted around in Monty's arms. "She doesn't care," she said to Monty. "Don't let anything bother you."

"I do think, however," Sue said, determining suddenly not to let Monty off too lightly, "I do think it would be better if you nullify that new will, Monty, and then you two get married." She walked out of the salon.

Jim and Stan were on deck. There were lights and boats everywhere.

They were both leaning over the rail, shouting, and didn't even hear Sue's inquiry as to what the lights meant. A big, very bright light approached them at top speed. It was dazzling. A voice came out of the light. "Search warrant," it yelled. "Stop! Charleston Harbor Police."

"I know," Stan said shortly. "We made very good time. When we could."

"Hey," Jim cried, "what do they mean, search warrant?"

"They mean search warrant," Stan replied. Both men were shouting against the stentorian voice coming from the approaching boat, which came very fast, stirring up white foam ahead of it.

"Why?" Stan shouted toward the boat. "What do you want?"

"Drugs, I'll bet," Jim said morosely. "If we've got any drugs we're in for it."

The enormous voice came nearer. "Dr. Smith. Warrant for his arrest. Stand by for boarding—"

"Stop the engines," Stan shouted at Jim, who leaped for the bridge.

The lawyer, Mr. Lawson, was the first man on deck.

Addie, by that time, was pressing forward also to look and gave a scream. "It's just like Juan! *Déjà vu!* Just like Juan!"

By this time the lawyer had pulled himself together. He

shot an angry glance at Addie and then allowed it to travel around the rest of them. Lalie cried, "But how—"

Monty stepped forward in a nicely dignified way and shook hands with Lawson. Lawson took Monty's hand without much enthusiasm. "Where is that man Smith? He damn near killed me."

"Why?" Not everybody said it, but it emerged as a single voice.

"Why! Because I knew he shot Juan. I'll tell you how I knew it. Not right away—that is—" The lawyer did look just faintly embarrassed. "After I had gone through the account of all the events here I began to sift through them—in my mind, you see—and suddenly I was sure that Juan had to have some urgent reason for returning to the yacht after someone had attacked him. I had felt that Juan was lying when he called it an accident. A hit over the head like that. So, what was his real reason for coming back? Because after Juan got over his scare, he persisted. He wanted something from one of you and intended to put on pressure. Blackmail struck me as a possibility. The next point was obvious. Who on this boat was most vulnerable to blackmail? Who would be most seriously hurt by some damaging fact? After some thought, taking you all one at a time, I felt that the doctor, owing to his status in a very sensitive profession, was the most vulnerable person and—" He adjusted his spectacles. "I was a fool! I decided to make a little test. I actually taxed the doctor with it. That is, I didn't say he murdered Juan. But I asked him when and where he had known him and that—that was enough." A red tide of anger swept his face. "He hit me over the head, and the next thing I knew I was in the water. I had been standing at the rail. Luckily, a cruise ship was in the area. I'm not much of a swimmer."

"The cruise ship picked you up?" Stan said.

"Certainly. And got me to land, and I've given a verbal account of the whole cruise to the police and—where is that doctor?"

Everybody told him. Everybody told the police. Addie murmured once, gently, that she hoped there were no sharks so near the coast.

The sun was setting in clear pinks and reds over the placid water. The sunset gun boomed out. The colors gently dropped.

Stan was in uniform again. Sue sighed, and Stan noticed it.

"Thinking of Monty?"

"Yes. Some."

"Miss him?"

"Yes. That is, not really. I'm thinking that the cruise began right here. Almost at this very table. We were having drinks, and you came by and Monty invited you—"

"My leave is up tomorrow. Another drink?"

"Tomorrow?"

"Sure. That's why I'm in uniform. Getting used to it again."

She turned her glass in circles. "Will you be gone long?"

"I don't really know. Depends on—oh, a lot of things."

"Oh, there you are," Lalie said happily, pulled up a chair, and sat down cozily between them. "Wanted to tell you. Celia just phoned. Everything is fine with them. Married and happy and have made up their quarrel."

"What quarrel?" Stan said crossly, as if interrupted in a serious conversation.

Lalie laughed. "Oh, I wondered if they had quarreled. Or something. Anyway, Celia said to tell you, Sue, Monty has destroyed that new will. But he's writing a new one and leaving something to your aunt. Just a friendly gesture, he said."

"That is very nice of him." Sue wished Lalie would leave.

Stan said, again rather stiffly, "What was their quarrel about?"

"I didn't know then. I thought he was just tired of Celia and—"

"What about?" Stan said.

"First, the yacht. Celia told him he paid too much for it. And then Sissy got into the act."

"Sissy—" Sue believed it. "What did Sissy do?"

Lalie giggled. "Seems last winter Monty got very fancy and bought himself a fur coat. Sissy took it into her head that it was a cat—no"—Lalie frowned—"too big for a cat. Anyway, I suppose that explains why she tore it up. Monty got mad, and as I understand it, one word led to another and—oh, well, they are all right again now. Married, too. But still have Sissy." She looked at Sue. "How are you making out with the great stone face here?" She nodded at Stan.

"Great—well, not at all," said Sue.

Lalie sighed. "Nobody can say I didn't try. Got nowhere. Better luck, Sue. I've got to go. Jim is waiting for me." She kissed her fingers lightly to them and sped away.

"Great stone face," Stan muttered. "Me!"

"Lalie . . . exaggerates. Sometimes."

There was a silence. Dusk was turning the waters of the Sound into a deep blue. There was the pleasant murmur of voices coming from the dining room. Nothing about the Club had changed. Yet undoubtedly life had changed in some degree for all the guests on the cruise.

Stan unexpectedly chuckled. "I drove out to your aunt's today. Thought I'd find you."

"I was in New York. Back at the hospital."

Stan said, "Oh."

Sue eyed the dark water. "Wiley seems to have quite an influence over Aunt Addie. She's completely stopped drinking since he came to stay with her."

Stan was not interested. "Really? They were most helpful and kind to us—those police, I mean."

"Have you heard? Did anybody ever find—"

"Nope. Not that I know. They sent out alarms to all boats in the vicinity. Nobody ever reported him."

Sue waited, thinking. "He'll turn up somewhere. I'm sure."

"Why?"

"Because he really was a great man."

"If you say so."

"And he knew he was a great man."

"Probably Napoleon felt the same thing. Look, Sue—I mean do you really plan to go back to work?"

"Yes. Why not?"

Stan tipped up his glass and looked intently into nothing at the bottom of it. "Oh, nothing. I was only thinking—of course, I don't have any money. Not like Monty—"

Sue's heart pounded so hard she felt that Stan must have heard it. "Stan! Do you really mean—"

"A navy wife doesn't have an easy time, you know."

"Oh, shut up," Sue said happily. "I'll have a wonderful time. I'll follow you around."

"Can't! At least, sometimes you can. Quarters and—what do you want?"

Sue was signaling the waitress, who came smiling. "The lieutenant wishes to order champagne."

Stan straightened his blue-clad shoulders with their proud gold-striped shoulder boards. "Sure, champagne. But I'm kind of dazed already. I mean—"

"Me too." Sue put her hand on the table so Stan could take it.

About the Author

MIGNON G. EBERHART's name has become a guarantee of excellence in the mystery and suspense field. Her work has been translated into sixteen languages, and has been serialized in many magazines and adapted for radio, television and motion pictures.

For many years Mrs. Eberhart traveled extensively abroad and in the United States. Now she lives in Greenwich, Connecticut.

In April 1971 the Mystery Writers of America gave Mrs. Eberhart their Grand Master Award, in recognition of her sustained excellence as a suspense writer, and in 1977 she served as president of that organization. She recently celebrated the fiftieth anniversary of the publication of her first novel, *The Patient in Room 18*.

15